CRITICAL PRAISE FOR

MATT BRAUN

"Matt Braun is a master storyteller of frontier history."
—Elmer Kelton

"Braun takes the big men, the complex personalities
of those brave few who were pivotal figures in
the settling of an untamed frontier."
—Jory Sherman, author of *Grass Kingdom*

"Matt Braun has a genius for taking real characters out of
the Old West and giving them flesh-and-blood immediacy."
—Dee Brown, author of *Bury My Heart at Wounded Knee*

"Braun blends historical fact with ingenious fiction . . .
A top-drawer Western novelist."
—Robert L. Gales, Western biographer

D1024144

Shadow Killers

Previously Published as *Bloodstorm*

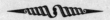

MATT BRAUN

St. Martin's Paperbacks

Shadow Killers was previously published under the title *Bloodstorm*.

This is a work of fiction. All of the characters, organizations, and events portrayed in this novel are either products of the author's imagination or are used fictitiously.

SHADOW KILLERS

Copyright © 1985 by Matt Braun.

All rights reserved.

For information address St. Martin's Press, 175 Fifth Avenue, New York, NY 10010.

ISBN: 978-0-312-97294-3

Printed in the United States of America

Pinnacle edition / February 1985
St. Martin's Paperbacks edition / February 2000

St. Martin's Paperbacks are published by St. Martin's Press, 175 Fifth Avenue, New York, NY 10010.

10 9 8 7 6 5 4 3 2

CHAPTER ONE

The three men reined their horses to a halt. High overhead, the sun beat down with a brassy glare. The landscape was barren, with windswept boulders dotted randomly among stunted trees. Westward, the Sangre de Cristo Mountains stood framed against a cloudless sky.

Ahead, the terrain sloped sharply upward. The men dismounted and one of them remained behind with the horses. Then, without a word, the other two pulled Winchester carbines from their saddle scabbards. The larger man was swarthy, with hawklike features and a droopy mustache. His companion was also dark-skinned, but clean shaven and somewhat less formidable in appearance. Their spurs jangled in the morning stillness as they walked forward.

The slope ended abruptly on a rocky escarpment. Some distance below was a narrow canyon, bisected by a small stream and a worn trail. The terrain rose steeply on the opposite side, sheltering the canyon north and south with sheer palisades. Only the faint gurgle of the stream broke the silence, and nothing moved. There was a foreboding sense of quiet, with time and motion stilled in a frozen tableau. The men stood there a moment, staring down.

Finally the larger one motioned to a craggy outcrop. His manner had about it an air of authority, and the second man moved as though on command. They seated themselves behind jagged boulders and dropped their sombreros on the ground. From his shirt pocket the clean-shaven one pulled out cigarette papers and tobacco. The leader hissed a sharp warning and shook his head. With a weak smile the man stuffed the makings back into his pocket. They settled down to wait.

An hour or so later the men suddenly tensed, their eyes alert. The sound of hoofbeats, growing steadily louder, echoed off the canyon walls. A rider appeared only a short distance downstream, his horse now held to a walk as the grade steepened westward toward the mountains. The men scrambled to their feet, staring intently into the gorge below. A moment passed while the larger one studied the rider with a look of watchful concentration. Then, as though in silent affirmation, he nodded to his companion. They shouldered their carbines, sighting on the rider.

Their shots cracked almost in unison. The rider seemed to jerk upright in the saddle, twin puffs of dust spurting from his broadcloth coat. Like a prolonged drumroll, the sound of gunfire reverberated endlessly along the rocky corridor. An instant later the rider toppled out of the saddle and his horse bolted, clattering away upstream. He hit the ground with a muffled thud, arms splayed outward. A shaft of sunlight reflected off what appeared to be the starched brilliance of a minister's dog collar. The darkish vermilion of blood slowly stained his shirtfront.

Grinning, the leader barked a command in guttural Spanish. The other man left his carbine behind and gingerly made his way down the face of the outcrop. On the canyon floor, he crossed the stream and knelt beside the body. He took the dead man's wallet, which contained less than twenty dollars in greenbacks, and a cheap pocket watch. As a final touch, he turned the dead man's coat and trousers pockets inside out. Then he rose and hurried back across the stream.

On top of the escarpment, he obediently handed over the wallet and pocket watch. The larger man examined the watch with a cautious expression, then he tossed it into the rocks. His mustache lifted in a sardonic smile as he thumbed through the wallet. He laughed and walked off toward the horses.

"Vamos! Hemos acabado el trabajo."

CHAPTER TWO

Braddock scanned the letter. So far he'd answered none of today's correspondence. The letter in hand, which was from a midwestern bank, was no exception. He dropped it into the wastebasket.

There was a light rap and the door to his office opened. Verna Potter, his secretary, stepped inside. Her pince-nez eyeglasses were perched on the end of her nose, and her expression was properly formal. She closed the door behind her.

"A Mr. Kirkland to see you."

"Frank Kirkland?" Braddock asked. "New Mexico?"

"I believe so."

Braddock checked his pocket watch. "Nothing like a punctual client. In fact, he's a little early."

Verna sniffed. "Perhaps Mr. Kirkland could teach you his secret."

"Spare me the lecture." Braddock grinned, pushing the correspondence aside. "C'mon. Chop, chop, Verna! Let's not keep him waiting."

Verna opened the door and motioned. "Won't you come this way, Mr. Kirkland?"

The man who entered was a natty dresser. Somewhere in his late thirties, he had pleasant features and dark hair that was flecked through with gray. He carried himself with a military bearing, and the immediate impression was of someone both distinguished and forceful, a man accustomed to issuing orders.

Braddock rose, extending his hand. "Welcome to Denver, Mr. Kirkland."

"Thank you." Kirkland shook hands with a firm grasp. "I presume you received my wire."

"Late yesterday." Braddock nodded. "Have a seat."

Kirkland took a wooden armchair. "Fortunately, my train was on time. I came straightaway from the depot."

Braddock lowered himself into the swivel chair behind his desk. He shook a cigarette from a half-empty pack and lit up in a wreath of smoke. He blew out the match, tossing it into an ashtray. His gaze was speculative.

"Your wire mentioned an emergency."

"Correct," Kirkland acknowledged. "Sorry the wording was so vague, but I had no choice. I couldn't afford to let anyone in Santa Fe know the purpose of our meeting."

"And what would that be exactly?"

"Murder."

Braddock slowly exhaled. "Tell me about it."

"Four days ago," Kirkland said grimly, "the Reverend John Tolby was killed. Someone ambushed him and shot him down in cold blood."

"Where?"

"Outside Cimarron," Kirkland replied. "That's the county seat of Colfax County. Reverend Tolby was the Methodist minister there."

"Is Cimarron near Santa Fe?"

"It's eighty miles or so to the northeast."

"Up somewhere around Raton Pass?"

"Yes."

"Which puts it fairly close to the Colorado border?"

"Colfax County abuts the Colorado line."

"Your wire said you're a lawyer."

Kirkland stiffened. "Are you questioning my credentials?"

"No," Braddock said quietly. "I was wondering why a lawyer from Santa Fe would be concerned with the murder of a preacher from Cimarron."

"I'm the attorney for the Cimarron Coalition. Reverend Tolby was one of the founders of the coalition. He was also a friend."

"Uh-huh." Braddock flicked an ash off his cigarette. "What's the Cimarron Coalition?"

"A citizens' organization," Kirkland informed him. "Businessmen and ranchers, even some small homesteaders. The better element of Colfax County."

"Why would they retain a lawyer so far away?"

"As you know, Santa Fe is the territorial capital. I represent their legal interests and lobby on their behalf."

"If you lobby for them"—Braddock paused with a quizzical look—"then you must lobby against someone or something."

"I do indeed."

"Who?"

"The Santa Fe Ring."

Braddock's ice-blue eyes were suddenly alert. "How come I get the feeling we just stopped talking about murder?"

"We haven't," Kirkland assured him. "There's every reason to believe the Santa Fe Ring was behind Reverend Tolby's death."

"I'd like a straight answer," Braddock said woodenly. "You didn't pick my name out of a hat, did you?"

"No."

"So," Braddock said, watching him carefully, "why me?"

"You were there the night Pat Garrett killed Billy the Kid."

"I'm still listening."

"By all accounts, the Kid was indirectly linked to Judge Owen Hough. Some people believe Judge Hough was the ring's man in Lincoln County. I understand you killed him."

Braddock had killed many men. He was regarded as the foremost manhunter on the frontier. Among others, he'd been involved in the downfall of such noted badmen as Dutch Henry Horn and Jesse James. His fame as a private detective had spread throughout the West, and the attendant publicity had destroyed his anonymity forever. These days he operated undercover, and always in disguise.

One of the first cases to bring him notoriety had occurred in Lincoln County, New Mexico Territory. There, working with Pat Garrett, he had been instrumental in the death of Billy the Kid. By happenstance, the case had pitted him against Judge Owen Hough. While no proof existed, Braddock had always believed that Hough was a political underling of the Santa Fe Ring. There was definite proof, however, that Hough had been responsible for the murder of a witness in the case. Her name was Ellen Nesbeth, and she'd been someone special in Braddock's life. He hadn't let her death go unavenged.

"You heard wrong," he said at length. "I killed Hough for personal reasons. It had nothing to do with the Santa Fe Ring."

"Perhaps," Kirkland allowed. "But one fact remains inescapable. He was their man, and you killed him. So far, that's the closest anybody has come to penetrating the ring."

"Wrong again." Braddock blew a plume of smoke into the air. "I linked Hough to a man by the name of Warren Mitchell. At the time, he was president of the Santa Fe Land and Development Company."

"He's still the president."

"Good for him," Braddock commented dryly. "But I never established any connection between the ring and Mitchell. It was pure supposition—no proof."

Kirkland leaned forward, staring earnestly at him.

"Nonetheless, you *believed* he was part of the ring, didn't you?"

"Let's get something straight," Braddock said flatly. "A man I respected told me about the ring. Other than his word, I have no knowledge that it even exists. Not a scrap of evidence."

"Oh, it exists all right!"

"Then you tell me," Braddock asked bluntly, "who belongs to the ring?"

"A great many men," Kirkland said, evasively. "Businessmen and politicians, bankers and lawyers and judges. The list would be endless."

"What are their names?"

"I have no idea."

"Who's the leader?"

"I don't know."

"Then what makes you so certain there is a ring?"

"Someone has an economic stranglehold on the territory. I'm talking about land and railroads, virtually every form of commerce. That wouldn't be possible without an organized conspiracy."

"Now you're dealing in supposition."

"To an extent," Kirkland admitted. "However, the people I represent are willing to pay to turn supposition into proof. We'd like to retain your services."

"I don't work for committees," Braddock said, no irony in his tone. "It only takes one loose lip to put my fat in the fire."

"You would report solely to me."

"That's another problem," Braddock remarked. "I don't make reports. I do the job my own way and at my own speed. The result speaks for itself."

Kirkland regarded him somberly. "Are you stating conditions or turning me down, Mr. Braddock?"

"Depends," Braddock said idly. "You started off talking about murder. Then you leapfrogged to the Santa Fe Ring. Which is it?"

"Both!" Kirkland's voice was heated and vindictive. "The

murder of Reverend Tolby is part and parcel of the greater problem. I'm convinced his killer will lead you to whoever's behind the conspiracy."

"Why was he killed?"

"Reverend Tolby used the pulpit as a public forum. He spoke out against the injustices visited on the people of Colfax County. His death was a warning to those who oppose the Santa Fe Ring."

"In other words, the Cimarron Coalition."

"Precisely."

Braddock stubbed out his cigarette in the ashtray. "You said his murder was part of a greater problem. Would you care to spell that out?"

"Of course," Kirkland said gravely. "At bottom, it amounts to a land-grabbing scheme by the Santa Fe Land and Development Company. Warren Mitchell performed the miraculous feat of transforming ninety-seven thousand acres into two million acres. And he did it virtually overnight!"

"How'd he manage that?"

"By outright bribery and political hocus-pocus!"

"Try to be a little more specific."

"To understand, you'll need some background information."

"The floor's all yours, Counselor."

"Very well."

Kirkland quickly warmed to his subject. Following the war with Mexico, all land north of the Rio Grande had been ceded to the United States. By the Treaty of Guadalupe Hidalgo, the American government agreed to respect the holdings of Mexican landowners. Yet the title to all property in New Mexico Territory had evolved from ancient land grants; the issue of who owned what was clouded by a convoluted maze of documents. At various times, land grants had been awarded by the King of Spain, the Republic of New Mexico, and the provincial governor. Ownership was often nine points physical possession and having the force to back the claim.

To compound the problem, many of the grants overlapped one another. Fraudulent land surveys further added to the confusion, and long legal battles seemingly resolved nothing. One such grant, the Beaubien-Miranda claim, was eventually acquired by the Santa Fe Land and Development Company. All too aware of the vagueness of the grant, the company hired the U.S. Deputy Surveyor to conduct an official survey. By virtue of the survey, the original 97,000-acre grant was swiftly converted into a 2,000,000-acre claim. At the same time, the company acquired other huge tracts of land throughout the territory. None was as large as the Beaubien-Miranda grant, which occupied a major portion of Colfax County. Overall, however, these holdings gave the company economic leverage in every county of New Mexico.

The company's position was strengthened when a deal was struck with the Santa Fe Railroad. The track line, which roughly followed the old Santa Fe Trail, traversed the land grant on the northern edge of Colfax County and proceeded on to the territorial capital. Yet there still remained the legal question of the original grant. In an audacious move, the company persuaded the U.S. Land Commissioner to establish an extraordinary precedent. Henceforth, a court decision based on an official survey would determine the validity of a claim. Shortly thereafter, a favorable court ruling declared the grant to be two million acres. The company had perfected a method by which New Mexico could be profitably, and legally, exploited.

Still, despite these devious maneuvers, trouble quickly erupted in Colfax County. Scores of settlers and ranchers had already staked out claims in the vicinity of Cimarron. By court edict, they were now declared trespassers on private property. The situation was further aggravated by the presence of several mining camps. The nearby mountains were rich with gold, and the miners now found themselves in the position of encroaching on company land. All the parties involved—ranchers, settlers, and miners—were ordered to vacate their claims or pay an exorbitant price for valid title. Colfax County quickly became a battleground between those with established roots and an organization that claimed prior ownership of the land.

The Santa Fe Land & Development Company was widely considered the offspring of the Santa Fe Ring. Warren Mitchell, president of the company, was thought to be a little more than a front man. Speculation and rumor fueled the belief that a powerful clique operated behind the scenes. The identity of the members was unknown, but their goal was obvious from the outset. Like feudal lords of ancient times, the Santa Fe Ring sought to control the economic lifeblood of an entire territory. The immediate response of ordinary citizens was the formation of the Cimarron Coalition, and open revolt in Colfax County began.

"We won't be budged," Kirkland concluded. "We've ignored the court order to vacate and we have no intention of paying them for the land. We're there to stay."

Braddock looked at him without expression. "I'd say you've got them convinced. Otherwise they wouldn't have resorted to gunplay."

"Assassins!" Kirkland said in an aggrieved tone. "We won't be intimidated either! Reverend Tolby's murder merely strengthened our resolve to hold out."

"What's the political situation?" Braddock ventured. "Any luck with your lobbying efforts?"

"I'm afraid not," Kirkland said glumly. "Territorial legislators have either been bought off or they're reluctant to oppose the ring. Our influence at the capital is practically nil."

"And in Colfax County?"

"Even worse!" Kirkland said with bitterness. "The courthouse crowd openly supports the land company."

"How do you explain that?" Braddock persisted. "Doesn't the coalition control enough votes to swing an election?"

"Not yet," Kirkland conceded. "We've been organized only a short time, and the next elections are still a year away."

"Sounds pretty bleak." Braddock paused, giving him an

evaluating glance. "So what're you asking me to do, Mr. Kirkland?"

"Find Reverend Tolby's murderer!" Kirkland said hotly. "And break the back of the Santa Fe Ring!"

"Let's be clear." Braddock's voice dropped. "Are you after evidence that will overturn the land grant? Or do you want an eye for an eye?"

Kirkland sensed the conversation was at a critical juncture. Braddock's reputation as a mankiller was unrivaled anywhere on the frontier. No lawman, certainly no outlaw, commanded such respect or outright fear. Yet it was common knowledge that Cole Braddock was not a gun for hire. He killed in the line of duty—or self-defense—but never for blood money. So now, acutely aware of what he'd been asked, Kirkland warned himself to proceed cautiously. He chose his words with care.

"There's no profit in revenge. Of course, considering the men we're up against, you may find it necessary to fight fire with fire. However, I would much prefer live witnesses, talkative witnesses. I want a case that will result in grand jury indictments."

Braddock stared at him for a time. He'd learned never to place any faith in a lawyer's double-talk. But the assignment intrigued him, for it was both broad in scope and something of a professional challenge. All the more so since his last encounter with the Santa Fe Ring had ended in a stalemate.

"I don't work cheap," he finally said. "The fee's five thousand out front and five thousand on delivery."

"Perfectly acceptable," Kirkland agreed. "I'll give you a bank draft on the coalition account."

"No," Braddock said slowly. "Write it out to yourself and let me have the cash. That way nobody in your bank will accidentally on purpose put out the word in Santa Fe."

"Very clever," Kirkland chortled. "I like the way you think, Mr. Braddock."

Braddock merely nodded reflectively. "I'll need a contact in Cimarron."

"Orville McMain," Kirkland said without hesitation. "He's publisher of the *Cimarron Beacon* and a moving force behind the coalition."

"How far can I trust him?"

"Completely," Kirkland observed. "McMain won't breathe a word to anyone. He's in some personal danger himself."

"Oh?"

"His editorials," Kirkland explained. "He's denounced the ring in no uncertain terms. We feel quite certain he's next on the assassins' death list."

"I guess he'll do," Braddock said, suddenly abstracted. "Have they hired a new preacher yet?"

"In Cimarron?"

"Yeah."

Kirkland shrugged. "Not to my knowledge. Why?"

"Have McMain put an announcement in the paper. Tell everybody a new parson's on the way." Braddock smiled cryptically. "The Reverend Titus Jacoby."

"Who's he?"

"You're looking at him."

"I—" Kirkland was bemused. "You intend to impersonate a minister?"

"A Bible thumper and a detective aren't all that different. We both listen to confessions and save souls—in our own ways."

"I see your point," Kirkland noted wryly. "One might even say you both perform the last rites."

"Your words, not mine."

"No offense meant."

"None taken."

"Well, now," Kirkland began, sensing he'd overstepped himself, "how shall we proceed?"

"How soon can you get your draft cashed?"

"No later than tomorrow."

"I'll leave when I see the money."

"Will you and I have any further contact?"

Braddock stood. "Not till the job's done."

Kirkland realized he'd been dismissed. He rose to his feet and shook hands. Then he walked out the door with a slightly dazed expression. He thought it ironic that Braddock would pose as a man of God.

And he wondered what sermon the Reverend Titus Jacoby would preach in Cimarron.

CHAPTER THREE

Braddock waited until the door closed. Then he moved to a large safe positioned against the far wall. He spun the combination knob and cranked the handle. From an inside shelf, he removed one of four ledgers. The cover was stenciled, "M–R."

The ledgers were a Who's Who of western outlaws and badmen. The contents were compiled from wanted posters, newspaper articles, and voluminous correspondence with peace officers throughout the West. A page was assigned to each desperado, and the dossier detailed every known fact regarding his past activities. The ledgers were cross-referenced by name and alias, as well as state and territory. Virtually everyone who was anyone, from horse thieves to gunslicks, was listed therein. The result was a comprehensive rogues' gallery.

The page on New Mexico Territory was a quick read. With the end of the Lincoln County War, a relative calm had settled over the territory. The names of Billy the Kid and most of his gang had been lined out, indicating they were no longer among the living. Yet New Mexico was not altogether a land of peace and brotherly love. One name stood out, and his place of residence was of immediate interest. He lived outside the town of Cimarron.

The man's name was Clay Allison. His dossier was a brief chronicle of violence and bloodletting. No outlaw, Allison was instead one of the more successful ranchers in Colfax County. Yet his quarrelsome nature, abetted by a hair-trigger temper, often put him afoul of the law. His first entry in the ledger involved a particularly brutal vigilante action. Allison led a mob which stormed the jail and lynched an accused murderer. Following the hanging, Allison then decapitated the man and put the head on public display in a saloon.

There were two other entries in the dossier. The first involved an argument over a horse race, resulting in a shootout. Allison killed his opponent and then exchanged insults with a friend of the dead man. The friend mysteriously disappeared and Allison was charged with murder. However, no body was recovered, and he was released for lack of evidence. Scarcely two years later, Allison went on a drunken rampage and terrorized the patrons of a dance hall. A deputy sheriff was summoned, and Allison killed him in a blazing gunfight. Although arrested and charged with murder, Allison was released. Witnesses swore the deputy had fired first.

Braddock closed the ledger. He lit a cigarette and stared off into space. From what Kirkland had told him, the Cimarron Coalition was composed of various factions. One of the factions mentioned was ranchers, and it was therefore logical to assume that Clay Allison was a member of the coalition. The dossier indicated that Allison was a violent hothead who seldom, if ever, considered the consequences of his acts. Such a man was dangerous to himself and anyone associated with him. He might fly off the handle at any moment, provoking trouble at an inopportune time. Or his temper might cause him to blurt out secrets when the situation demanded silence. In short, he was not to be trusted.

Normally when operating undercover, Braddock kept his own counsel. He told the client nothing of his plans and undertook the assignment in the most covert manner possible. All the more so since his notoriety—along with his photo in newspapers—made it necessary for him to operate in disguise. Yet, on the spur of the moment, he'd decided to take Kirkland into his confidence. Cimarron was a small town, and a stranger would immediately draw attention. A local contact was therefore essential; the publisher, Orville Mc-Main, would introduce him into the community and lend credibility to his cover story. The danger was that McMain might reveal his actual identity to other members of the coalition. It was a calculated risk, and he'd weighed it against the advantages of arriving in Cimarron under the guise of a preacher. But now he made a mental note to warn McMain to keep his lip buttoned and, in particular, to say nothing whatever to Clay Allison.

Crushing out his cigarette, Braddock rose and moved to the door. Verna Potter looked up from her desk as he entered the outer office. She was a spinster with plain features and hair pulled back in a tight chignon. His work as a detective was the focal point of her life, and she took a certain vicarious satisfaction in the number of outlaws he'd killed. His personal life, on the other hand, left her mortified. He spent his evenings in Denver's sporting district, and the woman who shared his bed was the feature attraction at a variety theater. Verna considered it all quite reprehensible for a man in his position.

Braddock paused at her desk. "I took the case. When you have a minute, check out the train schedules to New Mexico. I want the nearest stop to a place called Cimarron."

"Very well." Verna jotted it down on her notepad. "When will you leave?"

"In a day or so," Braddock said absently. "Kirkland's supposed to drop off five thousand in cash. Hold out a thousand for my expenses and deposit the rest."

"Why cash?" Verna peered over her pince-nez glasses. "I thought Mr. Kirkland appeared quite respectable."

"He's a regular prince," Braddock deadpanned. "But a

check leaves a paper trail. I'd prefer to keep the arrangement to ourselves."

Verna gave him an apprehensive glance. "Is the assignment that much more dangerous than normal?"

"Yes and no," Braddock said equably. "The stakes are bigger, and that tends to make people play rougher. I guess it all evens out in the end, though."

"In what way?"

Braddock grinned. "I'm not exactly a tyro myself."

"Don't brag!" Verna said sharply. "Everyone knows it brings bad luck."

"Are you superstitious"—Braddock cocked one eyebrow—"or just a worrywart?"

"Humph!" Verna averted her gaze. "Have you finished with today's correspondence?"

"There's nothing of interest," Braddock replied. "I dumped it in the wastebasket."

"I wonder that you read it at all!"

"Lock up for me." Braddock speared his hat off a hat tree. "The safe's open and a couple of ledgers are on the desk."

"Of course," Verna said with frosty disapproval. "I assume you won't return today?"

"You know what they say," Braddock called over his shoulder. "All work and no play . . ."

Verna watched him go out the door. Her waspish expression slowly dissolved into a faint smile. She thought him a devil and a roué, thoroughly incorrigible, yet late at night, alone in her cold spinster's bed, she forgave him everything.

He was her forbidden fruit, untasted.

Braddock walked toward the sporting district. Not without certain qualms, he had decided to approach the underworld czar of Denver. On occasion, they had been of service to one another. And while they were not colleagues, he'd nonetheless established an understanding of sorts with Lou Blomger.

On Larimer Street, he crossed into another world. The

Tenderloin represented a brand of civic betterment unique to westerners. Every imaginable vice, from the ordinary to the bizarre, was contained within an area of several square blocks. By municipal ordinance, all gambling dives, dance halls, bordellos, and saloons were restricted to the Tenderloin. Easterners found the concept at once fascinating and morally unconscionable. But to Braddock, who'd migrated to Denver by way of Texas, it seemed a wise and farsighted policy. Everyone benefited when whores and high rollers knew their place and stayed there.

As he strolled along Larimer, Braddock's thoughts turned to the town itself. Like many western settlements, its origins were linked to an enterprising form of avarice. Gold was discovered on Cherry Creek in 1858, and within a matter of months thousands of reasonably sane men hocked their worldly possessions and lit out for Colorado Territory. Some struck it rich, but most went away bedraggled and footsore, their quest for the mother lode a bitter memory. That same year a land speculator founded a town along the banks of Cherry Creek. He called it Denver.

Over the years, the town had reproduced itself a hundredfold. What was once a sad collection of log huts had spread and grown until finally a glittering metropolis had been created amidst the gold fields. By the early 1880s, Denver had become a cosmopolitan beehive, with theaters, opera, plush hotels, six churches, four newspapers, three railroads, and an entire street devoted to nothing but whorehouses. Vice was an organized industry in Denver, and the town's sporting district, known locally as the Tenderloin, was controlled by one man. His name was Lou Blomger.

Denver was also a peaceful, law-abiding town. By Lou Blomger's edict, no crimes of violence were tolerated within the Tenderloin. What highwaymen and robbers did outside the city limits was their own business. But those reckless enough to practice their craft in Denver proper were dealt a swift, brutal lesson in obeying the law. It was a lesson that

exacted absolute and final justice, without appeal or clem-
ency. Blomger's enforcers were skilled at performing neat,
workmanlike executions.

There was no sense of civic virtue behind Blomger's
edict. He was simply a pragmatic businessman, and the rackets were his business. He meant to insure that the Tenderloin operated without undue publicity or needless acts of
violence. Experience had taught him that the public was
blindly apathetic to almost any form of vice, so long as it
was conducted quietly and out of sight. The man in the street
wanted to know he could visit a cathouse or drop a few dollars at the faro tables in the evening. Yet he also wanted assurance that he wouldn't be waylaid by some hardcase on
his way home.

Whores and crooked gaming dens, even bunco games,
were condoned by Blomger. Still, he drew the line at spilling citizens' blood or forcibly separating them from their
wallets. He declared that any man who stepped over that line
would be judged an outlaw even among his own kind. With
his rise to power, peace had settled over Denver. The public
viewed the Tenderloin as a tawdry playground, and the rackets operated with blissful tranquility. Gunslingers, highwaymen, and thieves were welcome for as long as they cared
to sample the delights of Denver's heady atmosphere. But
only if they minded their manners and weren't tempted to
molest the local residents. Otherwise they were found float-
ing facedown in Cherry Creek.

Politicians and police alike hailed Blomger as a civic
benefactor. The foundation of his power, of course, was in
the fact that he controlled the rackets. The decision of who
got paid off, and how much, was his alone. Yet there was
more to it than mere payoffs. The Tenderloin cast the swing
vote in any election. Without Blomger's support a politician
never attained office, much less participated in the corruption
and graft. Slowly, always from behind the scenes, the tenta-
cles of his power reached outward and upward. When the
votes were counted after the most recent elections, the results

came as no surprise to Denver's political hierarchy. Lou Blomger owned city hall and the courthouse, and his name was spoken with reverence in the halls of the state capitol. His influence, however insidiously, extended to every level of government.

Braddock's visit was prompted by that very thought. He reasoned that a man with such widespread influence would have political connections beyond Colorado's borders. Since New Mexico joined Colorado on the south, it was conceivable that those connections extended all the way to Santa Fe. Or perhaps to the Santa Fe Ring itself. All of which raised the specter of yet another calculated risk. Lou Blomger might prove to be a valuable source of information. He might also represent a hazard, one with deadly consequences. Everything hinged on whether or not it was Blomger's ox that got gored.

Entering the Progressive Club, Braddock reminded himself to proceed with caution. Upstairs, where Blomger's office was located, he rapped on the door. The man who opened it was short and wiry, with the features of a ferret and a disposition to match. His name was Slats Drago and he was Blomger's personal bodyguard. He carried twin Colts snugged down tight in shoulder holsters, and his reputation was that of a cold-blooded killer. His attitude toward Braddock was one of amiable, albeit wary, respect. He nodded.

"Long time no see, Braddock."

"Hello, Slats. I'd like a word with Lou."

"Business or social?"

"Would it make a difference?"

Drago hesitated, then stepped aside. "Mr. Blomger, it's Cole Braddock."

Lou Blomger sat behind a massive walnut desk. He was a man of considerable bulk, with a rounded paunch and sagging jowls. His hair was flecked with gray and his eyes were deceptively humorous. His handshake was perfunctory, but he seemed genuinely pleased by the unexpected visit. He motioned Braddock to a chair.

"Have a seat, Cole. You ought to drop around more often."

"Well, you know how it is, Lou. No rest for the weary."

Blomger chuckled. "I know the feeling all too well. What can I do for you?"

"It's personal."

"Pay no mind to Slats. He's deaf and dumb where my affairs are concerned."

"No offense, but this time . . ." Braddock shrugged.

Blomger regarded him thoughtfully. After a moment, he glanced across at Drago. "Wait outside, Slats. I'll call if I need you."

Drago shot Braddock a dirty look. Then he opened the door and stepped into the hallway. When the latch clicked, Blomger slowly shook his head. "I think you hurt Slats's feelings. He considers himself a professional."

"No way around it. What I have to say has to be said to you alone."

"Oh? Why is that?"

"If it's repeated," Braddock said deliberately, "I'll hold you accountable."

Blomger's expression was impassive. He understood that the threat was made in earnest. Braddock was in effect offering him a chance to end the conversation, for once he gave his word, any breach of confidence would be taken as personal betrayal. No one, including Slats Drago, would then be able to protect him. Somewhere, somehow, Braddock would kill him.

"All right, Cole. Whatever you say stops here."

Braddock lit a cigarette. As he exhaled the smoke, he decided on the direct approach. "Have you got connections in New Mexico?"

"Political or otherwise?"

"Political."

"Not with anybody who carries any clout."

"How about a fellow named Warren Mitchell?"

"Never heard of him."

"I'm surprised," Braddock said casually. "He's rumored to be the head of the Santa Fe Ring."

Blomger loosed a rumbling laugh. "You've been hired to investigate the Santa Fe Ring?"

"I didn't say—"

"And you're asking me for the inside dope?"

"Yeah, something like that."

"Well, I'm sorry to disappoint you, Cole. I can tell you that the Santa Fe Ring exists, but nothing more."

"Why not?"

"Politics in New Mexico is a closed club. Outsiders aren't allowed to join, and insiders never talk."

"Then what makes you so sure the ring exists?"

"Because everybody's lips are sealed tight. When that many people get lockjaw, you can bet the rumors are true."

"That's it, nothing else?"

"A bit of friendly advice," Blomger replied. "Whoever operates the ring plays rough—damned rough. You'd do well to stay out of New Mexico."

Braddock smiled. "I've been there before."

"And lived to tell the tale. So you obviously intend to ignore my advice."

"I'll let you know—sometime."

"Fair enough. Until then, I'll just assume we never had this conversation."

"I'm obliged, Lou."

"Of course you are. I'm in the business of obligating people. And I always call the marker!"

Blomger's laugh followed him out the door. In the hallway, he traded a curt nod with Slats Drago. Then he turned toward the stairs and emerged a moment later on the street. Walking back uptown, he slowly put the day's business from his mind. His thoughts centered instead on tonight.

He wondered how Lise would react when he told her. And within a few steps, he stopped wondering. He knew.

CHAPTER FOUR

Braddock arrived at the Alcazar Variety Theater early that evening. The owner, Jack Brady, greeted him with effusive warmth. He was escorted to his usual table down front, and a waiter materialized with a chilled bottle of champagne. The bubbly, as always, was on the house.

In the sporting district, Braddock was looked upon as a celebrity. He was Denver's resident mankiller and as much an attraction as the stage show. The fact that he slept with Lise Hammond, the Alcazar's headliner, merely enhanced his reputation. Speculation among the theater's clientele was evenly divided between his affair with the girl and the actual number of men he'd killed. Still, for all their curiosity, no one broached such matters in his presence. He was a private man and tolerated few questions.

Apart from his reputation with a gun, his physical appearance also gave men pause. He was lean and tough, a strapping six-footer with shoulders like a singletree. His eyes were smoky blue and impersonal, set off by squared features and light chestnut hair. He had the look of a loner, and he did nothing to correct the impression. A similar streak of inde-

pendence extended to his professional life. Shrewd investments, which included a diverse portfolio of stocks and real
estate, allowed him to pick and choose his assignments. He
accepted a case for the challenge, because he took pride in
his craft. The money was simply the gauge of his worth as
an investigator.

"Good evening, Cole."

"Hello there, Daniel."

"Sorry I'm so late."

"Forget it." Braddock gestured to a chair. "Sit down and
pour yourself a drink."

Daniel Cameron was one of the few men Braddock invited to his table. A master gunsmith, he was stooped and
gray-haired, almost gnomelike in appearance. He kept Braddock's guns in perfect working order and often suggested
innovations calculated to give the manhunter an edge. One
such innovation was the cartridges Braddock carried in his
Colt.

The bullets sold over the counter were notoriously poor
man-stoppers. Though mortally wounded in a gunfight, an
outlaw would often live long enough to kill his adversary.
What Braddock needed was a bullet that would neutralize
the other man on the spot, stop him instantly. Daniel Cameron's innovation provided true stopping power.

The standard factory loading utilized a round pug-nosed
bullet. Cameron's design was a molded lead slug which gradually tapered to a flat nose. Going a step farther, he then
reversed the slug and loaded it upside down. The nose of the
slug was now seated inside the cartridge case, crimped tight
well above the sloping shoulders. The base, which was blunt
and truncated, was thereby positioned at the front of the cartridge.

The factory load normally achieved deep penetration. It
was not unusual for a standard pug-nosed bullet to plow
through a man, exiting virtually unmarred and still very
much in its original shape. What resulted was that the bullet expended the greater part of its energy drilling a clean,

somewhat symmetrical hole. The effect was not at all what Braddock wanted. A man dead on his feet frequently emptied his gun before dropping.

Cameron's imaginative innovation rather neatly solved the problem. The reverse-loaded slug achieved scarcely one-third the penetration of a factory load. Upon impact, the truncated base expanded, squashing the entire slug, from front to rear, into a mushroom-shaped chunk of lead. The result was that the mushroomed slug imparted its energy with massive shock, delivering a horrendous wound rather than drilling a clean hole. The effect was instantaneous, literally a man-stopper that halted an opponent dead in his tracks. On more than one occasion, the reverse-loaded slug had saved Cole Braddock's life.

"Happy days!" Cameron smiled over the rim of his glass. "You might be interested in why I was late."

"You'll tell me anyway," Braddock said genially. "So go ahead and get it off your chest."

A sly look crossed Cameron's face. "Tonight I put the finishing touches on a new Smith and Wesson forty-four."

"So?"

"Cole, it's unbelievable!" Cameron's eyes gleamed with pride. "I've honed the double-action trigger pull down to nothing. It almost goes off by itself!"

"C'mon, Daniel," Braddock groaned. "You tried the same thing on me when Colt came out with a double-action."

"This one's different," Cameron protested. "It's smooth as silk—smoother! And I still contend a double-action will shave time off your draw."

"Not with a cross-draw holster." Braddock patted the left side of his coat. "Figure it out for yourself, Daniel. By the time I pull and bring it up to fire, I've already got the hammer cocked. And a single-action trigger is a hell of a lot lighter than a double-action."

"Why cock the hammer?" Cameron insisted. "You could be squeezing a double-action as you align the sights. I say it would make you faster—much faster!"

Braddock shook his head. "Fast doesn't win gunfights. Take my word for it, Daniel. A quick man who's dead-on accurate will beat a speed demon every time."

"How about reloading?" Cameron countered. "A Smith and Wesson breaks at the top and ejects all the spent shells at once. The loading gate on a Colt takes twice as long, maybe longer."

"Well, I'll tell you," Braddock said with a sardonic smile, "I've never had occasion to reload. Your trick bullets stop the fight before it goes that far."

Cameron spread his hands in an exaggerated gesture. "It's 1882, Cole. Time marches on, and you, my friend, you're falling behind!"

"I'm still fogging a mirror." Braddock laughed and motioned toward the stage. "Drink your champagne and watch the show."

The orchestra thumped to life and the curtain swished open. Lise pranced onstage, her skirts flashing and her breasts jiggling over the top of her gown. At a signal from the maestro, the orchestra segued into a rousing dance number.

A line of chorus girls exploded out of the wings. Lise hoisted her skirts higher, exposing her magnificent legs, and led them in a high-stepping cakewalk. The tempo of the music quickened and the girls squealed and Lise wigwagged her underdrawers with bouncy exuberance. A spate of jubilant shouts erupted from men around the room.

In the midst of the routine, Lise moved downstage. Her bloomers were revealed in a showy step, and a spotlight enveloped her with dazzling brilliance. As the chorus line romped and cavorted behind her, she halted before the footlights. She dimpled her lips in a bee-stung pucker and blew Braddock a kiss.

The crowd went wild.

A shaft of light from the parlor lamp streamed through the bedroom door. Braddock lay sprawled on the bed, hands locked behind his head. His gaze was fixed on the ceiling and his expression was pensive. He pondered on the easiest way to tell her.

The bathroom door opened. Lise wore only a sheer peignoir and high-heeled slippers. She moved sinuously across the room and halted beside the bed. Her eyes were bright with excitement and a vixenish smile touched her lips. She shrugged out of the peignoir, letting it drop to the floor.

She was naked. The streamer of lamplight framed her in an amber glow, making her a vision of loveliness. She stood before him with sculptured legs and jutting breasts, her body rounded and supple. Her golden hair hung long and unbound, spilling down over her shoulders. A moment slipped past while she teased and tantalized, posing in the slatted light. Then, with a low, throaty laugh, she stepped out of the slippers and joined him in bed.

Braddock enfolded her in a tight embrace. Her arms went around his neck, and she kissed him with fiery passion. Her tongue darted into his mouth, and she shuddered convulsively, squirming closer. His hand went to the delta between her legs, and a murmur of feverish urgency escaped her throat. He rolled on top of her and entered her. Their mouths locked in union, his stroke gradually quickened and she drove at him until her body was wracked by jolting shudders. Her nails taloned his shoulders as she surged with violent contractions. Her mouth opened in an explosive cry.

"Oooh—oh, Cole. Oh, my God!"

Breathing heavily, they separated and his arm slipped around her waist. She clung to his hard-muscled frame, and for a long while time lost all meaning. Satiated with the musky smell of love, they rested, and after a period of silence, they kissed again, their bodies warm and their legs intertwined. Then she snuggled closer, her mouth pressed to his ear in a low whisper.

"Mmm. That was scrumptious, lover."

Braddock patted her bottom. "It'll have to last awhile."

"Oh?" She nuzzled his earlobe. "Why?"

"I accepted an assignment today."

"Damn!" She scooted around and sat upright. "When do you leave?"

"Tomorrow," Braddock said casually. "Maybe the day after."

"Where to this time?"

"New Mexico."

Her gaze sharpened. "What sort of job?"

Braddock was by nature a cynic. He trusted no one completely and he accepted nothing at face value. With time, however, he'd learned that his secrets were safe with Lise. What began as a sexual liaison had slowly ripened into an emotional bond. She shared his suite at the Brown Palace Hotel and she shared his innermost thoughts. She was his sole confidante.

"Someone was murdered," he said matter-of-factly. "Somebody else thinks the Santa Fe Ring was behind it. I've been hired to take a look-see."

"What's the Santa Fe Ring?"

"Good question." Braddock raised up on one elbow. "Some people believe it's an organized conspiracy involving politicians and crooked businessmen. It's so hush-hush nobody's proved it yet."

"You will!" She jiggled with excitement. "I just know you will!"

"I aim to do my damnedest."

She eyed him keenly. "It's big, isn't it? I mean really big—your biggest case."

"Yeah." Braddock gave her a wary look. "I suppose you could say that."

"Well, then"—she paused with a beguiling grin—"how about some help? I'm ready, willing, and available."

"No soap," Braddock said stolidly. "It's too dangerous."

"You need a new line!" She tweaked the hairs on his chest. "That's what you said last time, remember?"

"Save your breath," Braddock advised her. "You won't con me into it this trip out."

"Why not?" She mocked him with a minxlike smile.

"I had those lunkheads in Virginia City eating out of my hand. Without me, you wouldn't have solved the case! You said so yourself."

Braddock couldn't argue the point. She was a blond sexpot, a bawdy nymph with a body like mortal sin. She possessed a kind of bursting vitality, and she was the mental equal of any man he'd ever met. On his last case, she had accompanied him to Montana and played a one-week engagement at a Virginia City variety theater. Her natural talent for undercover work had quickly unearthed a vital lead in the investigation, a lead that he would never have turned up by himself. So her statement tonight was no idle boast. She had a flair for the detective business.

"Sorry," he said firmly. "New Mexico's a powder keg and somebody's already lit the fuse. I won't risk it."

"C'mon, lover!" She fluttered her eyelashes. "I handled myself all right in Virginia City, didn't I? And those boys weren't exactly kindergarten stuff!"

"No, they weren't," Braddock granted. "But you were offered a job there, and that gave you a legitimate front. We couldn't work the same dodge twice in a row, especially where I'm headed. It's a one-horse burg smack dab in the middle of nowhere."

"Excuses, excuses!" She lifted her chin defiantly. "Where there's a will, there's a way. And we both know it!"

Braddock wagged his head. "You might as well call it quits. The answer's no, and that's final."

"Jesus Christ!"

Lise bounced out of bed. She scooped up her peignoir and went storming into the parlor. Braddock listened to the clatter of glass on glass as she poured herself a shot from the brandy decanter. He'd never seen her lose her temper, and it bothered him more than he cared to admit. He slipped on a robe and walked from the bedroom.

Seated on the sofa, Lise looked like a sulky child. She took a slug of brandy and refused to meet his gaze. He moved forward and sat down beside her. Some things were difficult for him to articulate, and he now had to struggle for words. At last he let out his breath with a heavy sigh.

"Here's the score," he said softly. "If it was anyone else, I wouldn't give it a second thought. But it's not anyone else. It's you, and that makes a hell of a difference, from where I sit."

A lump formed in Lise's throat. Any open display of affection was foreign to his character, and she knew the words had cost him dearly. All his life he'd been an emotional nomad, allowing no strings and asking none in return. Tonight, in his own way he'd told her that his wanderlust was a thing of the past. He cared for her too deeply to put her in harm's way. Her eyes suddenly glistened and a tear rolled down her cheek.

"You must think I'm a spoiled brat."

"You're worth spoiling—in some ways."

"Are you mad at me?"

"One way to find out."

Braddock took her in his arms. He squeezed her in a crushing bear hug and the brandy glass dropped to the floor. She pulled his head down and kissed him with fierce abandon. When they finally parted, her tears were gone and the vixenish look had returned. Her eyes sparkled with a mischievous glitter.

"Cole."

"Hmmm?"

"If you should change your mind—"

"Holy crucified Christ!"

"—I'm still available, lover."

Her laugh was like wind chimes in a gentle breeze.

CHAPTER FIVE

Lise studied herself in the mirror.

Her mind was elsewhere as she slowly applied her stage makeup. Somewhat mechanically, she colored her cheeks with a magenta shade of rouge. Then she darkened her eyelids with kohl, spreading it in a fan-shaped pattern until her eyes seemed to blaze like opals set in dusky onyx. The last step was the tint on her mouth, which was accomplished with the same methodical motions. She painted her lips into a scarlet bee-stung pucker.

By now her evening ritual was performed largely by rote. She had spent a thousand nights, perhaps more, seated before a dressing-room mirror. As a stagestruck young girl, she'd hooked up with a traveling variety troupe. She began as a hoofer. Eager and naive, she had been determined to escape her family and the quaint boredom of midwestern life. From St. Louis she had toured virtually any city of consequence west of the Mississippi. Slowly she'd acquired stage presence, cultivated her voice, and moved out of the chorus. A headliner when the troupe finally folded, she had gone out on her own. And now, scarcely a year later, she had star billing at the Alcazar.

Tonight the glamor and excitement of her stage life somehow seemed trivial, even threadbare. Only an hour ago, Cole Braddock had caught the evening southbound train. Their parting had been short, without any great ceremony, for he hated good-byes. He'd simply kissed her with his usual look-for-me-when-you-see-me farewell, and walked from the hotel suite. She had only the vaguest notion of his destination and absolutely no idea when he might return. Sometimes an assignment ended quickly, but other times he'd be gone a month or longer. Worse, there would be no means of contacting him while he was away. Nor would he write her or even attempt to pass along a message through his secretary. She was effectively in a state of limbo for however long his assignment lasted.

For all his good intentions, she was still miffed about his current case. She appreciated his protective attitude and she understood that his concern was solely for her welfare, but she was nonetheless upset by the thought of being left behind. She'd said nothing more last night, and all day she had bitten her tongue in an effort to remain silent. She was determined that nothing would spoil their last few hours together. Further, she was resolved that he wouldn't leave with bad memories of their parting. Still, she felt piqued and just the least bit offended. All his logic in no way offset the substance of her argument. Working undercover, she could have rendered valuable assistance in New Mexico. And she could have done it without endangering herself or his precious assignment!

Staring into the mirror, she wondered if her anger stemmed from hurt pride. For despite the bond between them, she understood that he was still his own man. Her only assurance of holding him was in allowing him the freedom to come and go as he pleased. And to let him stay away, without so much as a note, for however long it suited his purpose.

Somehow the arrangement seemed a little lopsided. Yet she possessed the wisdom to understand that it would end if she ever attempted to smother him with demands. She genuinely believed that he never slept with other women, and while he wanted no strings attached to his life, he always returned to her. Not that he ever spoke of their relationship, for he was a man who seldom revealed his innermost emotions. He was more apt to cover his feelings with an offhand remark or a casual gesture of tenderness. When they were together, he *was* attentive and thoughtful and an ardent lover, but these damnable separations were sometimes more than she could bear. And she knew that her foul mood wouldn't improve with the passing of time. She was going to be very bitchy until he returned.

There were three sharp raps and the door opened. Jack Brady, owner of the Alcazar, stuck his head inside the dressing room. He was a florid-faced Irishman with a genial manner and a fondness for pretty women. Not without reason, he pampered Lise and treated her with the diplomacy befitting Denver's star songbird. He lived in constant dread that a competitor would pirate her away, and with her, the bulk of the evening trade. Her three shows a night made the Alcazar a veritable money tree. Now his face split in a broad grin as he jerked his head toward the stage.

"Five minutes till show time."

"Don't worry, Jack, I'll make it."

Brady's grin dissolved. "You look a little piqued. Anything wrong?"

"No. Everything's just hunky-dory."

"You sure don't sound like it."

"How I sound in here doesn't matter, Jack. It's how I sound onstage."

"Yeah, of course. I just thought if there was anything I could do. You know . . ."

"What you can do is shut the door on your way out. I'll be there when the curtain goes up, Jack."

"Uh—" Brady cleared his throat. "Well, give 'em a good show tonight. We've got a big crowd out front."

"Scram!"

Brady hastily closed the door. Lise regretted her tone the instant he'd gone, and almost called him back. But then on second thought, she changed her mind. She felt bitchy and she'd probably stay that way for the foreseeable future, and Jack Brady would just have to live with it!

She stood and slipped out of her dressing robe. Quickly she stepped into a spangled gown that was cut low on top and ended above her knees. After fastening the hooks, she checked her makeup one last time. Then she squared her shoulders and marched out the door.

Her face lit up with a bright, theatrical smile.

The curtain rang down on the first show. Lise walked off-stage to thunderous applause. She moved through a bevy of chorus girls crowding the wings and started toward her dressing room. Then, on the spur of the moment, she reversed directions.

As a rule, Lise remained backstage between shows. She had learned long ago that mingling with the customers was more bother than it was worth. But in the midst of her last number, she'd noticed Daniel Cameron sitting at one of the tables down front. And now, somewhat impulsively she decided to join the gunsmith for a drink. However loath she was to admit it, she simply couldn't stand her own company tonight.

A moment later she emerged from a door beside the orchestra pit. All the tables were full, and a buzz swept through the crowd when she started across the room. Hurriedly, ignoring a drunk who shouted her name, she made her way to Cameron's table. He was alone and pleasantly surprised by her sudden appearance. He scrambled to his feet.

"Good evening, Lise."

"Hello, Daniel. May I join you?"

"By all means."

Cameron held out a chair. Lise seated herself, and a waiter materialized at her elbow. She ordered a brandy, then turned back to Cameron. His wizened features were split in a wide smile.

"I can't tell you how delighted I am. I'm the envy of every man in the room."

"Aren't you the flatterer?"

"No, it's true. Frankly, I can't imagine why you'd pick an old reprobate like me. But I'm delighted all the same."

"To tell you the truth"—Lise cut her eyes around the room—"you're the only friend I see here tonight."

"Uh-huh." Cameron regarded her with a somber expression. "Forced to guess, I'd say Cole left town today. Would that be a safe bet?"

"You must be reading my mind."

"Hardly that. I'm just familiar with the symptoms."

"Symptoms?"

"Loneliness mixed with a dab of anxiety. Quite natural, given the circumstances."

Lise appeared puzzled. "I plead guilty to lonely. But what makes you think I'm suffering anxiety?"

"Cole," Cameron said reasonably. "I assume he's accepted another assignment. And knowing him, I would imagine it entails an element of danger."

The waiter reappeared with her brandy. When he walked away, she took a sip, watching Cameron over the rim of the glass. After a moment, she slowly shook her head.

"You're wrong, Daniel. I miss him, and when he stays away too long, I even begin to resent his work. But I never worry about him."

"Never?"

"Oh, I did at first. I suppose anyone would. After a while, though, I realized it was actually a little silly."

"Why?"

"For one thing, he's not the sort to get himself killed. I'm not saying he's infallible or walks on water. I just happen to believe he'll die with his boots off."

Cameron nodded. "I suspect you're probably right."

"And for another thing"—Lise paused, staring into her brandy—"Cole and I will never grow old together anyway. So why give myself heartburn?"

"Offhand I would say it's heartache rather than heartburn. Or else you're much more fatalistic than you appear."

"You're right on both counts, Daniel."

"How so?"

"I'm the one with heartache and Cole's the fatalist. He's not the least bit afraid of getting killed. And because he isn't, it'll never happen."

"Then why do you say you'll never grow old together?"

"Do you think Cole will ever make an honest woman of me?"

Cameron looked embarrassed. "Well, I'm hardly the one to answer that."

"We both know the answer, Daniel. He wouldn't stand to have his wings clipped, and I wouldn't try. Quite frankly, it's one of the reasons I fell for him."

"I see."

Cameron was clearly uncomfortable with the drift of the conversation. He swigged his drink, unable to meet her eyes. She laughed gaily and patted his hand.

"Oh, forgive me, Daniel. I'm making you play father confessor."

"No, no! Not at all."

"Let's talk about you. What's new in the gun business?"

"Well, I wouldn't want to bore you."

"Perish the thought. Go ahead, tell me all your secrets."

Cameron launched into the details of the experimental cartridge he had under development. He believed it would increase the knock-down power of the over-under Derringer which she always carried. Lise pretended rapt interest, listening attentively, but her thoughts, like windblown smoke, kept drifting back to personal matters.

She imagined herself returning alone to the hotel later that night to a cold, empty bed.

CHAPTER SIX

A brisk October wind whipped through Raton Pass. The town, which was just south of the pass, had been a way station on the old Santa Fe Trail. With the arrival of the railroad, Raton experienced a building boom, and its population doubled virtually overnight. It was now a mountain gateway to the far Southwest.

Braddock emerged from a ramshackle hotel. He'd arrived last night on the evening southbound from Denver. Now, with the sun barely an hour high, his appearance had undergone a startling transformation. His hair was dyed a dark brown, and fake muttonchop side-whiskers were plastered to his jaws with spirit gum. He wore a black frock coat and trousers and the stiff, turned-around collar of a minister. His greatcoat was equally drab, and the outfit was topped off by a flat-brimmed Quaker hat.

The frock coat was generously cut, and no telltale bulge betrayed the Colt .45 snug in its cross-draw holster. He was, to all outward appearances, a man of the cloth. And he called himself the Reverend Titus Jacoby.

Over the years Braddock had played a wide variety of

roles. Early on in his career, he'd discovered he possessed a streak of the actor. As his reputation spread, the gift had served him well. His face was known wherever he traveled, and so his very survival dictated that he operate in disguise. Every assignment differed, and his threatrical flair enabled him to create a character suitable to every occasion. By turn, he'd posed as a grifter and tinhorn, whoremonger and con man, and a veritable stock company of outlaws. He was, by necessity, a man of many faces, none of them his own.

Outward trappings, however, were merely an illusion. A magician employs sleight of hand to misdirect the eye, and Braddock used disguise in much the same way. For complete deception, the character he portrayed was rounded out with quirks and mannerisms and whatever lingo or speech pattern best fit the role. Experience had taught him that a touch of the bizarre enhanced the overall plausibility of the performance. A man who stood out in the crowd was somehow more believable than one who appeared ordinary and common. The final twist was to add a credible cover story to the disguise. So it was that he'd mastered the trick of submerging himself totally in the character of the moment. In these disguises Cole Braddock simply ceased to exist.

Reverend Titus Jacoby was no figment of the imagination. Braddock had grown to manhood in Texas, where religion was an everyday part of life. He'd worked his way up from cowhand to ranch foreman to range detective. From there, he had drifted almost by happenstance into the field of general investigation. In those early days, prior to the Civil War, he'd been exposed to the fire-and-brimstone brand of religion. Tent revivals and circuit preachers represented both salvation and entertainment to those who inhabited the remote backlands. The recollection of one evangelist was burned into his memory like a long-healed brand.

Titus Jacoby had been a man given to florid speech and thunderous quotes from the Scripture. The character Braddock had fashioned in his mind's eye was modeled on the good reverend. He remembered the bombast and the wild harangues, and he even recalled a fair amount of the Scripture. He thought it would make a whale of a performance in Cimarron.

All the same, a couple of things about the role gave him pause. Braddock enjoyed a sociable drink and a good smoke, but tobacco and demon rum were strictly taboo for any self-respecting member of the clergy. Along with blasphemous language and chasing women, these were strictures no minister would break lightly. So Braddock perceived a crown of thorns in the role he'd undertaken. While in Cimarron, he couldn't curse or drink, smoke the weed, or ogle the ladies. Any backsliding would be an instant tipoff that he didn't truly have the Lord's calling. He reminded himself never to play a preacher on future assignments.

Still, as of today he'd stepped into character. He looked the part, and henceforth he would act the part. He reminded himself that a minister seldom had two nickels to rub together. But unlike priests, no vow of poverty was involved. Protestant clergymen were simply underpaid, and the majority eventually turned into professional moochers. While none carried a beggar's cup, a handout or a free meal was never refused. The idea was to play on other people's sympathy, and talk poor-mouth.

Outside the hotel, Braddock walked south along the main street. He'd traveled through Raton several times before, both on personal business and while on assignment. Yet now he was struck anew by the natural wonder of the pass and the part it had played in the settling of the West. The Santa Fe Trail was pioneered some sixty years past by explorers turned traders. The jump-off point, where traders were outfitted for the trek westward, was Independence, Missouri. The initial leg of the journey led across boundless prairies to where the trail forded the Arkansas River. From there, it meandered on to Bent's Old Fort and then dropped into New Mexico through Raton Pass.

By 1824 caravans of freight wagons were crossing the plains. Fully half the trade goods hauled overland were funneled through Santa Fe and on south into Old Mexico. In 1846, with the advent of the Mexican War, Santa Fe became a frontier outpost of the United States. The volume of business along the trail increased enormously as freighters rushed to supply the government and private companies with contract goods. Then in 1878 the Santa Fe Railroad finally surmounted Raton Pass. Shortly thereafter, by way of Glorieta Pass, the end-of-track reached the New Mexico capital. With the coming of the Iron Horse, the Santa Fe Trail ceased to exist. Yet Raton Pass, the Trail's gateway through the mountains, prospered as never before. Once a remote stopover westward, it was now a major north-south artery on the railway line.

Walking past the depot, Braddock tipped his Quaker hat to a couple of ladies waiting on the platform. He was carrying a tattered carpetbag, which further enhanced the image of an itinerant preacher. But he was a preacher afoot and in need of transportation, for the railway didn't connect with Cimarron. Hopping a stagecoach was an option he'd already considered and rejected. He needed mobility, and a circuit rider could poke around almost anywhere without arousing suspicion. A horse was the logical solution, and he found what he was looking for on the edge of town. He turned into a combination livery stable and livestock dealer.

The owner was thick around the paunch and smelled of manure. He greeted Braddock with a slow once-over and a cautious smile. His name was Walt Suggs, and his attitude indicated he'd previously had bad experiences with preachers. He shook hands with studied reluctance.

"What can I do for you, parson?"

"I'm in the market for a horse, Mr. Suggs."

"How much was you aimin' to spend?"

"Well, not much," Braddock said lamely. "I might go as high as ten dollars."

"Ten—" Suggs stopped and shook his head with a pained expression. "You've come to the wrong place if you're lookin' for charity."

"God's work demands sacrifices of us all!"

"Mebbe so," Suggs grumped, "but I ain't no rich man tryin' to squeeze through the eye of a needle. And ten dollars won't get you nothin' but shank's mare."

"Perhaps. I could go twenty—with a saddle included."

"Tell you what," Suggs said testily. "If you ain't lookin' for speed, I got an old crowbait I'll let go cheap. Whereabouts you headed?"

"Cimarron," Braddock informed him. "I'm the new pastor for the Methodist church."

Suggs inspected him more closely. "Hope you're in real thick with the Lord, because the fellow you're replacin' got himself killed—and it weren't no accident."

"Yes, I heard." Braddock rolled his eyes heavenward. "But, then, we're all soldiers in the army of Christ. We go where we're called."

"Yeah, I reckon so," Suggs said without interest. "How's thirty bucks sound for the horse and a used saddle? I couldn't do no better."

"You are indeed a man of generous spirit, Mr. Suggs."

"Don't mention it, parson."

A few minutes later Braddock stepped aboard a dun gelding. The horse was swaybacked, with one walleye and the conformation of a mule. With his carpetbag strapped behind the cantle of the saddle, Braddock looked even more itinerant than he'd intended. His mount was fit for a pauper who traveled light.

Outside town, he turned onto a rutted wagon road. To the southeast lay Llano Estacado—the Staked Plains—and due east was the territorial juncture of New Mexico, Colorado, Texas, and no-man's-land. The wagon road dropped southwestward from mountainous terrain to a high, rolling plateau. A latticework of rivers and streams wound through grassland studded with rocky gorges and wooded canyons. Yet it was a land of sun and solitude, evoking a sense of something lost forever. The vast emptiness swept westward to where the spires of the Sangre de Cristo range towered awesomely against the horizon. Nothing moved as far as the eye could see, and the deafening silence was broken only by the low moan of the wind. There was an eerie sense that man was the intruder here. He felt like an alien presence, unwanted and uninvited, entering into a hostile land. It seemed to Braddock a presentiment of what lay ahead.

He reined his horse toward Cimarron.

The Sangre de Cristo range stood like a column of majestic sentinels. Several of the peaks topped 13,000 feet, and even those at lower elevations were capped with snow. Upper New Mexico was split by the range, which extended roughly on a north-south line. A few miles to the east, Cimarron was cloaked in the shadows of the mountains.

The town was small but prosperous. The countryside was dotted with ranches and small farms, and mining ventures were scattered throughout the nearby mountains. Stores and business establishments were ranked along either side of the town's main thoroughfare. The courthouse was situated in the heart of the downtown area, directly across from a bank and a hotel. Civic boosters were quick to brag that Cimarron was a hub of trade and commerce. Lately, however, its chief claim to fame was the Cimarron Coalition.

Braddock rode into town shortly before sunset. Upstreet from the hotel, he spotted the *Cimarron Beacon*. He reined to a halt before a hitch rack and swung down from the saddle. Someone lit a lamp inside the newspaper office as Braddock looped the reins around the post. His clothes were covered with grime from the long ride, and he took a moment to dust himself off. Then he mounted the boardwalk, moving to the door. He opened it and stepped inside.

There were two men in the outer office. One sat behind a desk, scribbling furiously on a sheet of foolscap. The other stood before a counter that ran the width of the room. He was attired in range clothes, with a Stetson tugged low on his forehead. A pistol was strapped to his hip and a shotgun was cradled across the crook of his arm. Braddock noted that the pistol was a Colt .41 Thunderer and the shotgun a lever-action Winchester, one of the latest innovations in firearms. He thought it a rather peculiar armament for a man who appeared to be a cowhand.

Closing the door, Braddock walked toward the counter. He nodded to the man with the shotgun, but the only response was a stoic watchfulness. Upon closer examination, he detected a certain strangeness about the man. An inch or so shorter than Braddock, he was lean and wiry and thickly corded with muscle. There was a tawny cast to his skin, set off by high cheekbones and a brushy mustache and jet-black hair. Yet his eyes were pale gray, which was somehow out of place with his overall appearance. He looked oddly like an Indian—except for his eyes.

"Good afternoon." Braddock stopped at the counter. "I'm looking for Mr. Orville McMain."

The man behind the desk glanced up from his scribbling. His eyes narrowed and he inspected Braddock's manner of dress. Then he rose and hurried forward with an outstretched hand.

"You must be the Reverend Titus Jacoby."

Braddock accepted his handshake. "And you must be Mr. McMain?"

"Call me Orville." McMain motioned him around the counter. "Come on back and have a seat. I've been expecting you."

Braddock took a wooden armchair beside the desk. McMain settled into a creaky swivel chair and leaned forward. His gaze burned with intensity.

"I don't mind saying you're a welcome sight, Mr. Braddock."

"Hold it!" Braddock halted him with an upraised palm. "Forget you ever heard that name. From now on, I'm Titus Jacoby—nobody else."

"I'll remember," McMain promised. "It won't happen again."

"Before we go any farther"—Braddock jerked a thumb over his shoulder—"who's your friend up front?"

McMain's face grew overcast. "The word's around that I'm next on the ring's death list. So the coalition members decided I should have a bodyguard. Buck got tapped for the job."

"Buck?" Braddock was bemused. "Is that a nickname?"

"I don't believe so," McMain said vaguely. "He goes by the name of Buck Colter. He's a hand on Isaac Coleman's spread."

"How'd he get picked for your bodyguard?"

"Because he's tough as nails," McMain confided. "Of course, I've never seen him pick a fight. He's quiet-spoken, real pleasant until he's pushed. Then he comes unwound like a buzz saw, and he never loses. Folks tend to give him lots of elbow room."

"Any idea how he came by that shotgun?"

"No." McMain looked puzzled. "Why all the questions?"

"Professional interest," Braddock said with a shrug. "Have you told anyone I'm on the case?"

"Frank Kirkland advised me to keep it quiet."

"Some people don't take advice," Braddock observed dryly. "Let's try the question again—have you told anyone?"

"No, I haven't." McMain made an empty gesture with his hands. "Not even my wife."

"Good," Braddock said with a measured smile. "Suppose you fill me in on the political situation. According to Kirkland, the ring pretty well controls the courthouse."

"That's true," McMain confirmed. "Top to bottom."

"Every county office?"

"The whole crowd," McMain said miserably. "Sheriff, county judge, tax collector—all bought and paid for."

"Who's the local kingfish?" Braddock asked. "The ring's front man?"

"Florencio Donaghue," McMain said scornfully. "He's part Mexican, part Irish. He walks both sides of the street, and that enables him to control the ballot box. Very crafty fellow."

"What's he do for a living?"

"He owns the hardware store."

"Have you been able to link him to Reverend Tolby's murder?"

"Fat chance!" McMain's tone was severe. "The sheriff investigated and said it was the work of robbers. The coroner's jury ruled it 'death at the hands of parties unknown.' Case closed."

"Where was Tolby killed?"

"Cimarron Canyon," McMain said gloomily. "It's the main road through the mountains. He made it a regular practice to visit the mining camps and hold services. Somebody bushwhacked him about twenty miles west of town."

"Somebody?" Braddock mused out loud. "Any idea who?"

"Only a guess," McMain said bitterly. "A good-for-nothing named Cruz Vega works for Donaghue. His principal job is to turn out the Mexican vote come election time. I'd say he's your man."

"But you've got no proof?"

"None."

"And there's nothing that connects Donaghue to the Santa Fe Ring?"

"Correct."

"One big mystery and no leads."

"That's why we hired you—Reverend Jacoby."

"So it is."

Braddock was silent for a time. He pulled thoughtfully at his earlobe and stared off into space. A stillness settled over the office while he weighed everything he'd heard. At length his gaze shifted back to McMain.

"Here's the way I see it," he said almost idly. "The whole ball of wax comes down to finding Tolby's killers. We have to catch them before we'll get a line on Donaghue or the Santa Fe Ring. So we'll take it one step at a time."

"Where do you propose to start?"

"I'll pick up where Tolby left off."

McMain raised an uncertain eyebrow. "I don't follow you."

"It's simple enough," Braddock remarked. "The killers have to be lured out into the open."

"I—" McMain hesitated, cleared his throat. "Are you saying you mean to use yourself as bait?"

"That's about the size of it."

"But how will you force them into the open?"

Braddock smiled. "Spread the word in your newspaper. The new preacher's arrived and he'll deliver his first sermon on Sunday."

McMain stared at him incredulously. "You plan to denounce them from the pulpit?"

"See you in church, Orville."

Braddock stood and walked around the end of the counter. He swapped nods with Colter as he moved to the door. Then, with his hand on the knob, he paused. He looked back over his shoulder.

"I'm curious about your shotgun."

Colter regarded him evenly. "What about it?"

"Why a lever-action?"

"Holds five shots," Colter said simply. "That's three more than a double-barrel."

"I notice you also carry a Colt Thunderer."

"Yeah?"

"Same question." Braddock angled his head critically. "Why?"

"It's double action and that saves cocking the hammer."

"You feel it's faster, then?"

"Wouldn't carry it otherwise."

"How about accuracy?"

Colter gave him a slow, dark smile. "I generally put 'em where they're meant to go. Why do you ask?"

"Curiosity." Braddock fixed him with a speculative gaze. "It's a lot of hardware—for a cowhand."

"Maybe." Colter returned his look steadily. "Course, you ask a lot of questions—for a preacher."

"I reckon that makes us even."

"How so?"

"Come to church Sunday and find out."

The door opened and closed. Outside, Braddock unhitched his horse and led it downstreet toward the livery stable. He now had a new mystery to add to the pot.

Why would a half-breed killer masquerade as a cowhand?

CHAPTER SEVEN

On Sunday the buggies and farm wagons began arriving early. An article in the newspaper, along with word of mouth, had spread the news throughout the countryside. Reverend Titus Jacoby would officiate at today's services.

The Methodist Church was located at the end of Main Street. It was the only Protestant house of worship in Cimarron, and therefore the pride of the community. The congregation was roughly half townspeople and half ranchers and farmers. Their economic and political interests were not always in harmony, but they were nonetheless united by their views on two very dissimilar topics. First, God and religion were central to their lives. And second, they considered the Santa Fe Ring an abomination, the spawn of Lucifer himself.

By ten o'clock the church was packed. All the pews were full and the crowd spilled out onto the front steps. The organ wheezed to life and the choir went into a stirring rendition of "The Old Rugged Cross." The deacons and their wives occupied a pew down front, and the remainder of the congregation seemed on the edge of their seats. An almost palpable sense of expectation filled the church, as though some momentous event was about to occur. Then, as the choir segued into another hymn, the door to an anteroom opened. The crowd strained forward for a better look.

Braddock walked to a chair midway between the pulpit and the choir box. He seated himself and crossed his legs, hands folded in his lap. His suit was freshly sponged and pressed, and a starchy collar encircled his neck like a white band of iron. His expression was somber but not sad, somewhat similar to an undertaker overseeing a high-priced funeral. His gaze was fixed on the middle distance, as if he were contemplating some profound matter known only to himself and God. He sat perfectly still and allowed the congregation to inspect their new pastor.

The last two days had been a time of preparation. Braddock had taken a room in the hotel and closeted himself with a Bible. He meant to deliver a stemwinder of a sermon, one that would singe the hair of anyone even vaguely connected with the Santa Fe Ring. Thus, he had read and reread both the Old Testament and the New Testament. Finally, after long deliberation, he'd chosen evil as his theme. His purpose was to incite anger in the ring leaders, and instill in them a dread that he would rally the coalition. He wanted someone to make an attempt on his life, and today's sermon was designed to set the stage. He would portray a zealot begging to be spiked to the cross.

Insofar as the congregation was concerned, Braddock hardly gave them a second thought. Orville McMain was a deacon as well as the moving force behind the coalition, and therefore a power in the church. No one would seriously question his selection of a new minister or the rather hurried fashion in which it had been arranged. Yet Braddock was all too aware that everyone present was there to hear the Reverend Titus Jacoby deliver his first sermon. Their former pastor had been brutally slain for openly challenging the Santa Fe Ring. They would expect his replacement to take up the standard and sound a similar battle cry. Braddock thought no one here today would go away disappointed.

The hymn ended and the choir took their seats. A hush settled over the church and the crowd sat motionless. Braddock rose from his chair and walked to the pulpit. He stood there a moment, staring out across the frozen tableau of faces. Then he squared himself up and raised his arms high overhead.

"Woe unto them that call evil good, and good evil!"

The crowd stared at him, instantly mesmerized. He paused, allowing the suspense to mount, and abruptly stepped away from the pulpit. His voice flooded the church, deep and resonant. His words hammered at them with a drumroll cadence.

"I say to you today what Paul said to the Ephesians. We wrestle not against flesh and blood, but against principalities . . . against powers . . . against the rulers of the darkness of this world . . . *against spiritual wickedness in high places!*"

Braddock strode back and forth in a tempest of oratory. He slammed his fist into his palm and punctuated his speech with wildly exaggerated gestures. He summoned up the specters of evil and injustice and innocent blood spilled. His eulogy to Reverend Tolby, most foully murdered!, left hardly a dry eye in the house. His damnation of the Santa Fe Ring sent a buzz of righteous anger sweeping back over the crowd. His fiery denunciation of land-grabbing rascals and corrupt politicians actually brought cheers. He combined demagogy with theatrics, and he held the congregation spellbound for nearly a half hour. At last, his voice raised in an orotund bellow, he marched back to the pulpit. He thrust his arms heavenward and shook his clenched fists.

"Take unto you the armor of God, that ye may withstand evil! Be strong and of good courage; be not afraid, for the Lord thy God is with thee. Glory hallelujah, brothers and sisters. Amen!"

A chorus of amens reverberated from the congregation. The choir broke out in "Onward Christian Soldiers," and Braddock stepped down from the pulpit. The three church deacons, one of them Orville McMain, joined him and soberly shook hands. The symbolism of their gesture was plain to read: the Reverend Titus Jacoby had been accepted as the new leader of the flock. Then, solemn-faced as owls, the deacons trailed Braddock up the aisle. Outside the church, McMain positioned himself beside Braddock on the steps. The congregation slowly filed out the door, and McMain performed introductions. Braddock shook every hand and modestly accepted their praise. The overall reaction confirmed what he was already thinking to himself. He'd put on a hell of a show.

When the crowd thinned out, McMain steered him toward a couple of men waiting off to one side. Their dress pegged them as ranchers, and their size commanded immediate respect. McMain, who was short and stocky, appeared dwarfed in their presence. The men were tall and rawboned, and looked tough as whang leather. Their features were pleasant enough and their smiles seemed genuine. Yet, curiously, there was no humor in their eyes.

"Reverend Jacoby," McMain announced, "I'd like you to meet Isaac Coleman and Clay Allison. These boys are the top cattlemen in Colfax County."

"Gentlemen." Braddock exchanged handshakes. "I hope you found the sermon worth the ride."

"A real barn-burner!" Allison beamed. "Goddamnedest thing I ever heard—if you'll pardon my French."

"Pay him no mind," Coleman interjected. "He's just tryin' to say you've earned your welcome, parson."

"I appreciate the sentiment." Braddock smiled politely. "Would I be correct in assuming that you men are members of the coalition?"

"Quite correct," McMain broke in smoothly. "Clay and Isaac were the first to join, and they helped me organize the coalition. Apart from Reverend Tolby, no one has contributed more in our fight with the ring."

"Some fight!" Coleman snorted. "All we've got to show for it so far is one dead preacher."

"Sonsabitches," Allison said viciously. "I'd shore like to lay my hands on whoever done it. We'd turn him into worm pudding muy damn pronto!"

"I wonder," Braddock said in a reflective tone. "Would killing him be the best policy? Or would we further our cause by persuading him to talk?"

"No harm in that!" Allison laughed. "We'll just string him up after he talks."

Braddock shook his head ruefully. "Vengeance is mine, sayeth the Lord. Not to mention the fact that a live witness might open all sorts of doors. Don't you agree, Mr. Allison?"

"Well, I'll tell you, parson." Allison studied him with a frown. "After that sermon, you oughtn't to feel so charitable. You're liable to need a bodyguard yourself."

"Amen to that," Coleman added seriously. "Whether you know it or not, you made yourself a target today. And we don't need another dead preacher."

Braddock exchanged a quick glance with McMain. Then he waved his hand in a casual gesture. "I'm gratified by your concern, gentlemen. But it's very unlikely I'm in any great jeopardy. The ring wouldn't risk public censure by murdering another—"

"Don't bet on it!" Allison cut him short. "Public opinion don't mean do-diddily to them. Otherwise they wouldn't've killed Tolby."

"Clay's right," Coleman pointed out. "Why d'you think we assigned one of my men to look after Orville? You'd be wise to listen, parson. No two ways about it."

"Have no fear," Braddock replied loftily. "The Lord will not forsake me in my hour of trial. I entrust myself into His hands."

Allison grunted sharply. "Orville gave us pretty much the

same argument. But he shore changed his tune after somebody drygulched Reverend Tolby."

"Which reminds me." Braddock turned to McMain with
a quizzical look. "Where's young Colter today? I don't recall seeing him at services."

"Oh, he was around," McMain said lightly. "Not much
on religion, but he sticks to me like glue. He's waiting right
over there."

Braddock followed the direction of McMain's gaze. He
saw Colter standing beneath the shade of a tree near the
street. The barrel of the shotgun gleamed dully in sunlight
filtering through the leaves. Colter dipped his head in a sign
of acknowledgment and smiled. Braddock understood that
the smile was something more than a courtesy. It had to do
with respect, mutual recognition.

He and Buck Colter were birds of a feather.

The pale light of a sickle moon bathed the Mexican quarter
of town. Late Monday night the central street was nearly deserted. Only a few horses lined the hitch rails, standing hip-
shot in the shadowed darkness. The faint strains of a guitar
drifted from inside a lamplit cantina.

Florencio Donaghue appeared, walking swiftly along the
street, looking neither right nor left. A large man, his features
were hawklike and tawny brown, indicating a fair degree of
Mexican blood. Yet he wore a vested business suit, with
glossy half boots and a brushed Stetson. He looked prosperous, and troubled.

Outside the cantina, Donaghue halted and peered through
the window. Three men, dressed in native clothing, stood
talking quietly at the bar. Off to one side, the guitar player
was perched on a stool, strumming a soft melody. At the rear
of the room, a lone man was seated by himself at a table.
Beneath a worn sombrero, his droopy mustache glinted in
the lamplight. He was drinking tequila.

Satisfied with the look of things, Donaghue entered the
cantina. He ignored the three men and nodded brusquely to

the bartender. Walking to the rear of the room, he stopped at the table. As he took a chair, the man seated there poured tequila into a clean glass. Donaghue waved it away with an abrupt gesture.

"For once, I see you're on time."

"*Buenas noches, mi jefe.*"

Cruz Vega spoke in a raspy, low-pitched voice. His mouth seemed curled in a perpetual smirk and his eyes were insolent. He took a swig of tequila and wiped his mustache with a thorny forefinger. He appeared sanguine, almost carefree.

"Listen closely," Donaghue informed him. "I have a job for you."

"I serve at your pleasure, *mi jefe.*"

Donaghue considered the flippant tone a moment. Then, deciding to overlook it, he went on. "You've heard of the new preacher, Reverend Jacoby?"

"But of course! Everyone knows of his sermon yesterday."

"What do they say about what he preaches?"

Vega smiled. "They say he speaks the truth. Now, me, I dunno. I never saw no conspiracy around here."

"Are you trying to be funny?"

"No, *mi jefe*! I am a very sincere man."

Donaghue frowned. "I could always find someone else to handle—these things."

"But never so well. I am very good at such work, is it not true?"

"Then save your humor for another time. I'm here to talk business."

"As you wish. I meant no disrespect."

"Very wise," Donaghue grunted. "Can you get hold of Cardenas tonight?"

"*Sí.*"

"Then see to it. I want you both on the job by tomorrow morning."

Vega cocked his head in a sly look. "Who are we to kill?"

"Who else?" Donaghue shrugged. "Reverend Jacoby."

"*Madre de Dios!* You want us to kill another holy man?"

"I want you to do as you're told."

"Have your superiors ordered this thing?"

Donaghue stiffened and gave him a hard look. "What do you mean by that?"

"Oh, nothing."

"Speak up. I asked you a question."

"Well, this Reverend Jacoby talks of a conspiracy. A great conspiracy, controlled by men in Santa Fe. It seems natural that they would order his death."

"Does it?"

"*Sí.* After all, it was they who ordered the death of the other one. The preacher called Tolby. Is it not so?"

"What makes you think that?"

"You do me a disservice, *mi jefe.* I am more than a simple *asesino.* I am a man of experience."

"Perhaps. But it is the assassin I pay. And I do not pay him to nose into my affairs. Is that clear?"

Vega realized he'd gone too far. He spread his hands in an elaborate gesture of deference. "Pardon my inquisitive nature, *mi jefe.* It was curiosity, nothing more."

Donaghue nodded. "Just keep your mind on business. Your business."

"Have no fear. I will make this Jacoby my personal business."

"I want it attended to quickly."

"Where do you wish him killed?"

"Outside town, if possible. But however it's done, it has to be done before next Sunday. We can't have him taking the pulpit again."

"Should it be made to appear a robbery, like the last one?"

"If time permits. Just don't let it drag on till the end of the week."

"Of course. And our arrangement will be as usual?"

"It will," Donaghue confirmed. "A hundred dollars for you and Cardenas. Payable when the job's finished."

"Consider him dead, *mi jefe.*"

"Don't disappoint me."

"Have I ever?"

Vega grinned and tossed off his tequila. Donaghue stared at him a moment, on the verge of saying something more. Then, with a heavy sigh, he hitched back his chair. He walked from the cantina into the dappled moonlight. His face was still troubled.

Early Tuesday morning, Braddock rode out of town. He turned the walleyed dun west and proceeded toward the mountains. Ostensibly he was off on his first tour of the backcountry circuit. His true destination was Cimarron Canyon.

Since church services on Sunday, he'd devoted considerable thought to his next move. The lapse of two days had provided sufficient time for word of his sermon to reach Santa Fe. By now a message would have been passed back in the opposite direction. Whether it had gone directly to Florencio Donaghue was open to conjecture. But there was every reason to believe that someone in Cimarron had been ordered to act. And it would be the same someone who had silenced Reverend John Tolby.

Braddock understood the mentality of killers. He also possessed a strong insight into the minds of those who ordered the killing done. His years as a manhunter had given him an uncanny sixth sense for the way they thought and how they would react when provoked. To a degree, he was able to put himself in their boots and view the situation from their perspective. While it was a warped perspective, it nonetheless lent a certain predictability to those who issued the orders. Violence, from their standpoint, was merely an instrument. A tool of business.

The Santa Fe Ring had embarked on a campaign of intimidation. The ultimate goal was to force the ranchers and homesteaders to abandon their landholdings. To that end, the leaders of the Cimarron Coalition were to be used as object lessons. Those who spoke out in open forum—such as Orville McMain and Reverend Tolby—were slated for death. Their untimely demise would serve notice that no one, whether a prominent newspaperman or a man of God, was immune to harm. And the ring, having killed once, would have no choice but to kill again. Otherwise their campaign of intimidation would simply fizzle out to nothing.

So Braddock felt confident he was now a marked man. Within the town limits he was relatively safe. Bloodshed on the streets of Cimarron was clearly a complication the ring wanted to avoid. Along with Buck Colter's shotgun, that was the major factor in McMain's continued good health. But outside Cimarron it was open season on coalition leaders. A murder in the high country could be rigged to look like robbery, even though the true motive was apparent to everyone. Hired killers were generally men of limited imagination, and Braddock had little doubt the same ploy would be used again. As he rode west, some inner conviction told him that Cimarron Canyon was where it would happen. Someone waited there to silence Reverend Titus Jacoby.

The noonday sun was at its zenith when Braddock entered Cimarron Canyon. In the west the snowcapped peaks of the Sangre de Cristo range loomed against an azure sky. According to his cover story, the first stop on his backcountry circuit would be Elizabethtown. The mining camp, located high in the mountains, was New Mexico's major gold producer. By all accounts, the camp was a scene of depravity and immorality, populated largely by whores and saloonkeepers. Quite apart from being a den of iniquity, Elizabethtown was also an outpost of opposition to the Santa Fe Ring. It seemed a logical forum for a preacher-turned-crusader.

Yet, as he moved deeper into Cimarron Canyon, Braddock thought the odds of reaching Elizabethtown were somewhere between slim and none. The canyon zigzagged through the heart of the mountains, with walls sweeping upward in craggy palisades. Here in the high country the landscape was forested with piñon pines and junipers, and rocky outcrops thrust skyward as the trail steadily steepened. Hummingbirds and goldfinches darted among the trees, and lazy dragonflies hovered over a swift-running stream that cut through the gorge. Overhead a sparrow hawk floated past on outspread wings, a dead rattler gripped in its talons. The bird settled on a boulder and cocked its head with a fierce glare at the horse and rider. Then, with lordly hauteur, it began feeding on the snake.

Braddock's nerves were strung tight. His every sense was alerted and his eyes were in constant motion. The clatter of the dun's hoofbeats echoed off the canyon walls, and the sound aggravated his feeling of being exposed and vulnerable to attack. The terrain was made to order for bushwhackers, and every switchback along the snaky trail was a natural ambush site. Yet, beneath the relentless tension, some inward composure steeled him to the task ahead. He'd set himself up as the lure with the express purpose of capturing a murderer. And he somehow knew today wasn't his day to die.

An hour or so later, as Braddock rounded a bend on a sharp upgrade, something caught his eye—a glint of sunlight on metal from a jagged outcrop directly in front of him. All thought suspended, he reacted on sheer reflex and threw himself sideways out of the saddle. A slug whistled past his ear, and in the same instant he heard the simultaneous crack of two rifle shots. He rolled toward a pile of boulders, pulling the Colt as he slammed up against the canyon wall. Spooked by the gunfire, the dun bolted and whirled away downstream.

Tossing his hat aside, Braddock thumbed the hammer on the Colt and inched his head around a boulder. Some thirty yards distant, twin puffs of smoke billowed from an outcrop near the top of the gorge. One slug pocked the dirt and the other whanged off the boulder, showering him with rocky shards. He saw two men, partially hidden behind the outcrop, frantically working the levers on their saddle guns. He picked the man on the left and drew a fine bead, laying the front sight shoulder-high. His finger touched the trigger and the Colt roared.

The man was jerked upright by the impact of the slug. He dropped his rifle and lurched sideways, arms windmilling like a scarecrow in a high wind. Then he lost his balance, teetering a moment on the edge of the outcrop, and tumbled into space. He bounced off the canyon wall and cartwheeled down the sheer slope. He landed headfirst and pitched forward on his back, the heels of his boots in the stream. He lay perfectly still.

A bullet plucked the sleeve of Braddock's coat, and he turned his attention to the second man. He thumbed the hammer and feathered the trigger, no more than a heartbeat between shots. He got off three rounds in the time it took the bushwhacker to jack a fresh cartridge into his saddle gun. The first and second shots, within a handspan of one another, kicked flinty sparks in the man's face. The third shot whumped into the stock of the rifle and blew it to splinters. The man yelped and let go of the rifle as though he'd taken hold of a hot poker. Then, seemingly galvanized, he took off in a wild scramble toward the top of the gorge. Braddock's last shot nicked his pants leg a moment before he vanished over the rim of the wall.

Stillness descended on the canyon. Nothing moved and the silence was tomblike, broken only by the gurgle of the stream. Braddock shucked empties out of the Colt and rapidly reloaded. All told, perhaps ten or twelve seconds had elapsed between the time he fired the last shot and the instant he stuffed the fifth shell into the cylinder. But as he snapped the loading gate shut, he realized there was no longer any need to hurry. From somewhere above, he heard the faint sound of hoofbeats and then nothing. The bushwhacker apparently knew the mountains and was by now long gone over some remote back trail. Any thought of pursuit was futile.

Braddock stood and moved around the boulders. Warily, the pistol cocked, he approached the fallen man. A single glance told the story, and he lowered the hammer with a sharp curse. His shot had gone where he'd aimed, shattering the man's collarbone. But the fall from the outcrop had undone his handiwork. The man's neck was broken, and his eyes stared sightlessly into the void of afterdeath. Instead of a witness, there was only a corpse. A crooked-necked dead man who would tell no tales.

For a moment Braddock examined the body with clinical interest. The man was Mexican, somewhere in his early thirties, with an old knife scar along his right jawbone. He would be easily identified, and his name might be linked to other names. Yet he was stone-cold, and by whatever name he was known, he would reveal nothing about the one who had escaped. Braddock jammed the Colt into its holster and turned away.

He walked off in search of the walleyed dun.

CHAPTER EIGHT

Sheriff Floyd Mather tilted back in his chair. He was a large man, with stern features and a sweeping handlebar mustache. His eyes were hard and his mouth was set in a dour expression. He stared across the desk at Braddock.

"Let's go through it again."

"Don't you believe me, Sheriff?"

"What I believe don't mean a hill of beans. I'm paid to get the facts, and we're gonna stick with it till I'm satisfied with your story."

"A commendable point of view."

"You tryin' to get smart?"

"Perish the thought!"

Braddock was walking a tightrope. Shortly before dusk, he'd ridden into Cimarron, the body draped across the back of his horse. By the time he halted outside the courthouse, word had spread along the street, and a large crowd quickly gathered. Several people identified the dead man as Manuel Cardenas, a familiar figure among the town's Mexican population. The sheriff was summoned, and he had immediately ordered the crowd to disperse. After inspecting the body, he waited until the local undertaker arrived. Then he'd marched Braddock into the courthouse.

The sheriff's attitude was one of ill-disguised skepticism. In his office, he had proceeded to interrogate Braddock at some length. The answers he got merely raised more questions in his mind. A look of disgruntled suspicion slowly settled over his features. For his part, Braddock hoped to learn more than he revealed. He was an old hand at the art of interrogation: he thought it quite possible the sheriff could be tricked into disclosing vital information. Yet his position was tenuous, for any slip-up would immediately destroy his cover story. And now, pinned by the sheriff's harsh stare, he warned himself to proceed with caution. A preacher who appeared too slick would only arouse further suspicion.

"All right," Mather demanded. "You say you were headed for the mining camps?"

"That's correct."

"What was your rush?" Mather persisted. "You'd barely took over as pastor."

"Where sin flourishes," Braddock said breezily, "there's not a moment to spare. I take my ministry where it's needed most—and miners are notorious sinners."

"Do tell?" Mather gave him the fish-eye. "So you're ridin' along and suddenly you get jumped out of the clear blue?"

"Exactly," Braddock affirmed. "No warning whatever."

"Who fired first?"

"Why, my assailants!" Braddock stared back at him with round, guileless eyes. "It's a miracle I wasn't killed outright."

"Some miracle," Mather grunted. "You've got two men takin' potshots at you, and you kill one and drive the other off. How'd you manage that?"

"Strictly the Lord's doing," Braddock replied innocently. "He stood beside me in my moment of peril."

"Sounds more like fast and fancy shootin' to me."

"On the contrary," Braddock corrected him. "The dead

man died from a broken neck. I was fortunate merely to wound him."

"What'd you wound him with?"

"I beg your pardon?"

"You weren't throwin' rocks, were you?"

"No, of course not."

"Then lemme see your gun."

Braddock sensed his troubles were about to multiply. He pulled the Colt from inside his jacket and handed it across the desk. The Peacemaker was chambered for .45 caliber, with standard sights and a 4 ¾-inch barrel. The finish was lustrous indigo blue and the grips were gutta-percha, custom-made, and deep brown in color. Apart from its distinctive appearance, the guts of the gun had been completely overhauled by Daniel Cameron. The sear had been honed, resulting in a trigger pull of scarcely three pounds, and a specially tempered mainspring had been installed. The end product was a weapon of incomparable artistry and silky-smooth action.

Floyd Mather's gaze narrowed. He hefted the gun, critically judging its balance. Then he unloaded it, dumping the shells on his desk, and closed the loading gate. He studied one of the blunt-nosed shells a moment, his brow wrinkled in a puzzled frown. At last he earred the Colt's hammer to full cock and gingerly touched the trigger. The hammer dropped with a crisp, metallic snap. He let out a low whistle under his breath.

"Judas priest," he said softly. "A hair trigger, hand-loaded shells, and a cross-draw holster. When you go heeled, you don't mess around, do you?"

"I'm pleased you approve."

"It's a lotta gun." Mather carefully laid the Colt on the desk top. "Why would a preacher carry a slick article like that?"

"Come now, Sheriff." Braddock kept his tone light. "Under the circumstances, it seems a normal precaution."

"What circumstances?"

"For one thing, my predecessor was murdered."

"He was killed by robbers. That's not exactly the same thing as murder."

"Would you characterize today's incident as the work of bandits?"

"Has all the earmarks." Mather looked him straight in the eye. "Why, you figure it was something else?"

"Oh, yes indeed!" Braddock said briskly. "I would say it fairly reeks of assassination."

"Why the blue-billy hell would anybody want to assassinate a preacher?"

"For the same reason Reverend Tolby was murdered."

"And what was that?"

"Are we playing cat and mouse, Sheriff?"

"I'm the one askin' the questions here!"

"Very well." Braddock spread his hands in a bland gesture. "Reverend Tolby was murdered because he publicly denounced the Santa Fe Ring."

"Bullfeathers!" Mather growled. "You've been listening to Orville McMain and his pipe dreams. There's no such thing as the Santa Fe Ring and never was!"

"How curious." Braddock deliberately goaded him. "Some people say this entire courthouse is controlled by the ring."

Mather flushed. "Are you accusing me of political shenanigans?"

"Are you denying it, Sheriff?"

"Goddammit!" Mather rasped. "I asked you a question. Are you accusing me or not?"

"If the shoes fits," Braddock said with a shrug, "wear it."

"Cute, aren't you?" Mather said with a flare of annoyance. "I suppose McMain's the one that told you all this hogwash?"

"Please, no names." Braddock paused with a smug grin. "Let us say the allegation has widespread currency throughout the community."

"That a fact?" Mather said gruffly. "Well, if you're so

smart, who's behind this so-called Santa Fe Ring? Suppose you tell me that."

Braddock took a chance. "I do keep hearing one name—Warren Mitchell."

Mather unwittingly blinked. His features screwed up in a tight grimace and his eyes went cold. "Who the hell are you anyway?"

"A servant of Christ," Braddock said humbly. "I spread the gospel and offer salvation to those who have strayed from the fold."

"You don't act like no preacher I ever met."

"Perhaps not." A smile shadowed Braddock's lips. "And all the more reason to look to your own salvation."

"That sounds the least bit like a threat."

"No," Braddock said without inflection. "It's more on the order of a prophecy."

"What's that supposed to mean?"

"A smart man abandons ship before it sinks."

"Get lost," Mather rumbled. "Take your fancy gun and don't let the door hit you in the ass."

Braddock retrieved the Colt and loaded it without a word. Then he holstered it and walked to the door. Abruptly, as though struck by an afterthought, he turned back.

"Oh, by the way," he asked casually, "the dead man, Manuel Cardenas, who was he?"

"Nobody special," Mather noted. "Handyman, jack-of-all-trades. He did odd jobs around town."

"Odd jobs indeed," Braddock commented wryly. "Who were his associates or friends?"

"Beats me."

"Does it really?"

"You callin' me a liar?"

"If the shoe fits . . ."

Braddock laughed and stepped through the door. On his way out of the courthouse, he mentally patted himself on the back. Floyd Mather had by no means told him all he wanted to know. But actions spoke louder than words, and for a moment the sheriff had been visibly unnerved. A telltale blink was brought on by the mention of a name.

Warren Mitchell.

A few minutes later Braddock strolled into the newspaper office. The pressmen were gone for the day and McMain was scribbling at his desk. Colter was stationed at his usual spot by the front counter.

"Howdy, parson."

"Good evening, Buck."

Colter smiled. "Hear you had a busy day."

"The Lord's work is never done."

Braddock moved around the counter and walked toward the rear of the room. McMain looked up and suddenly dropped his pen. His features were etched with concern.

"What happened?" he inquired nervously. "By the time I got to the courthouse, you were already inside with the sheriff. Were you really ambushed? How many were there?"

"All in good time," Braddock said as he got himself seated. "I'll tell you all about it later. But right now I need some information."

"Yes, of course," McMain agreed. "How can I help?"

"I got waylaid by two men. One of them got away and I sort of half-ass killed the other one. His name was Manuel Cardenas."

"I know," McMain said in a shaky voice. "It's all over town. People are talking about a preacher who carries a gun, and they're asking questions. I hope you have a good story in mind."

Braddock brushed aside the objection. "We'll worry about that later. What can you tell me about Cardenas?"

"Nothing." McMain gave him a blank look. "Oh, I've seen him around town. But Mexicans tend to stick to themselves. I've never so much as spoken to him."

"Who would know him?" Braddock insisted. "Someone we could trust to keep quiet?"

"I don't understand your urgency."

"Just humor me and put your thinking cap on."

"Well," McMain said, considering for a moment, "there's Bud Grant, the town marshal. He'd probably know more than anyone else."

"Would he keep his mouth shut?"

"I believe so," McMain said hesitantly. "In fact, I'm certain he would. Bud's always been neutral and never took sides, but he's a decent man. I respect him."

"All right." Braddock nodded. "Why don't you send Colter to fetch him? A town jail isn't much on privacy."

While they waited, Braddock recounted the day's events. He briefly described the shootout in Cimarron Canyon and related how Cardenas had died. Then he outlined the interrogation by Sheriff Mather, touching only on the highlights. But he declined to mention anything about Warren Mitchell or the sheriff's startled reaction. Some inner voice told him to stop short of the full truth.

Ten minutes later Colter walked through the door with Bud Grant. The marshal was a beefy man, with broad shoulders and the gnarled hands of someone accustomed to physical labor. He looked as though he would be more at home behind a plow than wearing a star. Colter resumed his post up front and Grant lumbered on back to the desk. After a round of handshakes, the men seated themselves.

McMain took an oblique approach. "Bud, we'd like your help on a certain matter. I've assured Reverend Jacoby"—his gaze shifted briefly to Braddock—"that you're no loose talker. So anything said here would be off the record and confidential."

"Sounds serious." Grant's features creased with worry. "I've always done my best not to take sides. I wouldn't want anybody to get the wrong idea."

"And no one will," Braddock cut in earnestly. "We wouldn't compromise your position, Marshal. All we want to do is ask a question."

The worry lines on Grant's forehead deepened. "Has it got to do with you being drygulched today?"

"You've already heard about that?"

"Cimarron's a small town, Reverend."

"Then you're probably aware I was jumped by two men. One of them was Manuel Cardenas."

"Are you fixin' to ask me something about Cardenas?"

"Yes." Braddock's eyes gave away nothing. "I understand you know most of the Mexicans in town."

"That'd be a fair statement."

"How familiar were you with Cardenas?"

"No more'n most," Grant said frankly. "He loafed a little and he worked a little. Sometimes he'd get likkered up and I'd have to put him in the cooler overnight. Not what you'd call a real troublemaker."

"No record of robbery or violence?"

"Nope." Grant met his gaze with an amused expression. "Course that don't include a few personal disagreements. Mexicans tend to settle things like that with knives. I generally overlook it, unless there's a killin'."

"Has he ever killed anyone?"

"Not so far as I know."

"Was there anyone in particular he chummed around with?"

Grant massaged his jaw. "I can't say as there was. Leastways, not outside of family."

"Are you talking about immediate family?"

"Yeah, sort of," Grant allowed. "He didn't have any brothers; just a passel of sisters. But he was pretty thick with one of his cousins, Cruz Vega."

Braddock swapped glances with McMain. "One last question, Marshal. Some folks believe Cruz Vega was behind the murder of Reverend Tolby. Have you heard anything that would link Cardenas to the killing?"

"Not a peep."

"There's speculation," Braddock ventured, "that Vega handles the dirty work for Florencio Donaghue. Would you have any information to that effect?"

"Well, I'll tell you, parson." Grant climbed to his feet.

"You've just crossed the line from fact to gossip. I try to steer clear of such talk."

"Anything else you would talk about, Marshal?"

"Nothin' I'd swear to."

The conversation ended on a cordial note. Bud Grant shook hands and walked from the newspaper office. McMain and Braddock watched in silence until he passed through the front door. Then McMain let out a gusty sigh.

"I guess we know who the second bushwhacker was."

"Knowing it and proving it," Braddock pointed out, "aren't one and the same. I couldn't place Vega at Cimarron Canyon today. Things were happening a little too fast for me to stop and take a look at his face."

"But it's obvious!" McMain protested. "Vega and Cardenas were there on Donaghue's orders. Who else would have sent them?"

"You ask tough questions, Orville."

"There's one way to find out."

"How?"

"Take Vega prisoner," McMain said sternly. "Threaten to hang him and he'll confess fast enough."

"What if he doesn't?"

"Then hang him!" McMain grated. "At least we'll have gotten Tolby's murderer."

"No dice." Braddock shook his head firmly. "For one thing, I don't deal in lynch law. For another, we're liable to spook Donaghue and force him to run. I want him handy when the right time comes."

"The right time for what?"

"When we need a songbird to whistle a tune on the ring."

"Are you saying we just wait—do nothing?"

"You wait," Braddock said, getting up. "I think I'll take myself a trip."

"Where to?"

"Santa Fe."

"Nonsense!" McMain grouched. "You won't learn anything in Santa Fe. It's *their* town!"

"Nothing ventured, nothing gained."

McMain rose as Braddock turned away. "I tell you it's madness!"

"Hold down the fort, Orville."

"But," McMain sputtered, "when will you return?"

"Look for me when you see me."

Braddock walked toward the front of the office. As he rounded the counter, Colter regarded him with an odd, steadfast look. Their eyes locked in a moment of silent assessment. Then the younger man cracked a smile.

"Off to convert some more sinners, parson?"

"Yea, verily, I give light to them that sit in darkness."

"Funny how they end up with powder burns too."

"God moves in a mysterious way, His wonders to perform."

"You performed a puredee wonder on Cardenas!"

Braddock let the remark pass. He grinned and waved and moved through the door. Colter clearly wasn't fooled by his masquerade or his glib way with Scripture. He reminded himself that he was already overdue for a talk with the young half-breed. But tonight his priorities were elsewhere, and he hurried off in the direction of the hotel. His thoughts turned immediately to Santa Fe.

And Warren Mitchell.

Isaac Coleman rode into town the following morning. His features were set in a tight scowl as he reined up before the newspaper. He dismounted and left his horse hitched out front.

Entering the newspaper, he greeted Colter with a dour nod. The stormy look on his face discouraged any attempt at conversation. So Colter merely watched as he marched toward the rear of the office. From the back of the shop, the pressmen barely glanced around.

Orville McMain braced himself. One look at Coleman's expression told him the reason behind the visit. He briefly wondered whether he was capable of carrying the charade any further. Then, remembering his promise to Braddock, he decided there was no choice in the matter. It was not yet time to reveal the detective's true identity.

"Good morning, Isaac."

"Mornin'."

"What brings you to town?"

"Our new parson."

Coleman took a chair. He tipped his hat to the back of his head and stared across the desk. McMain tried to look innocent.

"I see you've heard."

"Damn right I've heard! News like that travels faster'n scat."

"An unfortunate incident. But very much as you and Clay predicted. The reverend should have heeded your warning."

"Quit dancin' me around, Orville."

"I beg your pardon?"

Coleman jabbed the air with a finger. "You know goddamn well I'm not talkin' about them taking a shot at Jacoby. I wanna hear about him."

"Isaac, please." McMain darted a look toward the pressroom. "I suggest you lower your voice."

"The hell with 'em. You just gimme some answers—now!"

"What is it you want to know?"

"For openers, how come a preacher packs a gun?"

"Wouldn't you?" McMain gave him a conspiratorial smile. "Under the circumstances?"

"We're not discussin' me. We're talkin' about a minister."

"Are you saying a man of God forfeits the right to self-defense? No, Isaac, I think not."

"You're twistin' my words."

"Perhaps I didn't understand the question."

"All right," Coleman said testily. "I'll spell it out for you. Where'd a preacher get so good with a gun? Way I heard it, he did some mighty fancy shootin'."

McMain shrugged. "I suppose it was just one of those

things. Reverend Jacoby told me it was providential, a matter of luck."

"Bullshit!" Coleman snorted. "Takes more'n luck to walk away from that. The bastards had him cold."

"Maybe God was on his side after all. Stranger things have happened."

"And I suppose it didn't bother him the least bit, lettin' daylight through Cardenas. What happened to 'Thou shalt not kill'?"

"Are you condemning Reverend Jacoby for protecting himself?"

"Nope," Coleman said, wagging his head. "I'm just sayin' there's something funny here. None of it makes any sense."

"Aren't you being overly skeptical? After all, the Bible doesn't forbid any man—even a minister—the right to preserve his life."

Coleman pondered a moment. "What the hell was he doing out at Cimarron Canyon anyway?"

"As I gather it, he was on his way to Elizabethtown. He's a circuit rider as well as our parson, you know."

"Still goddamn curious." Coleman paused, staring at him intently. "You'd almost think he dared 'em to bushwhack him. Hell, he knew that's where they killed Tolby."

McMain willed himself to remain calm. A film of sweat popped out on his forehead and his mouth tasted dry. He forced a rueful smile. "You're imagining things, Isaac. Reverend Jacoby just happens to be a very determined man. He won't allow anyone to interfere with his mission."

Coleman hitched back his chair. He stood, tugging down his hat, silent a moment. Then he looked at McMain.

"Maybe I'll walk down to the hotel. I'd like to hear that story from the reverend himself."

"You're too late. I told you he's a determined man."

"What d'you mean?"

"I mean he won't be stopped. He rode out to complete the circuit. He plans to spread the word of God, no matter the risk to himself."

Coleman slowly shook his head. "You reckon he's a fool, Orville?"

"You've met him. You tell me."

"Looks to me like he wants people to think he's a fool. You know what I think?"

"What?"

"I think he's a goddamn liar."

"What's there to lie about?"

"I dunno. But I'm sure as hell gonna ask him when he gets back."

"Well, he won't return for a week or so. A backcountry circuit does take time."

"I can wait, Orville."

Coleman hesitated, as though about to say something more. Then he gave McMain an odd smile and walked away. Up front, he swapped nods with Colter and went through the door. A moment later he rode north out of town.

Orville McMain appeared shaken. He knew he'd been granted a short reprieve and nothing more. Sometime soon the truth would come out. And he dreaded that day.

Above all things, Isaac Coleman detested a liar.

CHAPTER NINE

Santa Fe was located on the banks of a stream that flowed southwesterly from the Sangre de Cristos. Its altitude was above seven thousand feet and the town itself was surrounded by several mountain ranges. The railway entered the valley from the southeast, through Glorieta Pass.

Braddock stepped off the train two days following the assassination attempt. Before departing Cimarron, he had arranged for McMain to publish a story in the *Beacon*. The Reverend Titus Jacoby, undaunted by his brush with death, was off on another tour of the circuit. With his absence explained, he'd then mounted the dun and ridden directly to Raton. There he had laid the good preacher to rest and spent the afternoon putting together another disguise. Late yesterday evening he had boarded the overnight train for Santa Fe.

Today, crossing the depot platform, Braddock looked anything but a preacher. He was attired in a broadcloth coat and striped trousers, with a flashy brocaded vest and a high-crowned Stetson. A pearl stickpin decorated his tie, and the pocket watch nestled in his vest was attached to a heavy gold chain. The muttonchop whiskers were gone, and his upper lip was now covered by a luxuriant soup-strainer of a mustache. His appearance was that of a wealthy high roller, and he had adopted the lexicon peculiar to Texans. His cover name was Elmer Boyd.

From the train station, Braddock walked uptown to the plaza. A broad square dominated by a cathedral and the governor's palace, the plaza was the town's center of activity. Built on commerce and politics, the territorial capital was the major trade center between Mexico and the United States. Formerly the terminus for the Santa Fe Trail, it was now served by railroad instead of wagon caravans. Trade goods were off-loaded there and stored for transshipment to all points of the compass. The plaza was crowded with shops and businesses and several open-air markets. The architecture was predominantly adobe, and the scene had a quaint atmosphere. For all its growth, Santa Fe still retained much of its native charm.

Approaching the plaza, Braddock was struck by a sharp sense of déjà vu. Not quite two years ago he had crossed the same plaza on his way to the territorial prison. There he had interrogated William Bonney—alias Billy the Kid—with regard to a murder and a gang of cattle rustlers. On that same day, he had happened across a secret meeting between Judge Owen Hough and Warren Mitchell. Only later had he come to suspect a connection between Mitchell and the Santa Fe Ring. The object of his investigation had proved to be Owen Hough, the political kingpin of Lincoln County. After killing Hough, he'd had no reason to delve further into the machinations of the ring. Nor had he ever met Warren Mitchell face-to-face. Today he planned to remedy that oversight.

One thought led to another as he walked toward the Capitol Hotel. He was reminded that he'd learned a vital lesson while investigating Judge Hough. At the time, he was still operating openly, using his own name. He'd made no great effort to conceal his movements or his whereabouts during the course of his stay in Lincoln County. Nor had he kept back any secrets from those allied with him in the investigation. The upshot was an attempt on his own life and the murder of several innocent people. One of those killed was a girl, and he'd never quite forgiven himself for her death. Yet he had profited by the mistake. Thereafter he operated on the principle that it was wiser not to let the left hand know what the right hand was doing. So he'd told McMain where he was headed, but nothing of what he planned. And not a word about the Texan named Elmer Boyd.

Braddock engaged a suite at the hotel. His manner was loud and vulgar, the perfect embodiment of a swaggering Texican. He overtipped the bellboy and went out of his way to act the part of a big spender. After lunch in the hotel dining room, where he pinched the waitress's fanny, he felt confident he would be remembered. Anyone inquiring about Elmer Boyd would be told of a brassy wild man who threw money to the winds. The tale would further bolster his cover story, for it contained a dash of the bizarre. He was just outrageous enough to be the genuine article.

Shortly after noon hour, Braddock crossed the plaza to the Mercantile National Bank. A long cigar jutted from his mouth, and he trailed a cloud of smoke as he entered a stairwell to the second floor. On the upper landing, several offices were ranged along a central corridor. He walked to the end of the passageway, where a suite of offices occupied one corner of the building. The top half of the door was frosted glass and the name of the firm was inscribed in gilt letters.

THE SANTA FE LAND & DEVELOPMENT CO.
WARREN F. MITCHELL
PRESIDENT

Braddock barged through the door like a conquering hero. A receptionist looked up from her desk with a polite smile. After introducing himself, Braddock demanded an interview with the head of the firm. His bluff air of assurance left her disconcerted, and she hurried off to an inner office.

Several moments passed, then the door opened and the receptionist reappeared. She beckoned him inside.

"Please come this way, Mr. Boyd."

"Thank you kindly, little lady."

Warren Mitchell rose to greet him as he entered. Braddock had the immediate impression of someone who was accustomed to having his own way and who was very seldom thwarted. Mitchell was tall and lean, quite distinguished-looking in a cutaway coat and a stiff wing collar covered by a black cravat. His gray mustache was neatly trimmed and waxed, and the overall effect was of confidence mixed with personal magnetism. He extended his hand in a firm grasp.

"Won't you have a seat, Mr. Boyd?"

"Call me Elmer. Everybody does!"

The office was furnished in dark walnut and lush chocolate leather. Braddock took a wing-backed chair, and Mitchell resumed his seat behind a massive desk. He gave Braddock's outfit a swift once-over, his appraisal cool and deliberate. A brief interval elapsed before he spoke.

"Well, now," he said pleasantly, "what can I do for you— Elmer?"

Braddock chortled, "Nobody does nothin' for nobody. Leastways not unless one hand washes the other. You follow my drift?"

"Vaguely." Mitchell gave him a blank stare. "Would you care to elaborate?"

"Glad to," Braddock said, munching on his cigar. "I came all the way from Fort Worth to offer you a proposition. You might say it's an everybody-wins proposition."

"I see," Mitchell said tentatively. "What did you have in mind, specifically?"

"The word around Texas," Braddock said with an oily grin, "is that you've got the Midas touch. I hear you make lots of money for your investors—tons of the stuff."

A fleeting look of puzzlement crossed Mitchell's face, then his expression became flat and guarded. "By investors, who do you mean?"

"Well, there was that deal you worked with the railroad. An acre for them and an acre for you and your crowd. Mighty slick little operation. And mighty profitable too."

Braddock had done his homework. Through a Colorado railroad baron, who owed him a favor, he had learned the details of the Santa Fe line's expansion into New Mexico. Warren Mitchell had been instrumental in obtaining the necessary right-of-way, part of which passed through Colfax County. Later it was whispered that, in return, the railroad had deeded to the ring a sizable portion of the federal land grant. Whatever the truth, the ultimate goal became apparent when the Santa Fe began laying track toward Los Angeles. Quite soon it would be the only railroad in the country with line extending from Chicago to the West Coast.

"Anyone else?" Mitchell asked. "Or are you just repeating rumors?"

"Don't believe me, huh?" Braddock's smile broadened. "How about that consortium you put together? The one with all them English and Dutch high rollers. I understand you made a hell of a killing!"

Mitchell's stare betrayed nothing. "You seem very well informed."

"I've got my sources." Braddock admired the tip of his cigar. "Course, what's important is what we can do for each other. I think you big financiers call it the quid pro quo."

"Hmmm." Mitchell considered a moment, then nodded. "I presume that brings us to your proposition."

"Yessir, it does!" Braddock said with cheery vigor. "You see, I made myself a right nice fortune in the cow business. But it's gotten to seem sorta boring, too easy. I'm ready to try my hand in a no-limit game."

"For the sake of argument," Mitchell replied, returning his gaze steadily, "let us say I was receptive to outside investors. What type of return would you expect on your money?"

"A fifty-fifty split on the profits."

"Aren't your terms overly generous?"

"A mite." Braddock blew a plume of smoke into the air. "But don't think you're dealin' with some addle-brained shit-kicker from Texas. I want to buy into your game and I'm willin' to make it worth your while. I'll settle for a divvy down the middle."

"Very astute," Mitchell said reasonably. "What size investment are we talking about?"

"Three million," Braddock said with a gravelly chuckle. "In case you think you heard wrong, that's a three with six big zeroes behind it."

A pinpoint of greed surfaced in Mitchell's eyes. "You talk extremely tempting figures, Elmer."

"I do more'n talk," Braddock told him jovially. "You show me a deal I like and I'll write you a check for three million simoleons. I come to play and I'm willin' to pony up for a piece of the action."

"I do believe you are." Mitchell regarded him thoughtfully. "I wonder if you'd care to join me for dinner tonight?"

"Why, I'd be downright honored, Mr. Mitchell."

"And, please," Mitchell said affably, "do call me Warren."

Braddock's grin was so wide it was almost a laugh. "Warren, I think we're gonna get along like a couple of turds in a teacup."

Mitchell winced. "I've no doubt of it, Elmer. None whatever."

After setting a time, Mitchell agreed to call for him at the hotel that evening. Braddock left the office in a jubilant mood, immensely pleased with himself. He'd salted the bait and it had proved an irresistible lure.

All that remained was to spring the trap.

Clay Allison dismounted in front of the newspaper. He looped the reins around the hitch rack, then stepped onto the boardwalk. Through the door he caught Colter's eye. He jerked his head for the other to come outside.

Colter hesitated a moment. After glancing toward the rear of the office, he leaned the shotgun in a corner. His gaze was neutral as he moved outside and crossed to the hitch rack. He nodded to Allison.

"What's up?"

"Want to ask you something."

"Yeah?"

"What d'you think of the new preacher, Jacoby?"

Colter pulled out some makings. He methodically built himself a smoke, saying nothing. At last he lit up and flicked the match into the street.

"I don't think about him too much. What makes you ask?"

"Isaac was here yesterday."

Colter exhaled slowly. "I saw him."

"Then you know he talked to McMain about the preacher."

"News to me. Isaac didn't say boo about nothin'. Same goes for McMain."

Allison gave him a sideways look. "How'd McMain act afterwards?"

"I don't get you."

"Well, you know. Did he act different? Do anything out of the ordinary?"

"Not so far as I saw. He went on back to work after Isaac left. Looked pretty ordinary to me."

"What about last night?"

"Same old routine. I saw him home and then went on to the hotel. Why all the questions?"

"Isaac thinks he lied."

Allison watched for a reaction. Even at the best of times, he found it difficult to be civil toward Colter. Something in the man's indifferent attitude rubbed him the wrong way. He was accustomed to a show of respect from hired hands.

Still, Coleman had warned him to go slow. Colter was not a man to be pushed or ordered about. Watching him now, Allison was nonetheless irked by his evasive manner. Some more direct method seemed in order.

"I get the feeling"—Colter paused, blew the ash off his cigarette—"you're askin' me if McMain lied."

"What if I was?"

"I'd tell you to go ask McMain. I don't even know what him and Isaac talked about."

"They talked about the preacher."

"Like I said, it's news to me."

Allison stared at him. "Lemme put it another way. What's your opinion of Jacoby?"

"I've got no opinion one way or the other."

"Why the hell not? You've been standin' around every time he comes to see McMain."

Colter smiled. "I try not to overhear other people's conversation. The less I know, the better I like it."

"All the same," Allison growled, "you're not deaf, dumb, and blind. You must've got some idea about him."

"Like what?"

"Well, for one thing, he's goddamn handy with a gun. 'Specially for a preacher."

"So?"

"So hasn't he ever said nothin' to you? Anything that'd give you a clue?"

"Nope. It's 'Hello, Buck,' and 'Howdy, parson.' We let it go at that."

"And you never eavesdropped on him and McMain? Just out of curiosity?"

"I reckon I ain't that curious."

"Goddamn peculiar, if you ask me. Only natural you'd wonder."

Colter took a long pull on his cigarette. He exhaled, eyes cold as glass. "You callin' me a liar?"

There was a moment of strained silence. Allison seemed to measure the other man with an appraising look. Then, for whatever reason, he let the remark pass.

"Nobody called you nothin'. But you could do me and Isaac a big favor."

"What's that?"

"Keep your ears open. We'd like to hear anything you hear."

"I'll let you know."

Allison started to question the cryptic comment. Then, on second thought, he decided to leave it there. He nodded, walking to his horse, and mounted. Without looking around, he rode out of town.

Colter grinned and turned back to the newspaper.

Warren Mitchell proved to be a genial host. He was urbane and witty, with a droll sense of humor. He was also a raconteur with a taste for the good life.

The meal that evening was meant to impress Braddock. Mitchell took him to Santa Fe's most exclusive restaurant, obviously a gathering spot for those of wealth and power. The maître d' greeted Mitchell effusively, escorting them to a reserved table. Several diners waved to Mitchell, and others stopped by the table to shake hands. Their attitude was at once friendly and servile, even though they were clearly men of substance themselves. There was a sense of nobles paying homage to a liege lord.

Fine cuisine was high on Mitchell's list of priorities. The dinner was a seven-course affair built around a superb trout almandine. From the wine cellar, Mitchell selected a delicate Chablis imported from the vineyards of France. Over dinner he pointed out various dignitaries seated around the room, mainly politicians and influential businessmen.

Then, with several glasses of wine under his belt, he related amusing anecdotes about their personal and professional lives. After the meal he ordered *aguardiente*, a fiery native brandy brewed by Franciscan monks. His stories about Santa Fe's elite soon took on a note of sardonic contempt.

Braddock was a rapt listener, suitably wide-eyed and attentive. Yet he slowly formed a new and disturbing impression of his host. He'd crossed paths with many of the West's most notable robber barons and political overlords. The experience had taught him a crucial lesson, one of his ironclad rules of conduct. A true overlord, a man secure in his own power, never stooped to petty criticism. Mitchell's anecdotes and catty stories were the stamp of an envious man, not a man who had ascended to the top rung of the ladder. But he was a man, nonetheless, who plainly commanded the respect of Santa Fe's upper class. All of which led Braddock to a conclusion too compelling to ignore. Some complex of deduction and gut instinct told him that Warren Mitchell was not the leader of the Santa Fe Ring. There was someone higher, a power behind the scenes. A czar who worked his will from the shadows.

The sudden realization brought Braddock up short. Then, from some dim corner of his mind, he recalled a lesson of a different sort. In conversation, a master bunco artist had once used an analogy to illustrate the art of fleecing a mark. He'd compared a con game to fishing for a wise old bass on the bottom of a lake. The idea was to dangle the bait until the bass was tempted to leave the safety of deep water. The next step was to jiggle the bait and pretend to withdraw it altogether. As the bait disappeared into shallow water, the bass would believe his meal was about to vanish for good. Finally, unable to resist the temptation, the bass would forsake the bottom for a quick strike. And presto! The bass was hooked and landed before he realized he'd outsmarted himself. A properly rigged confidence game operated on the same principle, and $3 million was very enticing bait. Braddock decided to try his luck in deeper water.

Mitchell avoided any mention of investments throughout the meal. Only when they were on their second glass of *aguardiente* did he broach the subject. He raised his brandy snifter in a toast.

"Here's to happy days," he said genially. "And a mutually profitable association."

"You damn betcha!" Braddock quaffed his brandy. "Course, I'm still waitin' to hear your deal. You got something against mixin' grub with business?"

"Not at all." Mitchell gave him a sly, conspiratorial look. "As a matter of fact, I've been considering several possibilities. The one that strikes me as most promising is Guadalupe County. I'm dickering right now on a land grant that covers almost ninety square miles. You could get in on the ground floor."

"Where's Guadalupe County?"

"Southeast of here, fifty or sixty miles."

"What makes this land grant worth buyin'?"

"Prime cattle country," Mitchell explained. "Watered by the Pecos River and perfect for leasing to some big rancher. Or we could split it into smaller parcels and sell it off."

"I dunno," Braddock said doubtfully. "I was lookin' to get out of the cow business. Guess I sorta had my mind set on something a little more civilized."

"How do you mean?"

"Well, for one thing, there's no railroad down that way. No towns to speak of either. It's just common, ordinary grassland."

"Hardly ordinary," Mitchell rejoined. "Cattlemen always need graze, and they're willing to pay top dollar. I visualize a quick turnover and enormous profits."

"Mebbe," Braddock allowed. "All the same, it don't set my mouth to waterin'."

"What would?"

"Like I said, something closer to civilization. Towns and people and a railroad. Something that's gonna grow."

"Elmer, you disappoint me. I thought you were a gambler."

"I am!"

"But you're asking to buy in on property that's already developed. The game doesn't work that way."

"And you're askin' me to buy a pig in a poke!"

"I beg your pardon?"

"Guadalupe County!" Braddock said hotly. "That land grant's likely got more holes than a sieve. You're liable to spend years proving it out in court."

"I assure you that won't happen. I've laid the groundwork with all the right people. The deal will go through without a snag, Elmer. You can take my word on it."

"Uh-huh," Braddock grunted. "So we're talkin' about connections. And where there's *right* people, there's a *right* man. Somebody that calls the tune."

"Your point escapes me."

"Well, looky here, Warren. I'm not questionin' your word, understand. But I'd just like to hear it straight from the horse's mouth. Suppose you set it up and lemme have a talk with the man himself."

"I'm afraid not," Mitchell informed him stiffly. "You'll have to rely on the assurances I've already given you."

"In that case"—Braddock tossed his napkin on the table—"why don't we shake hands and forget the whole thing? I'm plumb snake-bit when it comes to operatin' on blind faith."

Mitchell saw the three million vanishing before his eyes. There was a moment's calculation while he debated something within himself. Then he followed the bait into shallow water.

"All right," he said grudgingly. "I'll arrange a meeting."

"When?"

"In the next day or so."

"No money passes hands till I've met the *man*."

"Agreed."

"What's his name?"

"You'll have to wait for that, Elmer."

Braddock decided to push no further. He'd worked the con with finesse and time was on his side. He had played the gullible Texan with a fortune in cash, and the role insured that the meeting would actually take place. He counseled himself to patience, and raised his glass in a toast. His mouth split in a lopsided grin.

"Here's to you and me, Warren. And Guadalupe County!"

CHAPTER TEN

The next couple of days passed uneventfully. Warren Mitchell stalled, asking for time, and Braddock curbed his impatience. The only option was to walk away empty-handed.

Braddock nonetheless put the time to good use. He was reluctant to contact Frank Kirkland for fear of blowing his cover. But he spent several hours a day lounging about in saloons, playing the well-heeled Texan. He was quick to order a round of drinks, and the men he engaged in conversation never knew they'd been subjected to a subtle form of interrogation. He learned that the political climate in the capital was volatile, sometimes explosive. There was active, open opposition to the Santa Fe Ring.

The most vocal opposition was from the *New Mexican*, a small newspaper with limited circulation. The publisher, Max Flagg, used his editorials to blast the Republicans, currently the party in power. He branded everyone from the governor on down as tools of the ring, and his editorials fairly sizzled with righteous indignation. Yet his allegations were long on verbiage and short on substance. He wrote of cabals and conspiracies, but he offered nothing in the way of documentation. More than anything else, his newspaper appeared to be an organ for the opposition party. The Democrats were led by Francisco Chavez, a *jefe* within the Mexican community. He had the support of Flagg and the *New Mexican*, as well as the Anglo Democrats. Still, he was seldom quoted as saying anything of lasting significance. All of which was interesting, if not particularly enlightening. Braddock filed the names away for future reference.

On a personal note, he found Warren Mitchell a welcome diversion. In fact, their second evening together proved to be something of a revelation. Fashionable restaurants and the world of the social elite were Mitchell's natural habitat. Yet, for all his polished manner, there was a darker side to his nature. He was a womanizer, a connoisseur of the flesh, and he made no attempt to disguise it. Instead, he promptly introduced Braddock to Santa Fe's nightlife.

Though married, Mitchell seldom spent a night at home. He maintained a suite at the hotel, ostensibly for the purpose of entertaining business clients. Practically every evening he dined out and afterward strolled down to the sporting district. There he was a regular at the Tivoli Variety Theater, the town's swankiest dive. He had a fondness for roulette, and he generally spent an hour or so wagering modest bets. Then he retired to a table directly below the footlights and devoted the balance of the night to ogling showgirls. But even then, he was selective in his choice of company. He picked only the prettiest and the most voluptuous from the chorus line, and his invitations were never refused. He treated his guests to champagne and charmed them with his debonair manner. And he bedded them almost as a matter of routine.

Braddock thought this behavior revealed much about Mitchell's character. Here was a man of prominence and stature who took his pleasure with tawdry showgirls. A trait common to all libertines was that they were both self-destructive and not all that secure in their manhood. The fact that Mitchell found his sexual outlet on the wrong side of town indicated that his character was flawed in much the same way. There was, moreover, the element of moral bankruptcy. A pillar of the community by day, he became a randy satyr at night. All in all, it tagged him as a man of questionable scruples.

Still, Mitchell made no effort to hide his debauchery, and therein lay the problem. Braddock saw no immediate way to exploit the weakness. Nor would he have tried while awaiting a meeting with the leader of the Santa Fe Ring. Any overt move on his part would merely jeopardize the progress he'd made thus far. So he catalogued the information for some future time.

The wait ended late the third evening in Santa Fe. Braddock was seated with Mitchell at his usual table in the Tivoli. The curtain rang down on the final show, and Braddock assumed they would shortly be joined by a couple of girls. Quite unexpectedly, Mitchell paid the bill and suggested they take a walk. His manner was cryptic, and he offered nothing by way of an explanation. Outside the theater he turned uptown and led Braddock toward the plaza. Some minutes later they rounded a corner onto a side street and halted before a storefront office. A sign on the window was dimly visible in the glow of a nearby street lamp.

STEPHEN B. ELKTON
ATTORNEY AT LAW

Mitchell entered without knocking. The outer office was dark, but a shaft of light streamed from a door across the room. He closed and locked the street door and removed his hat. Then, nodding to Braddock, he led the way to the inner office. The interior was utilitarian by any standards, furnished with a plain oak desk and two wooden armchairs. The walls were covered with law books from floor to ceiling.

The man behind the desk was short and thick-set. Somewhere in his late forties, he had the girth of one who indulged himself in all the good life had to offer. He was clean-shaven, with round features and thin hair combed back over his head.

His eyes were deep-set and shrewd, and his smile was patently bogus. He rose as they entered the office.

"Elmer Boyd," Mitchell said as he motioned Braddock forward, "permit me to introduce Stephen Elkton."

"A pleasure, Mr. Boyd." Elkton pumped his arm warmly. "Warren has told me a great deal about you."

"You're one up on me," Braddock announced. "He hasn't said do-diddily about you."

Elkton laughed a fat man's laugh. "Warren does carry discretion to extremes. Won't you have a seat?"

Braddock doffed his Stetson and took one of the armchairs. Mitchell sat down beside him and Elkton lowered himself into a squeaky swivel chair behind the desk. There was an awkward moment of silence, then Elkton smiled.

"Warren tells me you're from Fort Worth."

"Thereabouts," Braddock said easily. "I do my bankin' in Forth Worth. My spread's southwest of there, down on the Brazos."

"Would I be familiar with your brand?"

Braddock was instantly alert. "You a cattleman?"

"No," Elkton said, a bit too quickly. "But from what Warren says, you've made quite a name for yourself."

"Circle B, that's my brand." Braddock regarded him with a level gaze. "Anybody that knows cows will tell you it's registered to Elmer Boyd. Now, lemme ask you one."

"By all means."

"You makin' small talk?" Braddock said bluntly. "Or are you questionin' my credentials?"

Elkton laughed indulgently. "We simply like to know who we're dealing with, Mr. Boyd. After all, we are discussing a very substantial investment."

"Only one trouble," Braddock said, a note of irritation in his tone. "You got the order of things all ass backwards. It's me puttin' up the three million, and that ain't exactly pocket change. So you've got to convince me—not the other way round!"

"A point well taken." Elkton smiled benignly. "I assume you're referring to Guadalupe County?"

"Betcher boots!" Braddock nodded soberly. "Warren claims there won't be no hitch with the land grant. He says we'll get valid title to ninety square miles."

"Quite true."

"To guarantee that"—Braddock's voice dropped—"you gotta have somebody real damn important in your hip pocket."

"True again."

"Who?"

Elkton favored him with a patronizing smile. "I hardly think that concerns you, Mr. Boyd. Nor could you reasonably expect me to be so—forthcoming."

"Wrong on all counts!" Braddock said brusquely. "You're asking me to bet without lookin' at the hole card. Nobody ever accused me of playin' dumb poker, Mr. Elkton."

"All I can say is that a court decision, based on a surveyor's recommendation, establishes valid title under the law. We have a survey and it coincides exactly with the original land grant. And we will—let me stress that again, Mr. Boyd—we *will* obtain a favorable court ruling."

"That a fact?" Braddock said skeptically. "You talkin' about a federal judge or what?"

"I've told you all you need to know, Mr. Boyd."

"Not by a damn sight!" Braddock croaked. "All that legal jabbering don't guarantee me nothin'."

"Then let me phrase it another way." Elkton smiled without warmth. "I've told you all I'm going to tell you. Some things must be taken on trust."

Braddock flipped a palm back and forth. "No offense, but why should I trust you? Warren tells me you're the he-wolf around these parts. So far, though, I haven't heard nothin' that'd make it a fact."

"I could pose the same question," Elkton replied succinctly. "Why should I trust you, Mr. Boyd? You're an absolute stranger."

"Hell's bells!" Braddock said with a baroque sweep of his arm. "Three million dollars buys a whole shitload of trust!"

Elkton gave him a frosty smile. "We haven't seen your money so far, Mr. Boyd."

"Don't worry," Braddock assured him earnestly. "I'm willin' to put my money where my mouth is and no two ways about it. But I'd sure like to hear something besides double-talk before I do."

"I regret there's nothing more I can say."

"Lemme ask you this," Braddock pressed him. "What's your part in Warren's land company?"

An indirection came into Elkton's eyes. "Suffice it to say I am an interested party."

"Yeah, but have you got any of your own money on the line?"

"You obviously have more questions than I have answers, Mr. Boyd. I suggest you use your own judgment as to whether or not it's a sound investment. Warren will be happy to accommodate you in any way possible."

Braddock knew he'd pushed it to the limit. Further questions would simply antagonize Elkton and accomplish nothing. Far better to leave the door open and play for a break. He looked from Elkton to Mitchell and back again. Then he slapped his knee and laughed.

"You would've made a hell of a horse trader, Mr. Elkton."

"I'll take that as a compliment, Mr. Boyd."

"Don't misunderstand me," Braddock said evenly. "I haven't bought into the game yet. I'll need a little time to study on it."

"Very well." Elkton stared at him like a stuffed owl. "I trust we can rely on your discretion. A word in the wrong ear might create problems for everyone."

"I get your drift," Braddock said with a waggish grin. "Nobody'll hear a peep out of Elmer Boyd."

"We'll wait to hear from you, then."

"Depend on it, Mr. Elkton."

Mitchell and Elkton exchanged a look. Something unspo-

ken passed between them, and Mitchell moved his head in
an imperceptible nod. Braddock caught the byplay as he
turned toward the door, and he needed no explanation. The
meaning was clear.

He would be watched while he was in Santa Fe.

Braddock departed with a cheery wave, and Elkton waited
until he heard the front door close. Then he stood and peered
into the outer office, satisfying himself it was empty. He resumed his seat.

"Boyd is hardly the bumpkin you described."

Mitchell shrugged. "I admit I'm surprised. He's sharper
than I thought."

"Perhaps too sharp."

"In what way?"

"Every way," Elkton replied. "For example, he was very
inquisitive about our judicial connections. How do you suppose he found out?"

"Not from me!" Mitchell said quickly.

"If not from you, then from whom?"

"All I said was that there would be no problem in obtaining a valid title. He apparently put the rest together for
himself."

"Are you saying he inferred all that from a single statement?"

"How else would he figure it out?"

"How, indeed?" Elkton mused. "We seem to have underestimated Mr. Boyd all the way round."

"I don't follow you."

"Come now, Warren! He obviously knows a good deal
about our operation. You said yourself that he'd somehow
learned of the railroad deal and the European consortium.
Isn't that so?"

"Well, yes, I did."

"Which means he's looked into our affairs rather thoroughly."

"Nothing wrong with that," Mitchell countered. "Anyone

who intends to invest three million would do the same thing. Besides, everything he's learned has been rumored for years. And printed in the newspapers, I might add."

"Perhaps," Elkton conceded. "But something about Mr. Boyd still bothers me. I distrust a man who has nothing to hide."

"Hide?"

"A man with no secrets. He seemed entirely too open about himself and his money."

"Some of that was an act. I've never met a wealthy Texan who didn't have larceny in his heart. They like to think of themselves as part buccaneer, part bunco man."

"Even so," Elkton remarked, "where does the act end and the man begin?"

"Hard to say."

"And all the more reason to check him out."

"We don't want to risk offending him. Why not wait until he gives us a draft for the three million? Then I'll put through a routine inquiry to his bank."

"Yes, that should suffice. Meanwhile, I want him followed. See to it."

"I'll talk with Johnson and Ortega."

"No rough stuff."

"Of course."

"Unless," Elkton went on, "we discover that Mr. Boyd does have secrets. Then, as the saying goes, he's fair game."

Mitchell nodded grimly. "I understand."

Early the next morning Braddock emerged from the hotel. His thumbs were hooked in his vest and a cigar was wedged into the corner of his mouth. He halted on the veranda and stood for a moment surveying the plaza. Then he went down the steps and strolled off at a leisurely pace.

Once across the plaza, Braddock turned onto a side street. His stride quickened and he walked rapidly to the distant corner. There he moved to the other side of the intersecting street and ducked into an alleyway. For the next half hour he followed a twisting path, frequently doubling back on himself, always looking over his shoulder. Finally, satisfied he wasn't being tailed, he headed for the west side of town.

Shortly before nine o'clock, Braddock walked through the door of the *New Mexican*. Overnight he'd concluded there was little chance of obtaining more information from either Mitchell or Elkton. In his own mind, he felt confident that Mitchell was indeed the front man for the Santa Fe Ring. He was equally convinced that Elkton was the shadowy mastermind who operated from behind the scenes. Yet it was apparent that the relationship was similar to a ventriloquist manipulating a dummy. On important matters, Mitchell only spoke when Elkton moved his lips, and the words were seldom his own. Therefore, Mitchell was unlikely to divulge anything of an incriminating nature.

All things considered, Braddock had decided there was nothing to lose by talking with Max Flagg. The publisher of the *New Mexican* was the avowed enemy of the Santa Fe Ring. His knowledge of the territorial capital and its inner political workings was undoubtedly first-rate. A Johnny-on-the-spot news hound was generally privy to all the juicy tidbits so seldom made public. The publisher might very well reveal something that would dovetail with what Braddock had already learned. In particular, Braddock was looking for inside dope on Stephen Elkton. The man was still very much a cipher, an unknown quantity.

Max Flagg appeared dubious from the outset. He was on the sundown side of forty, with a widow's peak hairline and a nose veined red from liquor. He wore steel-rimmed spectacles and his eyes had the canny look of a man who was surprised by nothing. His expression was unreadable when Braddock introduced himself as "a friend of Frank Kirkland." He closed the door of his cubbyhole office and offered Braddock a chair. Then he steepled his fingers and peered across the desk.

"What can I do for you, Mr.—?"

Braddock smiled. "The name isn't important."

"No?" Flagg squinted querulously. "You walk in off the street and tell me you're pals with Kirkland. Why should I take the word of a man who won't even give me his name?"

"The next time you see Frank"—Braddock paused to light a cigar—"ask him about the Gospel according to Saint Cole. He won't tell you my name either, but he'll vouch for the fact that we're all working toward the same end—the downfall of the Santa Fe Ring."

Frost's eyes were still veiled with caution. "How do I know you're not working for the ring?"

"Simple." Braddock took a draw on the cigar and his face toughened. "You mention me to anyone but Frank Kirkland and the ring will try to kill me. I'll look you up if that happens—and you'll wish I hadn't."

Flagg scrutinized him closely. Whatever he saw in Braddock's gaze, it convinced him the statement was no idle threat. Some swift-felt impulse also told him he was in the presence of an ally. He decided to accept the man with no name at face value.

"All right," he said at last, "mum's the word. How can I help you?"

"What do you know about Warren Mitchell?"

"Everything and nothing," Frost commented morosely. "He's the lightning rod for the ring. By that, I mean his land company provides a legitimate front for their schemes. He does the dirty work and he's very good at it. I would say he's indispensable to their operation."

"Who are 'they'—the ring members?"

"Do you want cold facts or warm gossip?"

"What's the difference?"

"In terms of cold facts," Flagg said in an aggrieved tone, "there's not an iota of proof against anybody. We're dealing with a secretive organization, and their methods are utterly ruthless. No one talks—ever!"

Braddock shrugged. "I guess I'll have to settle for gossip."

"The list is endless," Flagg confided. "The governor, the attorney general, the chief federal court judge, the surveyor general. Shall I go on?"

"You're saying all those men are members of the ring?"

"Not entirely." Flagg's voice was soft and troubled. "I believe the governor and the attorney general are almost certainly members. The others either accept payoffs or cooperate for political reasons. I've never been able to determine where one leaves off and the other begins."

"So far, all I've heard are allegations. Have you got anything concrete?"

Frost briefly outlined the turbulent nature of Santa Fe politics. Following the Civil War, local Republicans had gained control of the political apparatus. The White House, in concert with Congress, had initiated a program designed to punish pro-southern Democrats. Even now, almost twenty years later, the Democrats were still battling to restore a balance of power. But it was an uphill fight conducted largely against men who operated from the shadows. Only last year the territorial governor had been forced to resign when he fell into disfavor with the ring. The new governor, by all reports, had been selected principally for his amicable manner and his lack of curiosity. Allegations or not, Flagg concluded, the pattern of backroom politics was undeniable. New Mexico reeked of corruption.

"In other words," Braddock said pointedly, "you have no proof."

"If I did, I'd print it in banner headlines."

Braddock puffed on his cigar and blew a smoke ring. "Why do you place so much stock in rumors?"

"Stop and think about it," Flagg said grimly. "A single land company—presumably owned by one man—controls the economic lifeblood of New Mexico Territory. How is that possible?"

"I'm asking you."

Flagg gave him a weak smile. "The rumors say it's

possible because Warren Mitchell either owns or black-mails every politician in Santa Fe. I see no other conceivable explanation."

Braddock's eyes turned hard, questing. "Who owns Warren Mitchell?"

"I'm not sure I understand."

"Would you say Mitchell has the brains and the balls to pull all that off by himself?"

"To my knowledge"—Flagg lifted his hands in a lame gesture—"Mitchell has done exactly that. He's the power to be reckoned with, and he's the power broker. No one in pub-lic office got there without his stamp of approval."

"So I've heard." Braddock fixed him with a piercing look. "What do you know about Stephen Elkton?"

"Elkton?" Flagg repeated hollowly. "He's a widely re-spected lawyer and something of an intellect. I understand he's a student of Plato and Aristotle. The Greek school of thought."

"Wonder if he ever read Machiavelli."

"Pardon me?"

"A private joke," Braddock said woodenly. "Has Elkton ever been actively involved in politics?"

"Never," Flagg responded. "Apparently he's a very pri-vate man who devotes himself to his law practice. Why do you ask?"

"No reason." Braddock rose to his feet. "Just a shot in the dark."

Flagg eyed him keenly. "Should I inquire further? Per-haps I've overlooked something."

"Suit yourself," Braddock said with a tight smile. "When you see Frank, tell him I said hello."

"I still don't know your name."

"Let's leave it that way—for now."

Braddock nodded and stepped through the door. Once outside, he walked off with the cigar stuck in his mouth and his hands stuffed in his pockets. The conversation with Flagg had been a complete washout, and he mocked himself with sardonic bitterness. He'd played out his string in Santa Fe, and he was now at an impasse. Worse, he was assailed by a sense of time running ahead of him like an hourglass almost emptied of sand.

A short walk across town brought him to the train depot. He entered the station house and asked the telegrapher for a message form. Then he wrote out his instructions in a code known only to himself and one other person.

The wire was addressed to Verna Potter.

Slim Johnson tailed Braddock back to the hotel. He waited on the veranda, watching through a window as Braddock crossed the lobby to the stairs. Then he took off upstreet at a brisk pace.

Several moments later Johnson entered Warren Mitchell's office. In the anteroom, the secretary greeted him with a disapproving look. He was tall and lean, roughly dressed, and she thoroughly mistrusted him. But her boss kept him on the payroll and apparently valued his services. She showed him into the inner office.

Mitchell looked up from a stack of documents. He nodded to Johnson and then waited until his secretary closed the door. He didn't offer the other man a chair.

"What is it?"

"I followed Boyd," Johnson said, "like you told me."

"So?"

"I lost him."

"You dimwit!"

"And then I found him."

"Explain yourself," Mitchell ordered. "From the beginning."

"Well, he come out of the hotel a little before nine. He walks off, easy as you please, puffin' on a cigar. Acted like he had all day and nowhere to go."

"Get to the point."

"Sure thing, boss," Johnson said, hurrying on. "A couple of blocks from the hotel he turned a corner and *poof!*, he flat disappeared."

Mitchell gave him a withering look. "What happened then?"

"Nothin'. Leastways not for a while. Half hour or so later, I spotted him hotfootin' it across the plaza. So I tailed—"

"Wait," Mitchell interrupted. "Any idea at all where he might have been during that half hour?"

"Beats me, boss. Like I said, he gimme the slip."

"Where was Ortega? Why wasn't he helping you?"

"Well," Johnson began, hanging his head, "it didn't look to be that big of a job. Never figgered some peckerhead Texan would pull a fast one."

Mitchell suppressed a curse. He realized, not for the first time, that initiative was in scarce supply in his men.

Johnson and Ortega were hardened toughnuts, skilled killers, but there wasn't an ounce of imagination between them. He catalogued the thought for future reference.

"All right, go on."

"So anyway," Johnson resumed, "I tailed him down to the depot, waited till he sent a wire, then I followed him back to the hotel. He's there now."

"You saw him send a wire?" Mitchell demanded.

"Big as life."

"To whom?"

"Huh?"

"Who was it sent to?"

"I dunno. If you want, I'll go lean on the depot agent. He'd tell me pretty quick."

"No, never mind. Boyd might find out, and we can't risk that."

"Anything you say, boss."

"Stick with him, Slim. Don't lose him again."

"You damn betcha I won't!"

After Johnson left, Mitchell considered what he'd heard. None of it was particularly incriminating in itself. Losing a tail and sending a telegram were hardly grounds for pulling out of the deal with Boyd. Still, it was something to flag and file away for further study.

Upon reflection, Mitchell thought it wiser to keep his own counsel. He saw no reason to advise Elkton of the day's events.

Not just yet.

CHAPTER ELEVEN

━━━∽∿∽━━━

Braddock was seated in the lobby. The chair he'd selected faced the hotel entrance and was within earshot of the registration desk. He idly leafed through the morning newspaper.

Three days had passed since he'd wired Verna Potter. Yesterday, with Mitchell pressing for a decision, he had finally agreed to the Guadalupe County land deal. Contracts were now being drawn, and he had promised a check upon formal signing. He figured he had a couple of weeks, perhaps less, before the check bounced from the Fort Worth bank. The timing was critical, but he wasn't overly concerned. Verna had responded by wire, and her decoded message was very much as he'd expected. A new element would shortly be introduced into the game.

Braddock's vigil ended late that morning. His mouth sagged open in amazement as Lise Hammond sailed through the hotel entrance. Her hair, normally golden blond, had been dyed with henna. She was now something of a strawberry roan, the shade coppery red with auburn highlights.

Her coiffure had been changed as well; the style was now upswept with finger-puffs on top and masses of curls clustered high on her forehead. The dye job was professionally done and provided a startling contrast to her usual appearance. She looked brassy and brazen, an impression accentuated by her gaudy emerald-green dress. She had quite completely become someone else.

Lise spotted him the moment she entered the lobby. She lowered one eyelid in a quick wink and marched directly to the desk. A bellboy trailed along with her luggage, and the room clerk perked up noticeably when she requested accommodations with a bathtub. Braddock listened while she registered as Dora Kimble, and overheard the clerk announce her room number. Then, with the bellboy in the lead, she mounted the broad flight of stairs to the second floor. Braddock went back to his newspaper, waiting until the bellboy returned several minutes later. Then he rose and sauntered casually upstairs.

A worm of doubt still gnawed at Braddock. His wire summoning Lise to Santa Fe had been a last-ditch measure. Ever the icy realist, he knew he would uncover nothing more on his own. His investigation was at a dead end, and some bolder approach was needed to break the case. So he'd hatched a scheme whereby Lise would flimflam Warren Mitchell with sexual allure. Yet, despite her gift for guile and subterfuge, he remained more apprehensive than he cared to admit. Nor were his qualms wholly dispelled by the dye job and the striking change in her physical appearance. His concern centered on the man who orchestrated every facet of the ring's activities. One slip-up and Stephen Elkton would order her killed.

Upstairs, Braddock checked the hallway in both directions. No one was around and he walked swiftly to room 226. The door opened to his knock and he stepped inside. Lise closed it behind him, twisting the key. Then she threw herself into his arms. As she cupped his face between her hands, her kiss was warm and hungry. At last, with a final peck on the lips, she disengaged from his embrace and struck a pose, one hand to her hair.

"Hope you like redheads, lover."

"Well," Braddock began as he tossed his hat on the bureau, "I've always been partial to the cake, not the frosting."

"You old smoothy!" Her eyes gleamed with pleasure. "How do you think it will play in Santa Fe?"

"Pretty good," Braddock said, inspecting her closer. "You look like yourself and yet you don't. It'd fool anybody who doesn't know you personally."

"How about someone who's seen me onstage?"

"No problem," Braddock reassured her. "The color and the new hairdo turn the trick. I'm impressed."

"So am I." She tweaked his false mustache. "You're a regular chameleon when it comes to disguise."

"All part of the trade."

She looked at him with impudent eyes. "Your wire was something of a surprise."

"Yeah, well," Braddock mugged, hands outstretched, "things haven't gone exactly the way I'd planned."

"See?" Her lips curved in a teasing smile. "You needed me after all!"

"Don't rub it in."

"I'm just happy you sent for me, lover. And happier to be here!"

"Any trouble getting away from your job?"

"Not a bit." She threw back her head and laughed. "I told Jack Brady he could like it or lump it."

"How long have you got off?"

"However long it takes," she replied airily. "Brady couldn't replace me and he knows it! As you'll recall, I do tend to draw a crowd."

"No argument there," Braddock said absently. "Now all you've got to do is convince Ned Ingram. He owns the biggest dive in town, the Tivoli."

"I'm all ears."

Braddock took a chair and Lise seated herself on the edge of the bed. He briefed her on the assignment, starting with his impersonation of a minister in Cimarron. Then, step by step, he recounted what he'd unearthed during the course of the investigation. He frankly admitted he was stymied, with nowhere left to turn. A whole new dodge was needed to expose the Santa Fe Ring—something shifty and sly, perhaps even seductive. Which was why he'd sent for her.

"So that's it," he concluded. "I want you to put the whammy on Warren Mitchell."

A devilish smile played at the corners of her mouth. "What's he like?"

"A charmer," Braddock observed. "Educated, fancy manners, what the ladies call suave. He likes to think of himself as one of the big muckamucks, top-hat variety."

"Mmm." She uttered a low, gloating laugh. "Just my speed! The swells never could resist my brand of catnip."

"He's no dimdot," Braddock warned her. "So don't treat him lightly. You'll have to watch yourself every minute."

"Consider it done." Her eyes seemed to glint with secret amusement. "I'll have him eating out of my hand in no time."

"Overconfidence"—Braddock paused to underscore the word—"leads to mistakes. Keep that in mind or he'll tumble to you before you get started."

"Oh, pooh!" She lifted her chin slightly. "You said he likes naughty ladies, didn't you?"

"He likes them vulgar and cheap. The cruder, the better."

"Well, honey, you've never seen me at my wickedest. I can talk dirty with the best of them."

Braddock eyed her in silence for a moment. "He does more than talk. None of the girls at the Tivoli say no to him. You'll have to figure a way to hook him and hold him off—without losing his interest."

"You're looking at an expert." She wrinkled her nose and gave him a sassy grin. "I know every trick in the lechers' book. And I know how to string them along too!"

"You won't have any choice." Braddock opened his

hands and shrugged. "You'll have to buy time and somehow pump him for information. And you'll have to do it without mentioning Stephen Elkton. That would be a dead giveaway."

"But it's Elkton we're really after! How do I get the goods on him without using his name?"

"Good question," Braddock conceded. "And I wish I had the answer. What I do know is that Elkton plays for all the marbles. The least little tip-off and you won't get a second chance. Understand?"

Lise looked pensive. "Tell me a little more about Elkton."

"For openers, he's dangerous as hell. Mitchell had the jitters the entire time we were in his office."

"Maybe Mitchell scares easily."

"No." Braddock shook his head. "Elkton qualifies for the term 'sinister.' He's smart and he's a cold fish. No emotion at all. That's the worst possible combination."

"C'mon, lover. Don't tell me he got to you!"

"Let's just say I came away a believer."

"How do you mean?"

"I've been grilled by experts, but Elkton knows all the tricks and then some. He damn near pinned me to the wall."

"But you convinced him, didn't you?"

"I bought a little time, that's all. He's having me shadowed, and he warned me in no uncertain terms to keep my lip buttoned. Like I said, he plays for keeps."

"Are you saying he actually threatened you?"

"Not in so many words. He left it to my imagination what would happen if I spoke out of turn. I got the general drift."

"So you think he really would . . ."

"Kill me?"

"Yes."

"I don't think he'd bat an eye. To him, things tally out in dollars—not lives."

"I guess you're right. I mean, after all he did have a preacher killed."

"Exactly. And if you get careless, he'll kill you too."

"You sound like you're trying to scare me."

"I am." Braddock lifted a questioning eyebrow. "Just in case things go wrong, do you have your Derringer handy?"

"Handy enough," she said, patting her thigh. "I keep it stuck in my garter."

"Use it if push comes to shove."

"When do you want me to start at the Tivoli?"

"Tonight."

"Then we haven't a moment to spare."

Lise stretched voluptuously and held out her arms. He grinned and rose from his chair, moving to the bed. She pulled him down beside her and snuggled close in his arms. Her mouth found his and eagerly sought his tongue, and she kissed him with a fierce, passionate urgency. His arms tightened, strong and demanding, and she whimpered deep in her throat.

Her hand touched his belt buckle. . . .

Some two hours later Lise entered the Tivoli Variety Theater. One of the barkeeps pointed her in the right direction, and the afternoon crowd watched with appreciative stares as she sashayed toward the rear. She crossed from the barroom to the theater, switching her hips for their benefit. She went through a door to the left of a small orchestra pit.

The backstage area was empty and dimly lighted. Lise saw the glow of a lamp from a door near the alley entrance. She walked forward and halted in the open doorway. The office was small and musty and furnished somewhat like a monk's cell. There was a battered desk, flanked by a double file cabinet, and one straight-backed chair for visitors.

Up against the far wall was an overstuffed reclining divan. It was worn and threadbare and seemed perfectly suited for casting chorus girls. The man seated behind the desk looked nothing like a monk.

Ned Ingram was lean and wiry, with jutting cheekbones and sleek, glistening hair. His features were pasty and splotched with gray, and his eyes were opaque and curiously without expression. He glanced up from an accounting ledger and fixed her with a lusterless gaze. He slowly looked her up and down. He mentally undressed her and apparently liked what he saw. His mouth creased in a thin smile.

"Do something for you, girlie?"

"Are you Mr. Ingram?"

"No," Ingram said tonelessly. "My pa was Mr. Ingram. Most everybody calls me Ned."

"Pleased to meet you," Lise said brightly. "I'm Dora Kimble. I'd like to talk to you about a job."

"You a hoofer?"

"Only when I'm hungry," Lise quipped. "My specialty is ballads."

"A canary, huh?" Ingram shook his head back and forth. "Never had much luck with singers. The boys like to see the hot stuff—legs and bloomers."

"That's because they haven't heard my ballads."

"What's different about you?"

"I sing risqué," Lise said with a bawdy smile. "Or I sing dirty. All depends on the quality of your trade."

"Mostly low lifes." Ingram hesitated, considering. "Where've you worked before?"

"Pick a spot!" Lise said merrily. "Abilene, Dodge City, Leadville, Deadwood. I've played 'em all!"

"What brings you to Santa Fe?"

Lise regarded him with brash impudence. "I've always had my eye on San Francisco—the big time. So I'm working my way west."

"Uh-huh." Ingram nailed her with a stern look. "You're not in trouble with the law, are you?"

"Christ, no!" Lise yelped. "I'm strictly legit, Mr. Ingram!"

"Ned."

"Okay, Ned." Lise gave him a bright little nod. "Well anyway, like I was saying, I stay straight with the law."

"Lemme hear you sing something."

"What?"

"You said you're a singer, so sing."

"Without accompaniment?"

"The piano player don't come on till six."

"Oh." Lise cleared her throat. "You want it dirty or risqué?"

"Something in between."

Lise composed herself. The next few moments represented an acid test. She had started out as a hoofer and worked her way up from the chorus to a star headliner. Her husky alto voice was her trademark, and the way she belted out a ballad had brought her a degree of celebrity. Unlike her physical appearance, her singing style would be quite difficult to disguise. Early on in her career, however, she had conquered a pronounced nasal tone with the aid of a voice coach. By concentrating, she was confident she could again introduce that flaw into her style and still sing well enough to land the job.

The ballad she sang was a naughty ditty about an Indian maiden and a cowboy. The lyrics were ripe with sexual innuendo and peppered here and there with four-letter words. Once she began, she found she was actually enjoying it. A lady would never use such explicit language, but she was playing a wicked woman, and the taboos no longer applied. She sang through her nose, and while it offended her ear, the tonal quality masked her normal voice. To add sizzle to the ballad, she performed a simple dance routine, wiggling and jiggling in concert with the tune. She ended with her arms flung wide and her breasts thrust high.

"Not bad," Ingram remarked when she finished. "You ought to get rid of that twang, but I've heard worse. Besides, my band plays so loud nobody'll notice it anyway."

"I've got the job?" Lise squealed. "You're hiring me?"

"Hold your horses." Ingram's mouth lifted in a tight grin. "There's more to the job than what you do onstage. I've got certain rules."

Lise darted a glance at the divan. "What sort of rules?"

"Between shows, all my girls mingle with the customers and push drinks. Course, I don't allow no hanky-panky on the premises. But whatever arrangements they make after hours, that's their business."

"I've got nothing against pushing drinks."

"One other thing."

"Yeah?"

"Before I hire a girl"—Ingram's grin widened—"I generally get a little something on account. A sample of the wares."

"Well, Ned," Lise said in a teasing lilt, "I don't sell it and I don't sleep around. Not that I'm any lily of the valley! I just don't hop into bed with strangers, that's all."

"How long before somebody stops being a stranger?"

"Depends on the somebody." Lise laughed, her eyes dancing merrily. "A man who treats me nice wouldn't be sorry. I'm a regular wildcat when I do let go."

Ingram burst out laughing. "All right, you got yourself a job. But let's have it understood there's a condition attached."

"You and me?"

"One week," Ingram said with a smarmy grin. "Come across in one week or go back to working your way west."

"Ned, you're looking less like a stranger all the time!"

Ingram told her to report for work at six o'clock. She could then plan her act with the band and put together a costume from the stockroom. Lise thanked him profusely and wigwagged her hips as she went out the door. The condition he'd placed on the job bothered her not at all. One week or a hundred was immaterial.

Ned Ingram would be a stranger till hell froze over!

"There once was an Indian maid
Who said she wasn't afraid
To lay on her back
In a cowboy's shack . . ."

Lise stood center stage. She was bathed in a ruby-hued spotlight, and her smile was like naked sin itself. Her sumptuous figure was emphasized by a gown that was cut low on the top and high on the bottom. Her breasts threatened to spill out of the gown and her lissome legs flashed as she performed a cakewalk in tempo with the music. The song was the last number in her act and the raunchiest of the lot. Beyond the footlights, the theater was packed. Even the serious drinkers from the barroom were ganged around the entranceway. The band thumped louder as she ended the ballad with the dirtiest stanza yet.

Thunderous applause broke out even before the music stopped. The audience cheered and whistled and stamped their feet, all the while yelling for more. Lise took four curtain calls, bowing low enough each time to give the crowd a quick peek down the top of her dress. The last time out she let her gaze linger a moment on Warren Mitchell, who was seated at his usual table. She caught open lechery in his look during the instant their eyes met. Then she backed off stage, throwing kisses with both hands as a final wave of applause flooded the theater. The curtain closed only momentarily before the band segued into an upbeat number. A line of chorus girls pranced out of the wings.

Backstage Lise found a waiter with a message from Warren Mitchell. He explained that Mitchell was a Tivoli regular, a very big spender, and that she'd been invited to share a bottle of champagne. She looked properly impressed and followed him out front. From the back of the house, Ned Ingram caught her attention and signaled his congratulations with a circled thumb and forefinger. His expression was that of a cat spitting feathers, and she reminded herself to hit him up for a private dressing room. Then the waiter halted at Mitchell's table and pulled out a chair. She sat down with a vivacious smile.

"Thanks for the invite, Mr. Mitchell."

"I'm honored you accepted." Mitchell promptly filled her glass. "Allow me to toast your bravura performance."

Lise clinked glasses. "Here's mud in your eye! You really liked it, huh?"

"Yes, indeed," Mitchell said, leaning closer. "You're the hit of the evening, Miss Kimble."

"Why don't you call me Dora?"

"And you may call me Warren."

"Good!" Lise held out her glass for a refill. "Life's too short for starchy ways, right, Warren?"

"Quite so." Mitchell stared down the front of her dress while he poured. "Ned Ingram tells me you're new to Santa Fe."

"Fresh off the train," Lise said pertly. "And so far it's a pisser of a town. What an audience! Did you hear that applause?"

"I led the pack, my dear. Your performance deserved the warmest possible reception."

"Say, you're all right! I was afraid you'd be some kind of stuffed shirt. But you're a regular sport, aren't you?"

"Very regular," Mitchell said with a raffish smile. "Among my vices are wine and games of chance. And of course I have a congenital weakness for the ladies."

"I'm sort of partial to men myself."

"How nice." Mitchell cocked one ribald eye at her. "Tell me, are you as naughty as the songs you sing?"

"Sometimes," Lise said with a lewd wink. "It all depends on how the mood strikes me."

"Fascinating," Mitchell murmured. "And how would you characterize your mood tonight?"

"Well, you see, Warren, I'm not a one-nighter. I tend to pick a man and stick with him as long as I'm in town."

"And how does this process of selection occur?"

"Oh, I just *know*!" Lise simpered. "It might take a couple of nights to decide, but I always know when I've met Mr. Right."

"And does Mr. Right find the wait worth his while?"

"Why not find out for yourself?"

"An excellent suggestion," Mitchell said with a sanguine look. "As some philosopher once noted, anticipation is half the pleasure."

Lise knew then she had him gaffed. He was accustomed to girls who wilted before his glib line and urbane manner.

A girl who set a higher price on herself was clearly a novelty and a challenge. She touched both his vanity and his male pride. He would wait for the simplest of reasons.

He had to be the first man in Santa Fe to bed Dora Kimble.

CHAPTER TWELVE

———◆◆———

The Tivoli was packed with a rowdy crowd. Braddock stood at the bar, elbows on the counter and one boot heel hooked over the brass rail. He was nursing a whiskey and brooding on Lise Hammond. His expression was troubled.

Dora Kimble was now the toast of Santa Fe's sporting district. Her opening-night act had created a sensation, and everyone was talking about the lady who sang dirty ballads. On the second evening, Ned Ingram had wisely moved her into the headliner's spot. Her act had become the finale for each of the three shows presented nightly. The crowds had steadily grown larger as word of her racy performance spread through town. Tonight, which was her fourth night at the Tivoli, the turnout was little short of a mob scene. She was playing to standing room only.

Braddock watched her performance in the back-bar mirror. It was the last show of the evening, and she held the audience enthralled with the verve of her stage presence and the off-color lyrics of her songs. Yet Braddock scarcely heard the words, and his eyes followed her movements with only dulled awareness. His mind was focused instead on the events of the past few days. He found nothing to encourage him and a great deal to prompt his concern. He thought the risk to Lise was mounting at an alarming rate.

So far, Lise had uncovered nothing of value to the investigation. After the last show every evening, Warren Mitchell took her to his suite at the hotel for a nightcap. His sexual advances were rather mild in nature, and he'd made no attempt to force himself on her. To all appearances, he seemed content to bide his time. The platonic company of Santa Fe's newest stage sensation was, for the moment, a balm to his randier designs. He was attentive and entertaining, and it was obvious he reveled in squiring her around town. Her sudden fame also put him in the limelight, anointing him with a mark of distinction. For he was widely assumed to be Dora Kimble's lover.

Lise skillfully played on his vanity. She allowed him a kiss here and a squeeze there, and kept his ardor under control with promises of more to come. Her public display of affection also promoted the belief that she was his latest conquest. The envy of every man in town, he had arranged to show her off to some of his uptown friends. Only last night, he'd invited several of the chorus girls to an after-hours party at his suite. The gentlemen they were there to entertain included the attorney general, the territorial delegate to Congress, and a federal court judge. The party was a smashing success, with the politicos well oiled by the end of the night. One by one, they had disappeared with the girls to their own private hideaways.

Seizing opportunity, Lise had attempted to capitalize on the moment. Mitchell was mellowed by liquor and immensely pleased with the impression she'd made on his cohorts. She too had appeared impressed and exhibited a natural curiosity about his high connections in government. Her questions were subtle and worded in such a way as to appeal to his pride. Still, for all his mellow mood, Mitchell hadn't consumed enough whiskey to indulge in careless talk. His answers were limited to vague generalities, and he'd revealed nothing about his business or personal relationships with the men. Lise dared not press too far, and she had finally let the subject drop. Pleading the late hour, she'd then bid him good night.

Upon entering her room, Lise had found Braddock dozing on the bed. For the past three nights, he'd let himself into the room and awaited her return. The purpose was an exchange of information, and last night, like the nights before, had proved dismally unrewarding. Lise identified the men who had attended the party and went on to relate her later conversation with Mitchell. The upshot, as they'd both agreed, was of little consequence. That Mitchell entertained politicians with girls and booze proved nothing. Nor was there any hint of corruption or direct ties to the Santa Fe Ring. Their investigation, for all practical purposes, was going nowhere. But Lise had expressed a determination to stick with their original plan. She still believed she could dupe Mitchell into exposing his hand and establish a case against Stephen Elkton.

Braddock was no longer all that certain. Three nights in Mitchell's company had left Lise little to show for her efforts. It was possible, after introducing her to his cronies, that Mitchell might confide in her over a period of time. But Braddock secretly felt that he'd underestimated Mitchell's resolve and overestimated Lise's seductive powers. To compound matters, his own access to Mitchell had undergone a severe change. The land contract had been signed yesterday. With his check for three million in hand, Mitchell apparently saw no need to court him further. While he wasn't being snubbed, the dinner invitations had stopped and he was no longer Mitchell's guest at the Tivoli. Which pretty much eased him out of the picture. To see Mitchell, he now needed an appointment.

Tonight, as Lise finished her number Braddock was gripped by a sense of unease. He watched her take her bows and downed his drink as she hurried off stage. His gaze automatically shifted to Mitchell, who was seated at the table down front. His unease was suddenly replaced by a sharp stab of apprehension. He'd learned never to ignore his instincts, and some visceral compulsion told him it was time to try another tack. The feeling was reinforced when Lise appeared in her street clothes and joined Mitchell at his table. A moment later they walked from the Tivoli arm in arm.

Braddock watched them go out the door. His brooding abruptly ceased, and he decided that the danger to Lise had grown great enough for him to take action. Unless there was some sort of breakthrough, her charade would end tonight. Tomorrow he'd put her on the first train bound for Denver.

He rapped the bar for another drink.

"I really must insist, my dear."

"Honestly, Warren!" Lise shook a roguish finger at him. "You've been such a perfect gentleman. What's come over you?"

"Three nights of thinking about you—and gritting my teeth."

Lise was seated beside him on the sofa. When they'd entered the suite, she noticed there was something strange about his attitude. He had fixed their usual nightcap, but he'd been curiously silent. After a few sips of brandy, he had taken her glass and placed it beside his own on the coffee table. Then without a word he had wrapped her in a tight embrace and begun pawing her body. She'd wiggled loose only after a brief wrestling match.

"Why spoil things?" she said, looking at him now. "You agreed to let me decide in my own good time. Are you going to break your word?"

"Your own good time has the smell of forever."

"Oh, piddle!" She laughed and wagged her head. "Three nights isn't forever and you know it!"

"Haven't I treated you like a lady?"

"Yes."

"And haven't I exhibited both patience and restraint?"

"Of course."

"Then it's my turn for some consideration."

"Warren, all I'm asking for is a little more time."

"I need you now! Tonight!"

Mitchell seemed paralyzed by lust. His expression was somehow reminiscent of a tethered ram, and he stared at her with a look of glassy-eyed longing. He moistened his lower lip and the spell was suddenly broken. He grabbed her arms and pinned her to the corner of the sofa. She struggled, hammering at him with her fists in a vain attempt to escape. His hand slipped down the bodice of her dress and closed over one of her breasts.

A knock sounded at the door. Mitchell froze, his hand still cupping her breast. Then he sat erect and darted a glance at the door as the knock became louder. Lise straightened her disheveled dress and brushed a lock of hair off her forehead. He put a finger to his lips, signaling silence.

"Who is it?"

"It's me." A muffled male voice carried through the door. "Open up."

The voice galvanized Mitchell to action. He pulled Lise off the sofa and hustled her into the bedroom. He again cautioned her to silence and closed the door. The bedroom was dark, and as he turned away, Lise impulsively opened the door a crack. She put her eye to the slit and saw him tug his jacket straight as he crossed the parlor. He opened the hall door.

"Stephen!"

"You took your time about letting me in."

"Sorry."

"Are you alone?"

"Why, yes." Mitchell hastily closed the hall door. "What's wrong?"

"You're sure you don't have a woman in the bedroom?"

"Quite sure." Mitchell motioned with a casual gesture. "Have a look for yourself."

Elkton dropped into an armchair. "Where's the Kimble

woman? From everything I've heard, I halfway expected to find her here."

"She was," Mitchell said, seating himself on the sofa. "We had a brandy and then she went on to her room."

"So I see." Elkton studied the glasses on the coffee table. "Why didn't she finish her drink?"

"Well," Mitchell said as he fidgeted uncomfortably, "we had a slight misunderstanding, an argument."

"And she walked out on you?"

"No," Mitchell said defensively. "As a matter of fact, I asked her to leave."

"Good riddance," Elkton said in a sour tone. "I would have ordered you to break it off anyway."

"Come now," Mitchell bridled. "My personal life is my own, Stephen. I'll see her whenever I wish."

Elkton's brow furrowed. "Perhaps you'll change your mind when you hear what I have to say."

"I don't understand." Mitchell shook his head dumbly. "What possible interest could you have in Dora Kimble?"

"You ass!" Elkton said with a withering scowl. "Your infatuation with that bitch has brought us a world of grief."

"What are you talking about?"

"Tomorrow," Elkton replied angrily, "an editorial will appear in the *New Mexican*. Our old friend Max Flagg has blown the whistle on your party last night."

"Party?"

"Flagg termed it an orgy. His editorial charges that you used prostitutes and liquor to provide an evening of debauchery for the territory's leading politicians. He also names names—a complete guest list!"

"It's not true!" Mitchell protested. "I gave a party, not an orgy! Nothing improper took place. Nothing!"

Elkton fixed him with a jaundiced look. "You supplied girls and free liquor for men in public office. Whether or not they engaged in group fornication is immaterial. It has the earmarks of an orgy, and I assure you the label will stick."

"But"—Mitchell hesitated, groping for words—"I've thrown parties before, lots of parties. Why would Flagg ballyhoo this one?"

"In the past," Elkton said acidly, "you were discreet enough to include only other businessmen in the festivities. Does that answer your question?"

"You're referring to the political overtones."

"Exactly."

"How the devil did Flagg find out the names?"

Elkton arched one eyebrow and looked down his nose. "For a clever man, you're really quite naive, Warren."

"What do you mean?"

"I mean your personal life is an open book. You flaunt your mistress—the Kimble woman—in public. Then you use her to procure whores for your party."

"That's a lie!"

"No one will think so after reading Flagg's editorial. And it gets worse, much worse."

"In what way?"

"He implies that the men who attended your party are members of the ring. Then he goes on to speculate about your role." Elkton paused, and his voice rose suddenly. "He even hints that there's someone behind the scenes. Someone who directs the ring, masterminds it, using you as a front man."

"Good God!" Mitchell's face went ashen. "How did he get onto that?"

"How, indeed?" Elkton's eyes burned with intensity. "Whatever aroused his suspicions, they strike too close for comfort. I have no wish to see my name in print."

"What do you intend to do?"

"Serve notice," Elkton said with ominous calm. "I want Orville McMain killed. He was next on the list in Cimarron anyway."

"Why McMain?" Mitchell blurted. "Flagg wrote the editorial!"

"You are a fool," Elkton replied with cold hauteur. "Killing Flagg now would substantiate every charge he's made.

We'll take care of him once things have returned to normal. In the meantime, McMain's death will serve as a warning."

"I don't know, Stephen." Mitchell averted his gaze. "Won't that tend to stir up a hornest's nest? I mean, we've already killed one man in Cimarron—the minister."

Elkton gave him an evil look. "I wasn't soliciting your advice. Get hold of Donaghue and instruct him to take care of it. I want McMain dead by the end of the week."

Mitchell swallowed nervously. "If you're sure that's the best way . . ."

"Just do it!" Elkton said, rising to his feet. "Keep me informed of your progress."

Lise gently closed the bedroom door as Elkton prepared to leave. She moved swiftly to the bed and lay down with her back to the door. A few moments passed, then the door opened and Mitchell entered the bedroom. She rolled over, blinking in the glare of the light and sat up on the edge of the bed. Mitchell eyed her narrowly.

"Were you asleep?"

"Lemme tell you, honeybun." She laughed and walked past him into the parlor. "A working girl catches a snooze wherever she can. Why, did I miss something?"

"Nothing much." Mitchell was still watching her closely. "A friend with some personal problems dropped by looking for advice."

"Well, that's a relief!" She batted her china-blue eyes. "There for a minute I thought your wife had sicced the house detective on us."

"My wife!"

"You are married, aren't you?"

"I fail to see—"

"Don't worry, sweetie," she said with a vulpine smile. "I won't hold it against you. Nowadays it seems like all the good ones are married."

Mitchell took her by the shoulders. "You know I'm very fond of you, don't you?"

"Why, sure." She feigned surprise. "Why so serious?"

"A word to the wise," Mitchell said softly. "If you did overhear anything, then wipe it out of your mind. I wouldn't want anything—unpleasant to happen to you."

Her laugh was low and infectious. "Honey, where man talk's concerned, I'm deaf, dumb, and blind. You know, like the three monkeys—no see 'em, no hear 'em, no speak 'em!"

"I endorse the sentiment most heartily."

"And I'm bushed." She gave him a quick peck on the lips. "See you tomorrow night?"

"By all means."

"Sleep tight," she said with a coquettish grin. "And dream of yours truly."

Mitchell waited until the door closed. Then he walked to the sofa and flopped down. He felt reasonably certain she hadn't eavesdropped. But whether she had or not, Dora Kimble was the least of his troubles. He'd been ordered to arrange yet another man's death. And he thought it might very well be the proverbial last straw.

One murder too many.

Ten minutes later Lise stopped talking. Almost word for word, she had repeated the conversation between Mitchell and Elkton. Now, pausing to catch her breath, she awaited a reaction. Braddock seemed to look at her and past her at the same time.

"I think we'd better get you out of Santa Fe."

"Why?"

"You got lucky tonight," Braddock said quietly. "Mitchell's liable to sleep on it and change his mind."

"No chance!" Her eyes twinkled. "He's crazy about me!"

"Don't be too sure," Braddock cautioned. "You could put his head in a noose."

"That's the whole point!" She nodded vigorously. "I can testify to accessory to murder and conspiracy to murder. Put me on the witness stand and I'll hang them both!"

A stony look settled on Braddock's face. "Once before I

had a witness against a member of the ring. She was killed before she made it to the witness stand. I won't risk that with you." He stared straight at her. "Bright and early tomorrow, we'll sneak you aboard the train to Denver."

"I won't go!" she said stubbornly. "And that's final, Cole. So just save your breath."

"You'll go." Braddock's tone was harsh, roughly insistent. "You'll be on that train even if I have to hog-tie you."

"Like hell!" she flared. "I've earned the right to see this case through. And I'm staying, Cole! I mean it."

"Listen to reason," Braddock said with a stormy frown. "Your life's in danger, for Chrissake! Don't you understand that?"

"You want reason?" she replied with a charming little shrug. "All right, let's talk reason. Even with my testimony, you'd still try to drum up a corroborating witness. Am I right or wrong?"

"So?"

"So do it!" she chided him. "Find your witness and stop worrying about Mitchell. He's like putty in my hands! I'll just string him along until you're ready to move. You'll have to admit it makes sense, Cole."

"Only one trouble," Braddock said hesitantly. "All the other witnesses are in Cimarron."

"With or without me," she said in a hushed voice, "you'd still have to go back to Cimarron. You don't intend to let them kill McMain, do you?"

"I guess not," Braddock admitted grudgingly. "But I god-damn sure don't relish the notion of leaving you here by yourself."

"I'm a big girl." Her eyes sparkled with laughter. "And in a clutch, I've always got my Derringer. What could go wrong?"

"You want a list?"

"Stop fighting it, lover." She gave him a bright, theatrical smile. "You're going to let me stay and we both know it."

"Yeah, I reckon so," Braddock said uneasily. "All the same, I ought to have my head examined."

"I have a better idea."

"What's that?"

"Let's not talk any more—tonight."

Braddock smiled and took her at her word.

CHAPTER THIRTEEN

The northbound pulled out of Santa Fe at eight o'clock the next morning. Braddock was on board, still posing as a Texas cattleman. His eyes were grim, and he watched the town fall behind with a sense of reluctance. Some dark premonition told him he'd made a mistake.

Earlier, he'd hedged his bet with Mitchell. Before leaving the hotel, he penned a note, signing it Elmer Boyd, and hired a bellboy to run it over to Mitchell's office. The note stated he'd been called back to Texas on ranch business and would return shortly. Whether or not the bogus check bounced before he returned was a moot point. He'd covered himself for the moment, providing Mitchell with a plausible excuse for his sudden departure. He doubted anyone would bother to check the story.

Lise was another matter entirely. He'd allowed himself to be persuaded by the logic of her argument. Still, he couldn't shake the feeling that he would regret the decision. He was haunted by a vision of Ellen Nesbeth. The similarity was like a nightmare repeating itself. The ring had killed one woman to stop her from testifying, and it could easily happen again.

However careful, Lise was nonetheless a tyro in outwitting sharks like Mitchell and Elkton. He thought the odds were in her favor; otherwise he would never have agreed. Yet he was far from sanguine about the outcome. There was no way to hedge the bet where she was concerned. And that preyed on his mind.

The train chugged into Raton late that afternoon. A night's layover enabled Braddock to resurrect the Reverend Titus Jacoby. When he emerged from the hotel the following morning, he wore the muttonchop sideburns and the turned-around collar of a minister. He retrieved his horse from the livery stable, where he'd rented a stall the previous week. Then he turned the swaybacked dun onto the wagon road toward Cimarron. The long day's ride allowed him to consider the knotty question of Orville McMain. He was duty bound to save McMain from the ring's assassins. Yet he was equally determined to convert one of them—preferably Florencio Donaghue—into a star witness. Only then would he have the testimony to corroborate Lise's story. And that one thought was still uppermost in his mind. Whatever the cost, her safety superseded all else.

Dusk was falling as Braddock rode into Cimarron. The plan he'd formulated was tricky and dangerous. Somewhat refined, it was a variation of the dodge he'd used to mouse-trap the ring's hired guns in Cimarron Canyon. He was prepared for resistance on the part of McMain. There was every likelihood the publisher would simply refuse to go along. In the event reason failed, Braddock would then resort to some more drastic means of persuasion. He was also reconciled to the fact that he would have to deal with Buck Colter. The cooperation of McMain's bodyguard was essential, for without him the plan would never work. Braddock had him slated for a key role.

Orville McMain was again working late. Entering the newspaper office, Braddock exchanged greetings with Colter and walked on back to the publisher's desk. McMain was understandably startled by his sudden appearance. Braddock deflected his questions and launched into a quick recounting of events in Santa Fe. While he couldn't put his finger on the reason, he was still somewhat leery of telling McMain everything. So he made no mention of Lise or Stephen Elkton and thereby avoided any reference to the meeting in Mitchell's hotel suite. He related instead the contents of Max Flagg's editorial and the bombshell effect it had created in Santa Fe. Then he fabricated a story about Mitchell's reluctance to kill Flagg so soon after the editorial. He went on to explain Mitchell's ultimate decision, which involved direct orders to Florencio Donaghue. Orders to commit murder.

"You've been tagged," he concluded. "Mitchell wants an object lesson that'll get the message across, and you're it. Donaghue's hired guns will definitely try to kill you—no doubt about it."

McMain took the news with equanimity. "I suppose it was inevitable. As the leader of the coalition, I was a marked man anyway. Flagg's editorial just provoked them to take action now rather than later."

"Damn shame!" Braddock said fiercely. "I mean, it doesn't seem fair somehow. Flagg writes the editorial and you get shot at."

"One of life's inequities." McMain's smile was bleak. "I appreciate the warning, though. I'm very much in your debt."

"All part of the job." Braddock pursed his lips, considering. "What d'you aim to do?"

"Nothing," McMain said stoutly. "I won't run and I won't be intimidated. I intend to stand my ground."

"I admire your grit, Orville."

"Oh, it's not that," McMain said with false modesty. "I'm too bullheaded for my own good. I refuse to let the scoundrels dictate how I conduct my life."

"Suppose," Braddock began, scratching his jaw thoughtfully. "I'm only thinking out loud, you understand. But just suppose there was a way to beat them at their own game. Would you be interested?"

"Perhaps," McMain said slowly. "Do you have something in mind?"

"Yeah, after a fashion." Braddock leaned across the desk, his voice low and confidential. "All the way from Raton, I kept thinking how they've got us on the defensive. Then it occurred to me that it ought to be the other way round. It's high time we took it to them and attack!"

McMain nodded gravely. "The best defense is a good offense. It's one of the oldest maxims in warfare. But how do we go about it?"

"Deceit," Braddock said in a sidelong, conspiratorial glance. "What with me back in town, let's suppose a rumor pops up in the gossip mill. The word gets out that Reverend Jacoby really wasn't off riding the circuit. He was actually down in Santa Fe talking with the U.S. Marshal."

"Talking to him about what?"

"About the evidence you've got on Donaghue."

"Me!" McMain appeared bemused. "What evidence?"

"Evidence that Donaghue was behind the murder of Reverend Tolby."

"No such evidence exists!"

Braddock smiled. "You and me know that. But Donaghue couldn't take a chance. He'd have to assume it does exist, wouldn't he?"

"I imagine so," McMain said with an oddly perplexed look. "What would that accomplish, though?"

"Well, you see, that's where the second part of the rumor takes effect."

"The second part?"

"Yeah." Braddock regarded him with great calmness. "We let it slip out that the U.S. Marshal is on his way to Cimarron. It's all arranged for him to meet with you tomorrow night—here in your office—in secret. And at that time you'll personally deliver the evidence against Donaghue."

"But"—McMain frowned and shook his head—"it's all an invention. There's no evidence and no U.S. Marshal."

"True." Braddock grinned ferociously. "It's pure deceit, start to finish. Only, Donaghue won't know that."

"Good Lord!" McMain stared at him, immobile with disbelief. "It's another hoax, a trap, like the one at Cimarron Canyon. You're talking about using me as bait!"

"That's the general idea."

"And Donaghue will try to kill me!"

"You forget," Braddock reminded him, "Donaghue's already been ordered to kill you. So the attempt will be made no matter what we do."

McMain flushed and his voice went up a couple of octaves. "You left out one slight detail. I'd be sitting here like a staked-out goat. I wouldn't have a Chinaman's chance!"

"You're wrong," Braddock said flatly. "My way, we've got them on ground of our own choosing. We sucker them in and spring the trap and end up with some prisoners. In other words, we've got the edge."

"Pardon me if I take no comfort from the thought!"

"Consider the alternative." Braddock leaned forward, intensely earnest now. "You let them choose the time and place, and they've got the edge. They'll kill you sure as hell."

McMain blinked and swallowed hard. Then he very gingerly nodded his head. His voice was barely audible. "All right, we'll do it your way. I just hope you don't get too brave with my life."

Braddock sidestepped the objection. "I plan to capture whoever Donaghue sends to do the job. Then we'll offer him a deal to turn songbird and save his own neck. We ought to wind up with an open-and-shut case against Donaghue."

"And once we have Donaghue"—McMain smiled as though his teeth hurt—"we offer him a deal to testify against Mitchell. Is that it?"

"Why not?" Braddock said. "You hired me to bust the

Santa Fe Ring and Mitchell's the key. After we nail him, it's all over but the shouting."

"I'd be the first to say amen to that."

"One other thing," Braddock said almost as an afterthought. "We want the killers to think you're a sitting duck. Otherwise they're liable to play it safe and not take the bait. So we'll have to pull Colter off as your bodyguard."

"Hold on now!" McMain said, his voice clogged with apprehension. "You do that and I will be a sitting duck!"

An ironic smile tinged the corner of Braddock's mouth. "I'll be here with you, Orville. And I'm all the bodyguard you need."

"Try explaining that to Colter!"

"I intend to."

"How?"

"I've got a notion Colter and me speak the same language."

"I don't follow you."

"He will."

"God." McMain passed a hand across his eyes. "You ought to be a drummer. I think you just sold me a bill of goods."

Braddock chuckled and hitched back his chair. He walked toward the front of the office, circling around the counter. Colter stood like a gray-eyed monolith, the shotgun crooked over his arm. He nodded as Braddock halted a pace away.

"How's tricks, Reverend?"

"Not bad." Braddock kept his gaze level and cool. "You and me need to have a little talk."

"Fire away."

"I reckon you've already guessed I'm no minister."

"Now that you mention it," Colter said as he took a tug at his cookie-duster mustache, "I sort of had a sneakin' hunch along them lines."

"The reason I brought it up . . ." Braddock paused and stared at him for a long moment. "I'm in the position of having to take you into my confidence."

"That so?"

Braddock's eyes were very pale and direct. "I wouldn't take it kindly if you betrayed that confidence."

Colter's smile seemed frozen. "How would you take it?"

"Personal." Braddock underscored the word. "So personal you wouldn't like it the least little bit."

Colter barked a sharp, short laugh. "I've never been one to talk out of school. Whatever you've got to say, it stops here."

Braddock read no guile in him. "For openers, I'm a private detective."

"Figured you for a law dog of some variety or another."

"The name's Cole Braddock."

"No kiddin'?" Colter sounded impressed. "Not every day a fellow gets to meet a man with your reputation. Lots of talk about you around the bunkhouse."

"Don't believe everything you hear."

"Well, it's mostly what the boys read in the *Police Gazette*. Your name shows up pretty regular."

"Hope you took it with a pinch of salt."

"You mean it's not true?"

"Let's just say the *Gazette* tends to twist the facts."

Colter gave him a slow nod. "You still do work for the cattlemen's association?"

"Not for a while." Braddock appeared puzzled. "What makes you ask that?"

"I'm a cowhand," Colter said, grinning. "Heard you've run down some real bad hombres, rustlers and the like."

"Past history," Braddock said with a dismissive gesture. "I'm more concerned with McMain right now."

"What about him?"

"Donaghue's been ordered to punch his ticket."

"What else is new? We've been expectin' it ever since Reverend Tolby was killed."

"Suppose I told you the order came direct from Santa Fe?"

"Uh-huh!" Colter seemed to stand a bit taller. "Guess it's

time for me to get extra extra careful. Is that what you're tryin' to say?"

"Just the opposite," Braddock told him. "I want to pull you off the job."

"Leave him without a bodyguard?"

"Yeah."

"What the hell for?"

"You and me are going to do a little play-acting."

"Play-acting?" Colter said dubiously. "I wouldn't exactly call that my strong suit."

"Nothing to it," Braddock observed. "All you do is pretend you're something you're not. That ought to be second nature to you by now."

Colter stiffened. "You tryin' to tell me something?"

"You tell me," Braddock said with a hard look. "Why would a cowhand carry a double-action pistol and a fancy shotgun?"

"I carry the best I can afford. What's so peculiar about that?"

"Nothing." Braddock fixed him with an inquiring gaze. "Not by itself anyway. But when you add it to other things, it makes a man wonder."

"Other things?"

Braddock paused, staring him straight in the eye. "What was your momma—Cheyenne or Sioux?"

Colter stared back at him. "You oughtn't ask a man personal questions. It's not polite."

"Look at it this way," Braddock said casually. "I've told you who I am, and in a manner of speaking, I know who you aren't. You keep my secret and I'll keep yours."

"What makes you think I'm tryin' to hide anything?"

"Because you haven't told anyone."

"Says who?"

"It's what they don't say. A thing like that would be a pretty hot item. But nobody's put the bee in my ear, not a word. See what I mean?"

Colter wrestled with himself a moment, then shrugged.

"All right, you've got yourself a trade-off. What happens now?"

"We put on a play for the town gossips."

"How's it work?"

Braddock outlined the plan. The longer he talked, the better it sounded. Colter listened attentively and a slow grin spread over his face. He thought it entirely possible someone would get killed.

And he had a good idea who.

CHAPTER FOURTEEN

Warren Mitchell studied the note. His brow furrowed and a muscle twitched at the corner of his mouth. He dropped the slip of paper on his desk.

Yesterday he had questioned the bellboy at length. What he'd learned tended to confirm everything contained in Boyd's note. Elmer Boyd had boarded the morning north-bound, ticketed through to Raton. From there, according to what Boyd had told the bellboy, he intended to travel by stagecoach to Fort Worth. Apart from that, the bellboy had nothing to offer.

Hands locked behind his head, Mitchell tilted back in his chair. His nerves were on edge and his stomach churned with gassy discomfort. He'd read the note a dozen times, perhaps more. On the surface it all sounded very reasonable, very legitimate. Yet he couldn't shake the feeling that there was something more behind Elmer Boyd's abrupt departure. It boggled the mind that a man would so casually put a three-million-dollar deal on the back burner. What sort of ranching problems could be of such magnitude that it would send

Boyd scurrying back to Texas? No ready answer presented itself.

Still, Mitchell preferred to accept the note at face value. Elmer Boyd was an odd bird, albeit a rich one, and apparently a man of impulsive nature. Then, too, he was a Texan, and as everyone knew, Texans were a strange breed. Perhaps in Boyd's mind some sudden difficulty at the ranch took precedence over all else. The fact remained that the Guadalupe County deal had been clinched, and Boyd's check for three million had been deposited. There was nothing in Boyd's departure that would materially affect what amounted to an ironclad agreement. Unless . . .

Mitchell pushed the thought aside. The possibility that the check was no good seemed wildly irrational, absurd. Of course, if the problem in Texas was financial and Boyd needed to cover the check, that would certainly explain his departure. Or if sufficient funds no longer existed, Boyd was now beyond the reach of New Mexico courts. But all that was borrowing trouble, Mitchell told himself, and at a time when he was already juggling trouble enough. Which was one of the major reasons he hadn't mentioned Boyd's departure to Stephen Elkton.

In fact, he had studiously avoided Elkton since their meeting two nights ago. The passage of time had done nothing to diminish his overriding sense of apprehension. The more he pondered it, the more convinced he became that Orville McMain's death would merely inflame an already volatile situation. He considered Elkton's order to kill the newspaperman not just imprudent; it was a senseless provocation that would serve no useful purpose. Instead, it would act as a goad on the Cimarron Coalition and unite the various factions as never before. The upshot would be even stronger opposition, perhaps some organized form of retaliation. And worse, it would bring greater public support for the coalition.

It was this latter point that troubled Mitchell most of all. By nature, he was not a violent man. In truth, just the thought of shooting someone left him a bit sick. On occasion, at Elkton's insistence he had orchestrated the death of those who posed a direct threat to the ring. Yet it was not his style, and he'd always felt somehow sullied in the aftermath. He preferred intellect to brute force. His method was to finesse an opponent, not kill him.

And his intellect warned him that the death of McMain represented a monumental hazard. For now, the Cimarron Coalition was largely isolated within Colfax County. In turn, strong opposition from the Democrats was limited principally to Santa Fe. But another killing might very well bridge the gap and bring these two very disparate groups into formal alliance. Any ground swell of public support would then tend to create a wave effect throughout the territory. Once set in motion, such a populist movement could easily prove irresistible.

The end result, in Mitchell's view, might represent a symbolic death knell for the Santa Fe Ring. On a personal note, it would mean a finish to both the power and prominence he had attained in territorial business affairs. Yet, over the years he'd learned never to second-guess Stephen Elkton. The soft-spoken lawyer was a shrewd manipulator of men and events, with an uncanny insight into the forces that shaped ordinary people's lives. He was, moreover, a man of absolute amorality, without conscience or scruples. He considered violence, even murder, nothing more than an expedient in the normal course of business.

For good reason, then, Mitchell had decided to follow orders. To do otherwise would constitute an act of betrayal in Elkton's view. And Mitchell knew that, inexorably, such an act would lead to his own execution. All the more so since he was already in hot water over Dora Kimble. The *New Mexican*'s exposé on his "orgy for politicos" had rolled off the presses yesterday. As Santa Fe's newest variety sensation, the girl's name had received prominent mention. Which was still another reason why he had avoided Elkton. Out of sight was by no means out of mind, especially with his name publicly linked to a tart who sang dirty ballads, but low visibility seemed his best option for the moment.

As for the girl herself, he suddenly felt very much the fool. His campaign to seduce her seemed, in retrospect, a rather cruel joke. Elkton's talk of murder, with the girl secreted in the bedroom, had unsettled him more than he cared to admit. Since then, he'd displayed all the virility of an aging eunuch. Solely as a matter of pride, he had appeared at the Tivoli last night and brought her back to the hotel. But it was an act of sheer bravado, and overall a little demoralizing. He doubted that even Dora Kimble, on her finest night, could make him rise to the occasion.

Still, all things considered, the girl was the least of his problems. Yesterday he'd sent a telegraph message to Donaghue in Cimarron. The wire was drafted in the form of a business communication and signed with a fictitious name. It was a prearranged code, designed for no other purpose than to summon Donaghue to Santa Fe. The order he would pass along to Donaghue was not just personally distasteful. He thought it a mistake, and the potential repercussions seemed staggering to contemplate. Yet, given the circumstances, he could only play the cards as dealt.

His hands were sweating as he folded Elmer Boyd's note and stuck it in the desk drawer.

Florencio Donaghue stepped off the southbound train late that afternoon. He walked directly from the depot to the plaza, mingling with shoppers who crowded the boardwalk. He tried very hard to look unobtrusive.

A thick-set man, Donaghue was perspiring heavily. But it was neither exertion nor the westerly afternoon sun that made him sweat. All the way from Cimarron, he'd thought of nothing but the telegraph message. Only last month he had received a similar wire summoning him to Santa Fe. Upon arriving in Mitchell's office, he had been ordered to arrange the death of Reverend John Tolby. Today, he was worried that another wire meant still another death. He wanted nothing more to do with murder.

Donaghue loitered around on the plaza until sundown. As twilight deepened, he made his way to the Mercantile National Bank. There were few passersby and he turned, unobserved, into the stairwell. He knew Mitchell's secretary would have left for the day, and he felt relatively assured that the office would be empty. Upstairs he proceeded along the corridor to the Santa Fe Land & Development Company. He entered swiftly, without knocking.

"Someone there?" Mitchell called from the inner office.

"It's me," Donaghue answered.

"Lock the door."

Donaghue complied, then crossed the outer room. He found Mitchell, who was bathed in the glow of an overhead lamp, waiting with impatience. There was no offer of a handshake and he had expected none. He took a chair before the desk.

"I got your wire."

"So I see," Mitchell said tonelessly. "I assume you took the usual precautions?"

There was a patronizing undertone to the question. Accustomed to it by now, Donaghue knew that it had nothing to do with their business relationship. He was part Irish and part Mexican, and Mitchell looked upon him as an intelligent half-breed. He understood, and he took no offense. He merely nodded, and said, "I was not followed."

Mitchell shrugged. "How are things in Cimarron?"

"Pretty much routine. Just the usual problems."

"No more trouble from the new preacher, Jacoby?"

"He's out riding the circuit. So far as I know, he hadn't come back when I left. Any special reason you ask?"

"Just curiosity. What's new with Orville McMain?"

"Same old thing. He keeps folks stirred up with his editorials. Course, he's a windbag and nobody takes any of that stuff too serious."

"I do."

Something in Mitchell's voice alerted him. Donaghue felt the sweat puddle under his armpits. "You called me down here to talk about McMain?"

"Yes," Mitchell said evenly. "I want him—eliminated."

"Do you think that's smart?"

"Are you questioning my decision?"

"Not exactly. I just don't think it's a good move right now."

Mitchell stared at him. "I wasn't asking your advice. Nor is the matter open to debate. I want it done immediately."

For years Donaghue had been the political kingfish of Colfax County. Yet he was a big fish in a very small pond. Apart from the townspeople in Cimarron, the voting rolls were dominated by homesteaders and ranchers. There was little opportunity for corruption and graft and even less reason to bribe a politician. No one got rich serving in public office.

Then, operating in absolute secrecy, Mitchell's company bought the Beaubien-Miranda land grant. Prior to the public announcement, Mitchell recruited Donaghue into the organization. Along with Donaghue, he also got control of the Colfax County political machine. In time, with the help of shady federal officials, the land grant was expanded to two million acres. Donaghue and his courthouse cronies protected the ring's interests in the legal disputes that followed. Quite literally, they'd sold their souls for a chance at the brass ring, and betrayed their friends and neighbors in the process.

Even today, Donaghue still believed Mitchell to be the head of the Santa Fe Ring. He had dealt only with Mitchell throughout their long association. Like everyone else, he knew that Mitchell was the power broker in territorial politics and a man whose influence stretched all the way to Washington. It had never occurred to him that Mitchell too might take orders, parrot the commands of some higher authority. Had he been told the truth, he would have scoffed in open derision, for he believed Mitchell to be evil incarnate, one of the Devil's own. Were he to disobey an order, he hadn't the slightest doubt that his life would be forfeit.

"Mr. Mitchell," he said now, "I was only trying to warn you. We've killed one preacher and tried to kill another. Folks just won't hold still for—"

"Spare me the lecture! We'll deal with the coalition members as the occasion demands. In the meantime, I expect you to do as you're told."

"Why not let Ortega and Johnson handle it? Hell, at least they're professionals."

Donaghue's reference was to a couple of hired guns on the ring's payroll. Their talents had been employed to great effect in the Lincoln County War. But Mitchell preferred to use them only in the most extreme circumstances. He shook his head.

"I'm offering you a chance to redeem yourself. You and your men failed me with Jacoby. Outwitted and outfought by a preacher, no less! I suggest you exercise greater ingenuity with Orville McMain."

"You're the boss," Donaghue said with a resigned look. "I just hope it doesn't blow the lid off things."

"You worry too much, Florencio."

"Maybe it's because I understand common folks, Mr. Mitchell. They try to stick by the law, but they've got their limits. You push 'em too far and they'll push back."

"Very interesting. Suppose you catch the evening north-bound and get on back to Cimarron. I want this business finished quickly."

Donaghue understood he'd been dismissed. He rose with a nod and shambled out of the office. A key rattled in the lock, then the hallway door opened and closed.

Mitchell sat for a moment in the deepening silence. It occurred to him that Donaghue was a wiser man than Stephen Elkton. But, then, the wise seldom governed. In the end, might made right, and it was the strong who ruled.

The irony of it all had often amused him in the past. He wondered why he couldn't laugh tonight.

CHAPTER FIFTEEN

—————

Shortly before noon the next day, Braddock stopped by the newspaper office. A few minutes later he emerged with Colter at his side, and they walked toward the center of town. Passersby noticed that Colter was in a foul mood, and further, that he wasn't carrying his shotgun. The preacher was talking to him in a low voice, gesturing rapidly but with no apparent success. Colter's replies were sharp and surly, increasingly loud.

Uptown, they entered a café directly across from the courthouse. The noontime crowd, most of whom worked for the county, looked around in amazement. For almost a month, Colter hadn't let Orville McMain out of his sight. Wherever the publisher went, night or day, the shotgun-toting cowhand had been his constant shadow. Now, inexplicably, Colter was seating himself at a table with Reverend Titus Jacoby. All the more mystifying, Colter's expression was that of a mad bull hooking at cobwebs. Everyone within earshot leaned closer to catch the conversation.

"I don't care what you say, parson. He's plumb off his rocker!"

"Now, now," Braddock soothed. "You mustn't take it personally. Orville is simply doing what he thinks best."

"For my money, he's actin' like the town idjit!"

A waitress appeared and the conversation momentarily ceased. Colter ordered beefsteak and Braddock settled for the blue-plate special. The waitress went away and Colter sat lost in a glowering funk. Braddock clucked sympathetically, wagging his head.

"I do believe you're being too harsh on yourself—and Orville."

"Not by half," Colter grunted. "I should've talked him out of it. He's just not thinkin' straight!"

"You can only advise, Buck. In the end the decision is his alone."

"Oh, yeah?" Colter said in an abrasive tone. "Nobody in the coalition's gonna think so. I mean, there he sits with the evidence—"

"Lower your voice," Braddock admonished him. "We're in a public place."

"Sorry, parson." Colter leaned forward and went on in a froggy rasp. "Anyway, he's got the goods on the killers and he's just gonna sit there on his duff waitin' for the U.S. Marshal. It don't make sense!"

"Why not?" Braddock said, not asking a question. "I spoke with the marshal myself. He promised he would arrive no later than tonight. You know that."

"Course I know it!" Colter snorted. "But that don't justify Orville tellin' me to take a powder. Who's gonna look after him till the marshal shows?"

"Calm yourself," Braddock temporized. "You've performed sterling duty and Orville saw no need to impose on you further. Nothing will happen to him between now and tonight."

"Hope so, parson. I shore do hope so!"

"Set your mind at rest, Buck. He's perfectly safe."

The waitress, as though on cue, returned with their meals. Colter dug into his charred steak and Braddock took a bite of meat loaf. A look passed between them, and Colter got the message. All the lines had been spoken and their one-act drama had played to a receptive audience. It was now time to lower the curtain.

Braddock was pleased with himself. There had been no mention of Reverend Tolby or Florencio Donaghue. But to those sitting nearby, the murdered preacher and Cimarron's political kingfish were part and parcel of the conversation. Before the noon hour was over, the gossip mill in the courthouse would be churning at full speed. Word of McMain's meeting with the U.S. Marshal would spread, and with each retelling, the evidence would broaden in scope. By sundown Donaghue would have arrived at the only logical conclusion. Tonight was the night Orville McMain must be killed.

All in all, Braddock thought the ruse was a small gem. And he was vastly impressed by Colter's performance. Whatever his real name, there was no question about his gift for deception.

The young half-breed was a born ham.

The last step in the ruse was performed in public view.

After their noon meal, Braddock and Colter returned to the newspaper office. McMain, who was in a state of nervous agitation, questioned them at length. Braddock assured him that all had gone well at the café. The courthouse crowd had swallowed the story whole.

As Braddock turned to leave, Colter paused to collect his shotgun. McMain acted quickly, his movements momentarily obscured behind the counter. He stuffed a folded slip of paper into Colter's vest pocket, pushing it out of sight. He shook his head, forestalling questions; his eyes beseeched the younger man to say nothing. Colter hefted his shotgun and followed Braddock out the door.

From the newspaper, they walked down to the livery stable. There Colter saddled his horse, hesitating afterward on the streets for a brief handshake with Braddock. Then he mounted and rode north out of town. Everyone watching assumed his destination was Isaac Coleman's ranch, where he was employed as a cowhand. His departure was the clincher, visible proof that he'd been dismissed as McMain's bodyguard. It was, in fact, more truth than playacting. The young half-breed's offer of assistance had been refused yesterday and yet again on the noontime stroll to the café. Braddock preferred to work alone.

A mile or so outside town, Colter reined to a halt. He fished the slip of paper from his vest pocket and unfolded it. His eyes narrowed as he scanned the note. Hastily scrawled, it was a message to Isaac Coleman. It revealed Braddock's identity and the results of his undercover work to date. Then, in an apprehensive tone, it outlined the details of Braddock's plan for tonight. Fearful the plan would go awry, McMain asked Coleman and Allison to slip into town before dark. He cautioned them not to alert Braddock to their presence. Nonetheless, they were to keep a close watch on the newspaper office and await his signal. He wanted them near at hand at the first sign of trouble.

Colter tucked the note back into his vest pocket. With the reins looped around the saddle horn, he built a smoke and lit up. He sat there, his expression abstracted, mentally reviewing the situation. His immediate impulse was to ride back to town and inform Braddock. But that would compromise McMain, who had entrusted him to act in good faith. Then, too, there was the matter of his employer, Isaac Coleman. He owed a certain loyalty to the man who paid his wages.

Yet the whole thing stuck in his craw. Braddock had confided in him, enlisting his support. The detective clearly extended his trust to few people. Their handshake, in Braddock's view, represented an agreement, one man's bond to the other. In the strictest sense, delivering the message wasn't a betrayal of that trust. Colter had agreed to only one thing; not to personally divulge Braddock's true identity. It was the note that would actually let the cat out of the bag. He was nothing more than a message bearer.

Colter grunted to himself. While it wasn't betrayal, it wasn't altogether aboveboard either. But he was caught in the middle, pulled in opposite directions by McMain and Braddock. Whichever way he leaned, one or the other of them would feel he'd broken faith. So he couldn't win, for the simple reason that there was no way to satisfy everybody. Put in that light, the choice boiled down to no choice at all. His greatest loyalty was to the man who paid him top dollar to act as McMain's bodyguard. And the note was, after all, addressed to Isaac Coleman.

Gathering the reins, Colter gigged his horse into a lope. Only now, with the decision made, would he allow himself to consider what bothered him most. His uneasiness about the note centered to a large degree on Clay Allison. From all he'd seen, Allison was a loudmouthed braggart who bullied other people for the sheer sport of it. There was a mad-dog mentality about Allison, and that warped quality had resulted in the deaths of several men. Allison's only saving grace was that he'd somehow earned the respect of Isaac Coleman. Their friendship went back many years, and in certain ways they were closer than blood kin. Coleman treated him somewhat like a Dutch uncle.

A good listener, Colter had heard several variations of the same story. Allison and Coleman had first met in Texas, where they worked as cowhands for the legendary Charlie Goodnight. In 1870 they had teamed up as stock contractors, trailing a herd to New Mexico Territory. Their payment, taken in lieu of cash, was three hundred head of cattle. With breeder stock, they had then laid claim to a vast stretch of grazing land north of Cimarron. Later, after the operation had grown to a respectable size, they'd split the land and cattle down the middle. Their ranches, which abutted one another, eventually became the largest outfits in Colfax County.

Other stories, spoken of less openly, were also common bunkhouse fare. Before his Texas days, Allison was reported to have been discharged from the Confederate Army for emotional instability. The tale took on credence as his reputation spread for getting into drunken brawls and seemingly mind-less shooting scrapes. He was generally feared for his mur-derous temper, and local wisdom had it that he went a bit loony when antagonized. Whatever the truth of the rumors, there was no questioning his violent nature. He was known, with ample reason, as a mankiller.

The single moderating influence in Allison's life was Isaac Coleman. Still, in the extreme not even Coleman could control him. And that was what worried Colter most of all. Anyone who organized a lynching bee and later decapitated the guest of honor was a man who warranted concern. Some years ago, Allison had done precisely that and displayed the severed head in a Cimarron saloon. So his crazy streak made him dangerous, and not just to his enemies.

Colter's uneasiness ticked a notch higher. The note burned in his vest pocket like a red-hot coal, and he silently cursed Orville McMain. He rode north with the disquieting sense that he was headed in the wrong direction.

The ranch compound was located on a rise overlooking a wooded creek. The house was a sprawling adobe structure, faintly resembling a fort. Nearby were several outbuildings, the bunkhouse, and a large corral. The place looked deserted.

Colter checked the angle of the sun. It was going on three o'clock and he wondered if Coleman was out working with the other hands. Then, approaching the house, he spotted a horse standing hip-shot at the hitch rack. His edgy feeling took a turn for the worse. The mousy dun cow pony belonged to Clay Allison.

Coleman's wife met him at the door. She was a plain woman who looked older than her years. Her mouth was perpetually down-turned, and in answer to his question, she waved him along the hall. Walking to the end of the corri-dor, he paused in the doorway of Coleman's office. The ranch owner was seated at a rolltop desk, an open ledger spread be-fore him. Allison was slouched nearby in a leather armchair.

"Colter!" Allison's voice sounded surprised. "Where the hell'd you drop from?"

"Allison." Colter nodded. "Mr. Coleman."

Coleman motioned him forward. "C'mon in, Buck. How come you're not in Cimarron?"

"It's a long story."

Colter told it briefly. From Braddock's arrival yesterday to his own departure today, he covered the salient points. Throughout the recounting, he referred to Braddock as "Reverend Jacoby." It merely delayed the inevitable, but he felt he'd at least kept his word. He concluded by handing Coleman the note.

Coleman stiffened as he read McMain's words. He passed the note to Allison and looked around. "How long have you known about Braddock?"

"Yesterday," Colter said flatly. "He told me who he was after he'd talked to McMain. By then they'd already agreed on the plan."

"Plan!" Allison shouted. "Hell, that ain't no plan. It's goddamn suicide!"

"Hold on, Clay," Coleman interjected. "Let's take first things first. Buck, you say you only found out about Braddock yesterday?"

"That's right."

"You got any idea when McMain hired him?"

"Nope."

"Any notion at all of how he contacted Braddock?"

"Nobody said and I never asked."

Allison snorted. "Nobody has to say. It's got the smell of Frank Kirkland's work. Only a dumb-ass lawyer would waste our money on a dee-tective."

"Not exactly a waste," Colter observed. "Braddock's reputation speaks for itself. He generally gets the job done."

Allison peered at him. "You takin' sides?"

"I'm just stating a fact."

"Sounds to me like you and Braddock got real cozy."

"Allison," Colter said evenly, "how it sounds to you don't concern me. Savvy?"

Allison started out of his chair. Coleman jumped to his feet, arms outstretched. "You two pull in your horns! We haven't got time for personal arguments."

"Wouldn't take long," Allison grated. "I'd settle his hash lickety-split."

Colter just smiled. Coleman stepped between them, his expression somber. "Buck, what's your best guess? You think Braddock's scheme will sucker them into makin' a try on McMain?"

"If I was Donaghue," Colter allowed, "I'd figure it was tonight or never. Braddock laid the bait pretty slick."

"How much faith you got in Braddock? Any chance they'll get past him and kill McMain?"

"I reckon there's always a chance. But if I was a bettin' man, I'd say the odds favor Braddock."

"Why's that?"

"Just a hunch. He strikes me as the kind that don't make mistakes. In his line of work, he can't afford it."

"Yeah," Coleman mused almost to himself. "I suspect you're right."

"Wouldn't hurt to play along and find out."

"Tell you what, Buck. Joe Phelps and Jack Noonan are workin' the north fork. They're pretty handy boys when push comes to shove. Go fetch 'em for me and hotfoot it on back here."

"You mean to let Braddock make his play?"

"Why not? Like you said, it's his line of work."

After Colter was gone, Allison rose from his chair. He cocked one eye at Coleman. "I hear the wheels turnin'. What you got in mind, Isaac?"

"We'll hide and watch. See what Braddock flushes out of the weeds."

"Go on, there's more to it than that."

"Well, the worst that could happen"—Coleman paused, his mouth razored in a crafty smile—"is that poor ol' Orville will get his ass shot off. And it wouldn't bother me a whole hell of a lot if he does. Wasn't right, him not tellin' us about Braddock."

"And whatever happens, we end up a step closer to Donaghue. Is that it?"

"We might just get the goods on Donaghue. We're shore as hell due a change of luck."

"You're one sly son of a bitch, Isaac. I like it, like it a lot."

"Yeah, but there's a hair in the butter. We don't wanna get ourselves crosswise of Braddock."

"Comes down to it, you let me handle that. I talk the kind of language he understands."

"Just keep your head, Clay. Don't go off on one of your— spells."

"Goddammit, you know better'n that, Isaac. When'd I ever cause trouble 'less it was necessary?"

Coleman thought it prudent not to answer. He slapped the other man on the shoulder and went off in search of his wife. Allison stared after him, grinning strangely. His eyes were fixed in a faraway look.

As though from a great distance, a voice spoke to him and he laughed softly to himself. Tonight seemed a long time to wait.

CHAPTER SIXTEEN

The moon went behind a cloud. For a moment the alley was cloaked in inky darkness. Then the cloud scudded past and the town was bathed in spectral moonlight. A dog barked somewhere in the distance.

On the street lampposts flickered like guttering candles. The supper hour had come and gone, and the street itself was virtually deserted. Farther uptown, the sound of a piano and laughter drifted faintly from the saloon. Then a ghostly stillness settled over Cimarron.

The front window of the *Beacon* was lit by the glow of a single lamp. The alleyway directly beside the newspaper separated it from a dry goods emporium. The newspaper had no side windows, but a door opened onto the alley. Opposite the door a narrow loading platform jutted outward from the emporium's stockroom.

Braddock stood hidden in the shadows. He was pressed back against the loading platform door, which was recessed slightly into the wall. A lamppost lit the mouth of the alley, and toward the rear of the buildings the far end was dappled with moonlight. All the more important, directly across from him was the side door of the newspaper. It was the reason he'd chosen this particular spot.

The plan had gone off smoothly. After Colter's departure, Orville McMain spent the afternoon at the newspaper and continued working into the evening. With nightfall, Braddock had left his hotel by the rear entrance and made his way to the alley. There he'd taken up a post on the loading platform, all but invisible in the shadowed doorway. He'd long ago mastered the skills essential to a stakeout or a manhunt. He stood perfectly still, loose and relaxed, avoiding any movement that might betray his position. He thought it would be a short wait.

Under normal circumstances, Braddock knew the killers would have delayed until McMain left the newspaper. Then, on his way home the publisher would have been shot down on some dark side street. Yet the circumstances tonight were anything but normal. A. U.S. Marshal was expected, and the killers would have to strike before McMain had a chance to surrender the evidence. Their attempt would almost certainly be made by the side door; the risk of being spotted on the street was much too great. So, exactly as he'd planned, Braddock waited on ground of his own choosing. The killers had lost the edge.

Shortly before ten, the crunch of dirt underfoot sounded at the end of the alley. Braddock's every sense alerted, and his hand snaked inside his suit jacket. The footsteps were slow and stealthy, and his ears told him there was only one man. Several moments later a figure emerged from the shadows and halted at the side door. The light from the street lamp glinted on gun metal as he took hold of the doorknob. Braddock pulled his Colt and thumbed the hammer.

"Don't move or you're dead!"

The man froze rock-still. Braddock crossed the loading platform and stepped to the ground. He quickly disarmed the man, stuffing the pistol in his waistband. Then he rapped out a sharp command.

"Inside! The door's unlocked."

Braddock followed him through the door and slammed it shut. McMain was standing behind his desk, watching intently as they moved from the darkened pressroom into the office. Braddock nudged the man forward and shoved him down in a chair. In the light from the desk lamp, his features were angular, with the swarthy complexion of a Mexican. His mouth was down-turned beneath a droopy mustache, and his eyes were black as obsidian. His expression was stoic.

Braddock holstered the Colt. "How about it, Orville? Do you recognize him?"

"Certainly," McMain replied. "His name is Cruz Vega."

"Well, now." Braddock nodded, smiling. "We met once before, didn't we, Vega?"

"No, señor," Vega said with a guttural accent. "I believe you are mistaken."

"Cimarron Canyon," Braddock reminded him. "We swapped lead out there not too long ago."

"I know nothing of that, señor."

"Course you do," Braddock said matter-of-factly. "That's the day I killed your cousin—Manuel Cardenas."

Vega's eyes shuttled away. "I know you killed Manuel, señor. But I was not there."

"You're here tonight, though."

"Sí."

"And you were sent here to kill Mr. McMain."

"How could you prove a thing like that?"

"You had a gun in your hand."

"A very small crime, señor. Verdad?"

The front door abruptly burst open. Clay Allison and Isaac Coleman trooped into the office. The ranchers were followed by Buck Colter and two more men who had the look of cowhands. Allison and Coleman moved around the counter and stopped before the desk. Allison glared at McMain.

"You were supposed to signal us, Orville."

"I haven't had a chance."

"Well, it's a damn good thing I had somebody watchin' the window. We could've grown beards waitin' on you."

"Hold it," Braddock interrupted. "What's going on here?"

Allison chuckled and flashed a wide grin. "Orville figured you could use some help—and we're it!"

Braddock turned to McMain. "Is that true?"

"Yes." McMain gave him a hangdog look. "I wasn't convinced you could do it all by yourself. So I asked Buck to carry a message for me."

"Colter told them?"

"No," McMain amended hastily. "I wrote a note explaining the situation."

Braddock's frown deepened. "How much do they know?"

"Everything," McMain said with a weak smile. "I couldn't ask them to help and leave them in the dark. Besides, they're members of the coalition. They have a right to know."

"That wasn't part of our agreement."

"Simmer down," Allison broke in. "We're all workin' toward the same end. No need to get your nose out of joint."

"Stay out of it, Allison!" Braddock's jaw set in a hard line. "Your help's not needed and I don't want it. Take your men and vamoose—now!"

A moment elapsed while they stared at one another. Then Allison let go with a rolling laugh. "Well, I'll tell you how it's gonna be, Mr. Detective. You've got our help whether you want it or not. What d'you say to that?"

"I say clear out"—Braddock's eyes hooded—"and do it damn quick."

"By jingo!" Allison said with a mirthless smile. "You talk like the cock o' the walk when you ought to be listenin' with both ears. Whyn't you take a peek and see what Isaac's holdin' on you?"

There was a metallic whirr as Isaac Coleman eared back the hammer on his six-gun. Braddock turned his head and saw the snout of the pistol centered on his chest. Allison relieved him of the Colt and the revolver jammed in his waistband, and dropped them on the desk. Then he moved past

Braddock and halted in front of Vega. He spoke to McMain over his shoulder.

"What's the greaser told you so far?"

"Nothing," McMain said blankly. "He refused to admit anything."

"Do tell!" Allison spit on his hands and rubbed them together. "Well, I got some medicine that'll open his mouth lickety-split."

"Allison!" Braddock's voice stopped him. "Vega is my prisoner. Touch him and you'll answer to me."

"Isaac, keep our detective friend covered. I'm gonna give this greaser a taste of knuckle sandwich."

Allison laughed a wild, braying laugh. Then his fist lashed out in a blurred movement. The blow connected with a sharp crack, and Vega slammed backward in the chair. A bright fountain of blood jetted from his nose, spilling down over his mustache. Before he could recover, Allison clubbed him on the side of the jaw and his head bounced off the wall. He slumped forward and Allison caught him with a looping roundhouse that knocked him out of the chair and onto the floor. Allison took a step back and kicked him in the pit of the stomach.

Vega's mouth snapped open in a whoofing whoosh of breath. He doubled over and clutched his midsection, eyes bulging with pain. His nose was broken and a jagged cut had been opened over his right eyebrow. He grunted as Allison lifted him bodily off the floor and propped him up in the chair. His mustache glistened wetly and the whole right side of his face was covered with blood. Allison took a handful of hair and wrenched his head back against the wall. The rancher's gaze was dulled and out of focus.

"Had enough?" Allison shook him like a rag doll. "You ready to gimme some straight talk, amigo?"

Vega coughed raggedly. *"No hablo inglés."*

"Whoo-ee!" Allison cackled. "You are some tough pepper-gut! Wanna think it over, change your mind? Give us just a few words!"

"No sé."

"You'll savvy before we're done, greaser."

Allison backhanded him across the mouth. Vega brought his arms up, attempting to protect himself, but Allison grabbed him by the lapels of his coat and pinned him to the wall. Supporting him with one hand, Allison then administered a brutal beating. His right arm worked like a piston, and the blows were delivered with methodical ferocity. Vega's features dissolved into a pulped mass that looked something like a freshly butchered side of beef. A final punch broke off his front teeth at the gum line, and he sagged sideways into a chair. Allison gripped his hair, jerking him upright.

"Last chance," Allison said in a jovially menacing voice. "Talk to me or I'll beat you to death where you sit."

Vega gagged and spit out a mouthful of teeth. The stumps left a bloody gap in his gums, and his lips were like puffed mush. His left eye was swollen completely shut and the split over his right eyebrow had been widened to a raw wound. He took several deep breaths, frothing bubbles from his mouth like a goldfish. Then he slowly nodded his head.

"That's the ticket!" Allison crowed. "Just to show you there's no hard feelin's, we'll start with something simple. You remember Reverend Tolby, don't you?"

"Sí."

"And you killed him, didn't you?"

"Sí."

"Who helped you?"

"Manuel Cardenas."

"He's dead," Allison scoffed. "Who else?"

"Pancho Griego."

"Who's he?"

"Mi compañero," Vega mumbled. "A friend. He did not help kill Reverend Tolby, but he help us other times."

"He live in Cimarron?"

"No."

"Where's he from?"

"Rayado."

"That little burg south of here?"

"*Sí.*"

"All right," Allison said with a vinegary satisfaction. "You're whistlin' the tune I wanna hear. Now we'll get down to the important stuff. Who paid you to kill Reverend Tolby?"

"No one."

Allison cuffed him across the mouth. "You're not listenin', amigo. Who was it that hired you?"

"We robbed him, señor. Only the two of us; no one else. *Es verdad.*"

"The truth, hell!"

Allison drew his pistol. He placed the tip of the barrel under Vega's nose and slowly cocked the hammer. His mouth zigzagged in a cruel grimace.

"One more time," he snarled. "And if the answer don't suit me, I'm gonna blow your fuckin' head off. Who hired you?"

Vega looked petrified. His one good eye widened and beads of sweat glistened on his forehead. His lips barely moved.

"Donaghue," he sputtered. "Florencio Donaghue."

"What'd he pay you?"

"A hundred dollars."

"For all three of you?"

"*Sí.*"

"Cheap bastard," Allison said in disgust. "Why'd he want Tolby killed?"

"He did not say, señor."

"Was it because Tolby was preachin' against the Santa Fe Ring?"

"I think so."

"Bullshit!" Allison jabbed the gun muzzle into his nose. "Talk to me about the Santa Fe Ring. Who does Donaghue get his orders from?"

"Madre de Dios!" Vega shook his head wildly. "I was told nothing, señor. Nothing!"

Allison studied him with a mocking scowl. "Well, it don't surprise me. I wouldn't've told you neither." He lowered the hammer and bolstered his gun with one quick motion. "Just for the record, Donaghue sent you here tonight, didn't he?"

"Sí, señor."

"I reckon that does it." Allison turned away, his mouth set in an ugly grin. "One of you boys run fetch your lariat. We're gonna hang ourselves a greaser."

Braddock tensed, on the verge of objecting. Isaac Coleman stilled him with a warning look and a wave of his gun. While one of the cowhands went for a rope, Colter and the other man were assigned to guard Braddock. Allison collared Vega by the scruff of the neck and waltzed him outside. Coleman and McMain exchanged a glance, then fell in behind. Colter and his sidekick, with Braddock wedged between them, brought up the rear.

"Sorry," Colter said in a low voice, "I was obligated to carry McMain's message."

"Why?" Braddock demanded. "Because you work for Coleman?"

"A man pays my wages, he buys my loyalty too."

"You sell yourself awful cheap, Buck."

"I kept my word," Colter said with a wooden expression. "I didn't say nothin' about what you told me. All I did was carry a message."

"Who are you trying to convince—me or yourself?"

Colter fell silent, stung by his tone. As they halted on the boardwalk, Allison and Coleman already had Vega positioned beneath a lamppost. The cowhand trotted back from the saloon, where his horse was tied to the hitch rack. He gave Allison the lariat, and Vega stood with a look of pop-eyed terror while the loop was cinched around his neck. Then Allison tossed the coiled lariat over a crossbar on top of the lamppost.

Upstreet several men were bunched in a knot outside the saloon. Bud Grant, the town marshal, separated from the crowd and hurried down the boardwalk. He stopped a couple of paces away, scanning their faces. His gaze finally settled on McMain.

"What's the problem, Orville?"

McMain shifted uncomfortably. "Vega tried to kill me. He also confessed to the murder of Reverend Tolby."

"Then press charges," Grant said forcefully. "Let the law do its job."

"The law!" Allison said with a sourly amused look. "Hell, everyone knows who runs the courthouse. You really think Donaghue would let him swing?"

"That's up to a jury."

"We're the jury!" Allison said vindictively. "We tried him and found him guilty—and he's gonna hang!"

"You've lynched too many men, Allison. Turn him over to me and I'll see to it that he stands trial. Otherwise your coalition's nothing but a gang of vigilantes."

"Yeah, and it's high time we started cleanin' house. There's a whole goddamn list of people that need their necks stretched."

"Start somewhere else," Grant ordered. "I won't let you hang him in my town."

"You won't, huh?" Allison's eyes blazed. "Turn around and walk away, Grant. 'Cause if you don't, I'll put a leak in your ticker. That badge don't mean shit to me."

Bud Grant was no coward, yet he was a realist and readily conceded he was no match for Allison. A gunfight would end with Cimarron looking for a new town marshal. At last he concluded Cruz Vega wasn't worth getting himself killed for. He turned and walked back toward the saloon.

Allison still had the loose end of the lariat in his hand. He suddenly stepped off the boardwalk and hoisted Vega a few inches into the air. Coleman leaped to help, and together they hauled the thrashing Mexican to the top of the lamppost. Allison took a couple of quick hitches around the base of the post and tied off the lariat. Then he moved back to watch the show.

Vega died hard. He dug at the lariat, gouging long welts down the front of his neck. His walnut features slowly turned purple and then black as the noose cut deeper into his throat. He kicked and danced as though searching for a foothold, and his heels drummed frantically against the lamppost. Several minutes passed, with the men watching in silence, before he choked to death. His struggles gradually weakened, then his body went slack and there was a noxious stench as his bowels voided. He dangled open-eyed at the end of the lariat.

A strained stillness fell over the group. Allison continued to stare up at the corpse with a dopey smile, but the others looked away, their expressions showing embarrassment. No one spoke, and the creak of the lariat was like a scratchy metronome in the silence. After a time, Braddock brushed Colter and the other cowhand aside. His eyes were stone cold and his hands were knotted into fists. He walked straight toward Allison.

"You'll recollect that I said you'd answer to me."

CHAPTER SEVENTEEN

"You're a regular rooster, aren't you?"

Allison backpedaled to the middle of the street. Braddock stepped off the boardwalk and followed him without a break in stride. Something told Allison he'd offended the wrong man. He threw up his hands as though warding off evil spirits.

"Whoa, hoss! I got no fight with you!"

"Fight or get whipped—your choice."

"No sense to it!" Allison reversed directions, circling toward the boardwalk. "I done told you we're on the same side."

"We were," Braddock said coldly. "Not anymore."

"You're gonna fight me over a stinkin' greaser?"

"Quit running and let's get to it."

"No siree bob!" Allison pulled his pistol, holding it loosely at his side. "I don't allow no man to lay hands on me."

"What's the matter?" Braddock said with wry contempt. "You acted mighty tough with Vega."

"Goddammit, he had it comin'!"

"So do you." Braddock continued advancing on him. "And it's time to pay up."

Allison cocked his pistol, leveling it. "Hold 'er right there! You take another step and I'll kill you deader'n hell."

"Allison!"

Colter's shout was like a thunderclap. Braddock stopped and saw the young half-breed move away from the other men. His pistol was extended at arm's length, pointed at Allison. He halted on the edge of the boardwalk.

"Drop your gun, Allison."

"God a'mighty!" Allison darted a quick glance over his shoulder. "What's got into you, Buck?"

"I don't hold with killin' unarmed men."

"You gonna turn Judas for him!"

"Drop it," Colter said with dungeon calm. "Or I'll drop you."

There was a stark silence. A sense of suppressed violence hung in the air, and the men seemed frozen in a stilled tableau. Colter's eyes were hard and deadly, and Allison regarded him with a look of wary hostility. At last Isaac Coleman broke the spell. He took a step toward Colter.

"Don't!" Colter warned him. "You try anything and Allison's a goner."

"Listen to me," Coleman said in a shaky voice. "You don't wanna do this, boy. The man's an outsider!"

"I just switched sides."

"For Chrissake!" Coleman took another step. "I treated you like a son, Buck. You owe me!"

"I'm not funnin', Isaac." Colter sighted along the barrel. "You or anybody else makes a move and Allison is cold meat."

"You'll double-damn regret it all your days!"

"Maybe." Colter's finger tightened on the trigger. "What d'you say, Allison? I'm through waitin'."

Allison muttered an unintelligible curse and gingerly lowered the hammer on his pistol, dropping it at his feet. A strange light came into his eyes, and he abruptly laughed. He tossed his hat on the ground, spit on his hands. Then he cocked his fists and waved Braddock forward.

"All right, you sorry son of a bitch. Come and get it!"

Braddock shuffled toward him, arms raised. He feinted with a left, then a right, and let go a stinging left hook. Allison shook off the blow and popped him on the chin. Braddock went down, losing his hat as he landed flat on his back. He was stunned by the power of the punch and was vaguely surprised to find himself on the ground. The brassy taste of blood filled his mouth and pinwheels of light flashed through his head. Allison sensed victory and moved to end the fight with a rough-and-tumble stomping. His first kick missed as Braddock rolled away, but he was uncommonly agile for a big man, and he lashed out with his other boot. Braddock took the force of the kick on his side, and for an instant he thought his rib cage was shattered. Then his head cleared and he caught his wind. He scrambled crablike to his feet.

Breathing heavily, he circled Allison with a new respect. The man was clearly a barroom brawler of some experience—and dangerous. Braddock gave ground as Allison waded in, windmilling with both arms. Bobbing and weaving, Braddock absorbed most of the blows on his arms and shoulders. But a looping overhead right got through his guard and caught him flush on the jaw. A shower of sparks rocketed before his eyes and the whole left side of his face went numb. He instinctively crouched, slipping inside the flurry of punches, and clinched Allison in a tight bear hug. The shooting stars and swirling dots slacked off a bit, and the groggy sensation passed. He allowed Allison to manhandle him and roughly shove him away. The tactic gave him a brief respite, room to maneuver.

Braddock dimly realized he wouldn't last. Allison was a punishing scrapper, and the sheer volume of blows would eventually beat him down. To win, he would have to end it fast, outfox rather than outmuscle him. He backed off, his guard lowered, acting wobbly and disoriented. Allison advanced on him, fists cocked, snarling an oath as he ambled forward. Braddock retreated a step farther, looking slow and clumsy, inviting a move. The ruse worked, and Allison went for a quick kill. His shoulder dipped, faking a straight left, then he launched a murderous haymaker. Braddock ducked under the blow and buried his fist in Allison's crotch. The big man roared like a bull elephant and doubled over, clutching himself as violent spasms knifed through his groin. Shifting slightly, Braddock grabbed the back of his head and kneed him squarely in the face.

Allison hurtled backward as if he'd been shot out of a cannon. He tripped over his own feet and sat down heavily in the dirt. His face was splattered with blood, and he retched, his mouth puckered in a pained oval. Yet he was far from whipped, and he shook his head, gulping great lungfuls of air. He rolled onto his hands and knees, struggling to maintain his balance. Then, his back to Braddock, he planted one hand on the ground and slowly levered himself upright. He stood and turned around.

Braddock was waiting. He exploded a short left hook to the jaw, followed by a chopping right cross to the temple. The splintering combination sent Allison reeling backward in a nerveless dance. He slammed into the lamppost, jarring it with the impact of his weight, and stood there as if transfixed. His eyes went blank, then his knees buckled and he settled to the ground on the seat of his pants. Overhead the corpse of Cruz Vega swayed beneath the shimmering light.

Brushing himself off, Braddock collected his hat and walked forward. His side ached, one of his molars was loose, and his ears rang with a faint buzzing sound. He glanced down at Allison and decided he wouldn't care for a repeat performance. He felt he'd been run through a gristmill.

Colter was still holding a gun on the other men. Braddock mounted the boardwalk and stopped beside him. McMain kept his gaze averted, looking somewhat shamefaced. But Isaac Coleman was having no part of humble pie. His eyes were smoky with rage.

"Don't change a thing," he said angrily. "We're gonna do what's got to be done."

A vein pulsed in Braddock's forehead. "I take it one hanging just whetted your appetite?"

"Damn tootin'!" Coleman glowered at him through slitted eyes. "Before we're done, we'll hang Griego and Donaghue, and anybody else that don't toe the line. We only just started!"

Braddock regarded him with an odd, steadfast look. "You're a fool, Coleman. A goddamn simpleton."

"Here now!" Coleman squared himself up stiffly. "You watch your mouth or I'll—"

"No, you won't." Braddock fixed him with a cold stare. "You mess with me one more time and I'll bury you. The same goes for Allison."

"That'll be the day!" Coleman hooted. "You try him with a gun and you're in for a surprise. It's you that'll get buried!"

"When he wakes up, you give him my message. Just steer clear—or else."

"Oh, I'll tell him. But you better find yourself a hole and pull it in after you. That goes for Judas Iscariot there too."

"If you're talkin' to me," Colter said, his voice flat, "you and Clay get off the street when you see me comin'. We're quits from here on out."

"You goddamn ingrate! You haven't heard the last—"

"Yeah, he has," Braddock said brusquely. "Take Allison and be on your way. I won't tell you a second time."

Coleman gave him a dirty look. There was a prolonged silence, and the rancher appeared on the verge of saying something more. Then he changed his mind and motioned the cowhands forward. They moved to the lamppost and, one on either side of him, hefted Allison off the ground. With his toes dragging in the dirt, they walked in the direction of the saloon. Coleman turned and stalked along behind them.

"You know," Braddock said, watching after them, "it occurs to me that Coleman's not the only fool around here."

Colter looked puzzled. "How's that?"

"I'm not heeled," Braddock said sardonically. "All that

big talk and my gun's still inside. Guess it's a good thing Coleman didn't call my hand."

"You had him buffaloed," Colter noted. "He wasn't gonna push too hard. Not after the way you cleaned Allison's plow."

"I hear you're pretty handy with your dukes too."

"Fair to middlin'."

"You ever tangle with Allison?"

"Nope," Colter said, smiling. "He left me alone and I returned the favor."

"Wish I'd done the same." Braddock rubbed his jaw. "Couple of times, he damn near tore my head off."

"I got the feelin' you enjoyed yourself."

Braddock laughed. "I would've enjoyed it a hell of a lot less without you to back my play. I'm obliged."

"I owed you one." Colter looked down at his boots. "Wasn't for me, they wouldn't've showed up here tonight."

"Hell, forget it." Braddock turned toward the office door. "Hold on a minute and I'll go get my gun."

Neither of them had acknowledged McMain's presence during the conversation. As Braddock entered the newspaper, McMain edged around Colter and hurried inside. Colter followed him through the door and stopped near the counter.

Braddock collected his pistol off the desk. Out of habit, he checked the loads, lowering the hammer on an empty chamber. Then he holstered the Colt and picked up Vega's gun. He glanced around as McMain approached.

"Here you go, Orville." He extended the gun. "A keepsake of your lynching bee."

"No, thanks." McMain bowed his head. "I'm not proud of tonight, Cole. It was just . . . necessary."

"How do you figure that?"

"Vega deserved to hang! After all, he murdered Reverend Tolby. We were within our rights to exact retribution."

"An eye for an eye?"

"Yes, exactly!"

"Why not let the law do it for you?"

"Don't be absurd!" McMain said with sudden vehemence. "Vega would never have gone to the gallows. Not in Colfax County."

"You could've requested a change of venue."

"To what end!" McMain asked cynically. "Every official in the courthouse is on the ring's payroll. We wouldn't have gotten an indictment, much less a conviction."

"Maybe not." Braddock dropped the gun on the desk. "Well, see you around sometime, Orville."

"Wait!" McMain appeared confused. "Where are you going?"

"I quit," Braddock said evenly. "I'm off the case."

McMain stared at him, aghast. "But you can't do that. We've already paid half your fee!"

"You got your money's worth."

"I beg to differ," McMain said promptly. "We retained you to perform an investigation. A full investigation!"

"Who're you kidding?" Braddock looked at him impassively. "You hired me to do your dirty work. I should've caught on sooner."

"I don't know what you mean."

"Yeah, you do," Braddock rebuked him. "Frank Kirkland conned me good when he showed up in Denver. Investigating the ring was strictly back burner, wasn't it?"

"No."

"C'mon, admit it!" Braddock said crossly. "What you really wanted was revenge for Reverend Tolby. You hired me to do your killing."

"You're mistaken."

"And you're lying, Orville. You sicced me on Donaghue the minute I hit town. You wanted him dead and out of the way."

"That's ridiculous!"

"Is it?" There was open scorn in Braddock's gaze. "With Donaghue dead, you and your coalition could've taken over Colfax County. You probably justified it by telling yourself he was behind Tolby's death. But it was perfect timing where your political plans were concerned. So you sent Kirkland out to hire you a killer."

"Why would I do that?" McMain waved his hand as though dusting away the accusation. "Allison and Coleman are quite capable along those lines. Tonight proved it."

"You lost control tonight," Braddock said with a short look. "You pulled the cork and then you couldn't put the demon back in the bottle. A bullet was the only thing that would've stopped Allison once he'd sniffed blood. And you don't have the guts for it, do you, Orville?"

McMain was caught up in a moment of indecision. His eyes drifted to the gun on the desk, and he studied it with a somber expression. Then he shrugged and looked up at Braddock.

"We had no way of knowing Vega would come alone tonight. I was afraid for my life, Cole. I honestly believed you needed help. That's the only reason I sent for Allison."

Braddock rocked his head from side to side. "I reckon the joke's on you, Orville. You let Allison out of the bottle and all you got for your trouble is a dead Mexican. Not much, is it?"

"I regret the whole affair."

"You'll be even sorrier before it's over. The marshal hit the nail square on the head. Before Allison's done, your coalition will be known as the Cimarron Vigilantes. I doubt that'll win you too many votes at the ballot box."

"It's not too late," McMain said hastily. "You could still complete your assignment."

"Wishful thinking," Braddock replied. "Donaghue probably skipped town before Vega was cold. He'll run even faster—and farther—with Allison on his trail. So it appears we're fresh out of witnesses."

"What about Pancho Griego, Vega's accomplice?"

"Same thought holds for him."

"Wait, Cole." McMain's voice was low and urgent. "Allison's a rancher, not a professional manhunter. Suppose you were able to capture Griego or Donaghue before he got to them? Then we'd still have a case, wouldn't we?"

"You talking about the Santa Fe Ring?"

"I am how," McMain assured him. "All you need is one witness to make a case against Warren Mitchell. And I know you could beat Allison to Donaghue. I'm certain of it!"

Braddock seemed to look through him. "You're switching horses in the middle of the stream. What you really wanted was Donaghue's scalp, and now you're hot to bust the ring. Why's that?"

McMain's lips peeled back in a weak smile. "I made a mistake and I'm willing to admit it. You've shown me the light, Cole."

"Uh-huh." Braddock nodded, digesting the thought. "You've lost control of Allison, and Donaghue's off to who knows where. So all of a sudden I'm your last-ditch chance. Wouldn't that about cover it?"

"Aren't you being a tad too skeptical?"

"I try never to stub my toe in the same place twice. I'm still waiting for an answer."

"Very well," McMain said sheepishly. "You are my last chance. The coalition won't survive if Allison gives it a black eye. You're the only one who can stop that from happening."

Braddock silently congratulated himself on his foresight. He'd been wise to make no mention of Lise or Stephen Elkton. He saw now that McMain was both slippery and ambitious, a man with political aspirations who dealt in expediency and raw pragmatism. He was not one to be trusted.

"Tell you what, Orville," he said at length. "I'll go along with you on two conditions."

"Anything you say, Cole."

"First, I'm only interested in the ring. Whether or not your coalition survives is immaterial to me. If busting the ring helps you in some way, that's fine. If not, then it's tough titty."

"And the second condition?"

"Even more personal," Braddock said with a hard grin. "You agree not to switch horses again. That includes Allison or any other cute ideas that might pop into your head. Because if you double-cross me again, I'll kill you."

"You're not serious!"

"Dead serious," Braddock said coolly. "You could've gotten me killed tonight. I won't stand for any more tricks."

"That's a rather harsh condition, isn't it?"

"Say no and I'll head on back to Denver. It's your chestnuts in the fire, not mine."

"In that event"—McMain bobbed his head—"I have no choice but to agree."

"Looks like I'm back on the case."

"Where will you start?"

"I'll let you know . . . sometime."

Braddock walked forward and circled the counter. Colter fell in beside him, and they went out the door. On the street he paused a moment, looking toward the saloon.

"Buck, why don't I buy you a drink?"

"I've got nothin' better to do."

"Let's do it, then."

Cruz Vega's dead eyes stared down as they turned upstreet.

CHAPTER EIGHTEEN

~~~⚡~~~

The crowd in the saloon was unusually subdued. Townsmen for the most part, they were discussing the lynching in low voices. Allison and Coleman were nowhere in sight.

Conversation abruptly stopped as Braddock and Colter walked through the door. The men ranked along the bar had witnessed the hanging and the bloody slugfest that followed. Their stares were bemused, filled with undisguised curiosity.

The man they knew as Reverend Titus Jacoby was by now a total enigma. Scarcely a fortnight past, he had killed a robber in a pitched gun battle. Tonight, employing the tactics of a seasoned brawler, he had beaten Clay Allison to a pulp. Speculation was rampant, and few of them any longer believed he was a preacher. Still, the obvious question would not be asked directly. None of them was feeling especially foolhardy.

Braddock led the way to a rear table. The barkeep hustled back, and Braddock ordered a bottle of rye with a water chaser. After they were served, he took out his handkerchief and dipped it into the water pitcher. He dabbed at his split lip and wiped the caked blood off his face. Finished, he wadded the handkerchief into a ball and dropped it in a spittoon. Then he uncorked the bottle and poured. He raised his glass, smiling at Colter.

"Happy days."

Colter sipped, watching him quietly. Braddock downed the whiskey in a single draught and slowly lowered his glass. He waited for the rye to hit bottom, then eased back in his chair. He jerked his chin toward the bar, where the townsmen were conversing in low monotones. His smile widened into a broad grin.

"I'd bet they never saw a Bible thumper take it neat."

"What the hell!" Colter chuckled softly. "You've already killed one man and whipped the daylights out of another. I reckon nothin' would surprise 'em now."

"Probably not." Braddock refilled his glass. "I might as well retire this preacher's outfit. The word's sure to get out by tomorrow anyway."

"Or sooner," Colter added. "McMain won't have no choice but to 'fess up. There'll be a regular parade of busybodies through his office."

"You got a smoke?"

Colter dug into his pocket and tossed the makings across the table. Braddock curled a paper between his fingers and spilled tobacco out of the sack. He rolled the paper with one hand, then licked it lightly and twisted one end. Colter gave him a match, which he popped on his thumbnail. He lit the cigarette and took a long drag.

"Hard habit to break." He exhaled, snuffing the match. "I'm glad it's over and done with. Acting like a preacher puts a real crimp in things."

"I can see how it would. You were mighty convincing, though. I even bought it myself—till you killed Cardenas."

"I meant to capture him." Braddock studied the fiery tip on the cigarette. "If I had, the case would've been wrapped up by now. Damned inconsiderate the way he went and broke his neck."

"Yeah, it was." Colter began building himself a cigarette. "You roll a smoke like you've had experience."

"Some," Braddock acknowledged. "I used to be in your line of work. Smoked roll-your-owns for a lot of years."

"Where was that?"

"Texas," Braddock remarked. "I started out on the Rio Grande and ended up in the Panhandle. Toward the last, I was foreman for the LX spread."

"How'd you get into the detective business?"

"Long story." Braddock flicked an ash into the spittoon. "I worked as a range detective for about seven years. Then people started offering me different types of assignments. So I finally opened my own agency."

Colter struck a match and puffed. "You ever ride for the International?"

Braddock caught something in his voice. The International Cattlemen's Association was an organization comprised of stockgrower associations throughout the western states and territories. Detectives who worked for the International were noted for their ruthlessness toward cattle rustlers and horse thieves. Summary execution, without due process of law, was standard policy.

"I turned them down," Braddock said casually. "Figured I was better off on my own. What makes you ask?"

"No reason." Colter idly blew a smoke ring. "Why'd you turn 'em down?"

"I hire my services but not my gun. That didn't fit in with their method of operation."

"Oh." Colter seemed to lose interest in the subject. "I forgot to mention it a minute ago. Clay Allison's a Texan too. His stompin' grounds was somewheres over around Fort Belknap."

Braddock played along. "Any idea why he moved his outfit to New Mexico?"

"I heard he got himself in some sort of scrape."

"Figures," Braddock said with heavy sarcasm. "He strikes me as a natural-born troublemaker."

"The worst," Colter said, smiling. "Folks say he could start a fight in an empty room."

"How long have you known him and Coleman?"

"Four months or thereabouts."

"What's your opinion?" Braddock asked. "Do you think they'll be satisfied with hanging Vega? Or will they go after Donaghue?"

"Well, first off"—Colter paused to drain his glass—"I overheard part of what you told McMain, and you're right. Donaghue wouldn't stick around town, not after tonight."

"Any idea where he'd head?"

"Your guess on that would be as good as mine."

"Which brings us back to Allison and Coleman."

"I'd bet they've already checked around town. They had plenty of time while you were talkin' with McMain. So it's likely Donaghue skipped out and they know it."

"What would they do next?"

"Go after Vega's compadre—Pancho Griego."

"Tonight?"

"Probably not," Colter said after a moment's reflection. "You whipped Allison pretty good. They'll more'n likely lay over at his place tonight and let him lick his wounds. I'd judge they won't hit the trail before mornin'."

"So you think they'll head for Rayado?"

"Vega said that's where Griego lives."

"How far south is it?"

"Fifteen miles, maybe a little less."

Braddock mulled it over a minute. "You told me Coleman's threats were all hot air. What about Allison?"

"How do you mean?"

"Let's suppose I cross paths with him again. Would he try gunplay or not?"

"Only if he got the drop on you. His bark's a lot worse'n his bite."

"I thought he'd killed a couple of men in shoot-outs?"

"Way I heard it, he took 'em by surprise. Course, there's no question he's a killer. But that don't make him a gunhand, not in my book."

"Is that why he gave you a wide path?"

"I don't follow you."

"Allison's no dimwit," Braddock commented. "He knows a dangerous man when he sees one."

"Who, me?" Colter said blandly. "What makes you think that?"

"Why were you picked to guard McMain?"

"Coleman offered me double wages."

"Yeah, but why?" Braddock pressed him. "Coleman must've had a reason. He didn't just pick your name out of a hat."

Colter's stare revealed nothing. "What're you tryin' to say?"

"You're evidently no slouch with a gun. So it sets me to wondering whether you're a cowhand—or something else."

"I'm no hired gun!" Colter declared. "Besides, what difference would it make anyway? I'm nothin' to you."

"You weren't," Braddock amended. "Not till you saved my bacon tonight."

"Why do I get the feeling you're leadin' up to something?"

A moment passed, then Braddock shrugged. "I could use some help on the case. Interested?"

Colter was visibly surprised. "What kind of help?"

"For one thing, I don't know the country too well. You'd be a big help tracking down Griego and Donaghue."

"I'm still listenin'."

"From what you said about Allison, it wouldn't hurt to have somebody watching my back. I could use an extra set of eyes."

"Extra eyes or an extra gun?"

"Whichever's needed."

Colter sipped his whiskey, peering over the rim of his glass. "I got to admit the idea interests me. Somebody should've taken Allison down a peg or two way back when."

"Only one thing."

"What's that?"

"I don't ride with a man until I know something about him. You'd have to come straight with me."

"On what?"

"For openers," Braddock said firmly, "you could start by telling me your real name."

Colter gave him a quick, guarded glance. "You got a lotta brass. What makes you think I changed my name?"

"Tell me I'm wrong and we'll let it drop."

"Why should I tell you anything?"

Braddock eyed him with a steady, uncompromising gaze. "One way or another, I'll find out who you are. A half-breed on the run isn't all that hard to identify." He paused, lending emphasis to the thought. "Why not just spill it? Whatever you say stops here."

"How do I know that?"

"I owe you," Braddock said simply. "And I always pay my debts. You might need a friend somewhere down the line."

A blanket of silence enveloped the two men. Colter stared off into the middle distance and seemed to fall asleep with his eyes open. Presently he blinked and took a couple of quick puffs on his cigarette. He looked back at Braddock.

"I got crosswise of the law last summer."

"Where?"

"No-man's-land."

"What happened?"

"I killed some men."

"How many?"

"Ten."

"Jesus Christ." Braddock looked startled. "You killed ten men by yourself?"

"It wasn't hard."

"Sounds like you declared war on somebody."

"I had reason."

"Why don't you tell me about it?"

"It started a long time ago, in Colorado."

Colter stubbed out his cigarette and began talking. His Cheyenne name was An-zah-ti, Little Raven. Like many squaws, his mother had been sold as wife to a white mountain man. After only one winter the trapper rode away, never to return, and a few months later a boy was born. At the naming ceremony, the boy was called Little Raven, for he had coal-black hair and strange gray eyes. He lived eight winters with the Cheyenne, growing strong and sturdy. Their village was on a remote backwater known as Sand Creek.

The Pony Soldiers came on a cold, blustery morning. There was no warning, no attempt to identify the village as peaceful or hostile. Another Cheyenne band had raided a white settlement, and swift retribution was demanded. That the village chief was Black Kettle, a friend to all white men, made no difference whatever. The battle cry was "Nits make lice," and the Pony Soldier leader ordered his men to kill anything that walked. What followed was a slaughter; the snow turned crimson with the blood of the Cheyenne. Little Raven saw his mother raped and then finished off with a bullet through the head. He also caught a glimpse of the Pony Soldier leader, laughing and goading the troopers on in their butchery. It was a face the boy never forgot.

Afterward, the slaughter was called the Sand Creek Massacre, and there was a great outcry from white men of conscience. The Pony Soldier leader, Colonel John Covington, was relieved of command and soon disappeared from Colorado. Little Raven, along with other captured children, was sent to a Quaker missionary school in Indian territory. There he was taught the white man's way. The Quakers prepared him well, wiping out the Cheyenne intonation from his speech and opening his mind to the customs of a world apart from his childhood. Some years later, grown to a strapping youth of eighteen, he put the reservation behind him. Though tawny-skinned, he passed himself off as white, growing a bushy mustache to complete the disguise of his pale gray eyes. Thereafter, he walked the white man's road.

A wanderer, he drifted from one ranch to another, working

his way up from horse wrangler to cowhand. He called himself Buck Colter, and he spent three years learning his new trade. Then, shortly after turning twenty-one, he saw Colonel John Covington's name in a newspaper. The leader in a movement to open public lands, Covington had been instrumental in settling no-man's-land. Colter quit his job and rode north out of Texas, bent on revenge. He hired on with a cattle outfit and spent the next three years awaiting an opportunity. Not an eye for an eye, but white man's justice. Some legal means of bringing about a final settlement of accounts.

"Three years," Braddock observed thoughtfully. "That would've been last summer."

Colter nodded. "Things didn't work out the way I'd planned. Covington was head of the Stockgrowers' Association, and he used all kinds of tricks to discourage farmers from settlin' on rangeland. But he kept his nose clean where the law was concerned."

"So you got tired of waiting?"

"Nope." Colter caught his eye for an instant, then looked quickly away. "I hooked up with a farm girl and started hearin' wedding bells. We even staked out a piece of land."

"What stopped you?"

"The association had a hard and fast rule. No cowhand was allowed to own stock while he was still ridin' for an outfit. The idea was to stop little operations from springin' up."

Braddock lit another cigarette. "And you broke the rule?"

Colter's expression became somber, then pensive. "I wanted to build a spread of my own. Whenever trail herds would pass through, I'd buy a few head. All legal and aboveboard."

"Let me guess," Braddock said, exhaling smoke. "You thumbed your nose at the association, and Covington got his bowels in an uproar. He probably had somebody rough you up or stampede your herd."

"Worse'n that," Colter said with a quick swipe at his mustache. "He bribed a cattle inspector and got me railroaded for rustlin'. I was convicted on nothin' but trumped-up evidence."

Braddock searched his eyes. "Were you a hundred percent innocent?"

"Damn right!" Colter flared. "I aimed to get married. I was walkin' the straight and narrow."

"What happened after the trial?"

"I escaped." Colter wrapped his hands around his whiskey glass. "I cornered the cattle inspector and tried to get him to change his story. He made a fight of it."

"Was he the first one you killed?"

"Yeah," Colter mumbled. "Then Covington brought in a hired gun, fellow by the name of Doc Ross. One night Ross and some of Covington's men waylaid me at the girl's house. I got away without a scratch."

"And the girl?"

Colter looked into his drink as though he might find revealed there the answer to life's mystery. "She was killed."

Braddock smoked in silence a moment. "I take it that's the night you declared war?"

"Wasn't nothin' left to lose. I rode out to Covington's place, but he wasn't there. So I walked into the bunkhouse with my shotgun and cut loose. All seven of the bastards was the same ones that'd been at the girl's house."

"Seven at a whack." Braddock slowly shook his head. "That explains why you use a lever-action shotgun."

"It gets the job done."

"Was Doc Ross in the bunkhouse?"

"No," Colter said, poker-faced. "I rode directly from there into town. Covington and Ross were in the saloon, celebratin'. They thought I was dead."

"You showing up that way must've been a real shock."

A smile touched Colter's lips. "Froze the sonsabitches in their tracks. They thought they were seein' a ghost."

"How'd you kill them?"

"I used the shotgun on Ross. Covington didn't deserve no

more chance than a mad dog. All the same, I gave him an even break with pistols. He lost."

"Were there witnesses?"

Colter's smile turned grim. "Witnesses weren't no help at that point. Killin' that many men in one night just naturally tagged me a murderer. Covington being the head of the Stockgrower's Association only made it worse."

"When you mentioned Covington, it sort of jogged my memory. I recall reading about it now."

Braddock briefly explained his rogues'-gallery file. Shortly after the killings, the International Cattlemen's Association had circulated a dodger on Colter. The reward was five thousand dollars, and he was wanted dead or alive.

"I'm curious," Braddock concluded. "Why aren't you using a phony name?"

Colter shrugged. "The International's detectives won't ever stop doggin' my tracks. I decided to lay low and only work for small outfits. That way there's less chance of being recognized. But I won't change my name—not again."

"Are you talking about the missionary school?"

"Yeah." Colter's brow puckered in a frown. "For better'n ten years, the Quakers called me Sam Raven. I picked my own name when I lit out from the reservation. It's the one I aim to stick with."

Braddock gave him a quizzical side glance. "Aren't you asking for trouble?"

"Maybe," Colter said with a fatalistic look. "I suppose the Quakers halfway turned me into a white man's Injun. But when it's all boiled down, I'm still Cheyenne. I won't turn tail just to avoid a fight."

"One man against the International makes it pretty long odds. Sooner or later their hired guns will track you down."

"The Cheyenne Dog Soldiers had the right idea. Before they went into battle, they'd say, 'Today's a good day to die.' I reckon I never got that out of my blood. It's as good a way as any to live—or die."

Braddock marked again that the young half-breed was prodded by strange devils. Yet, given the circumstances, Braddock's admiration was stirred. The code by which Colter lived was one of courage and absolute fearlessness. A quiet acceptance that death was preferable to cowardice.

"What now?" Colter said at length. "You sure you want to associate with a common murderer?"

"I never go back on my word, Buck."

"You're liable to wind up on the International's list yourself."

Braddock laughed. "Then I'll tell them what I told 'em when they offered me a job as a bounty hunter."

"What's that?"

"Stuff it where the sun don't shine!"

CHAPTER NINETEEN

—◆—

The morning sky was overcast. A chill wind whipped down out of the north, and there was a touch of dampness in the air. All the signs pointed to a hard winter.

There was no road as such between Cimarron and Rayado. A washboard trail stretched south across a vast emptiness. The terrain sloped gently downward, leveling off into flatland broken occasionally by arroyos and dry creek beds. It was inhospitable country, and the few ranches south of Cimarron were scattered far apart. As they had for generations, Mexicans subsisted on what they could coax from the flinty soil.

Braddock and Colter sighted Rayado shortly before nine o'clock. Earlier, almost at the crack of dawn, Braddock had awakened the proprietor of the livery stable in Cimarron. After haggling briefly, he'd swapped the swaybacked dun and thirty dollars for a blaze-faced roan. He knew he'd been cheated, but the press of time hadn't allowed for prolonged dickering. The roan was sound of wind, and in the event his search for Pancho Griego turned into a manhunt, he needed a horse built for endurance. He was also prompted by a greater and even more pressing urgency. He had to beat Clay Allison to Rayado.

The town was little more than a wide spot in the road. There was a general store and a cantina and a small church with a bell tower. The church looked more like a fort, and had probably doubled as a defensive stronghold during the Apache wars. Clustered around the town's main buildings were a crude collection of adobe houses. Indistinguishable in appearance, the adobes resembled a handful of dice tossed randomly onto the bleak landscape. The inhabitants of Rayado were poor, if not impoverished, typical of Mexicans who lighted a candle to the Virgin and prayed for a brighter tomorrow. Their goats and runty pigs wandered at will in and among the dwellings.

On the edge of town, Braddock reined to a halt. He traded glances with Colter and neither of them appeared any too cheerful. There were four horses hitched outside the cantina.

"What do you think?" Braddock inquired. "Anybody we know?"

" 'Fraid so," Colter said dourly. "The same bunch we tangled with last night. Allison and Coleman and the two hands."

Braddock let out his breath in a sharp grunt. "Looks like Allison has more staying power than I thought. That whipping doesn't seem to have slowed him down any."

Colter nodded in agreement. "They must've been on the road long before daylight."

"Wonder why he didn't bring more men?"

"Maybe he figures we're off chasing Donaghue."

"Whatever his reason, we played into luck."

"How do you figure that?"

"Four against two." Braddock smiled, staring at the horses. "Sounds like pretty decent odds."

"What've you got in mind?"

"You take the back door and I'll take the front. We do it fast enough and nobody'll get any foolish ideas."

"And if somebody does get foolish?"

"Then I guess we'll have to explain it to the coroner."

"You fight my kind of fight, Cole."

Braddock grinned and shrugged out of his greatcoat. He was no longer wearing the turned-around collar, but he was still dressed in the funereal minister's suit. He pulled his pistol and stuffed a sixth cartridge into the empty chamber. Colter, meanwhile, slipped his shotgun from the saddle boot. A quick crank of the lever jacked a shell into the breech and cocked the hammer.

Behind the nearest adobe, they dismounted and left their horses tied to a scraggly tree. A Mexican woman appeared at the window and Braddock motioned her back inside. Then they circled around several houses and crossed the road in line with the cantina. Colter peeled off and hurried toward the rear of the building. Braddock walked to within a few feet of the door and flattened himself against the front wall. On the count of ten, he stepped away from the wall and cocked his pistol. He pushed through the door in one swift stride.

The cantina was empty. Braddock stood for a moment with a mildly bewildered look. Then a door at the rear of the room opened and a sleepy-eyed Mexican emerged with his hands overhead. Colter nudged him forward with the nuzzle of the scattergun. The Mexican saw Braddock and his eyes suddenly turned wary. Colter moved to the side and stopped.

"He's got living quarters out back. Nobody else but his woman and a litter of kids."

Braddock arched one eyebrow. "You're sure those horses belong to our friends?"

"No two ways about it."

"You talk Mexican?"

"Some."

"Ask him if he's had any visitors this morning."

Colter addressed the Mexican. *"Habia hombres aqui hoy?"*

"Sí, señor."

"Fueron americanos?"

"Sí." The Mexican nodded rapidly. *"Polícia americano."*

Colter glanced at Braddock. "They've been here, all right. Allison told him they were lawmen."

"Figures," Braddock said with a trace of irony. "Ask him where they are now."

Colter turned back to the Mexican. *"Adonde van después de salir de aqui?"*

"A casa de Pancho Griego."

"Usted le dio la direction?"

"Sí."

"Donde esta la casa de Pancho Griego?"

"Al otro lado de la calle." The Mexican pointed out the door. *"Vaya detrásde la tienda. Vive en la tercera casa."*

"Gracias."

Colter dismissed him with a wave of the shotgun. He looked from Colter to Braddock, clearly confused by the sudden invasion of Anglo *pistoleros*. Then he swallowed his curiosity and trudged on back to his sleeping quarters. Colter turned to Braddock.

"They're at Griego's house."

"Where's he live?"

"Behind the store and three houses down."

"Maybe we got here in time. If he was dead, they'd already be gone."

"One way to find out."

"Let's go."

Braddock led the way through the door. Outside they crossed the road and skirted around the store. Turning south, they were both struck by the absence of people. No one was about, including women and children. Upon closer examination of the houses, they noticed that the doors were closed and the windows shuttered. It seemed the people of Rayado had locked themselves in, or locked someone out. Then, faintly, the morning stillness was broken by a muted scream.

The cry came from the third house down. While the door was shut, the window shutters were open, and the keening moan of a man in pain sounded from within the house. Braddock and Colter increased their pace, covering the door as they approached. At the corner of the house, they wheeled sharply right and moved toward a side window. Colter waited while Braddock removed his hat and eased his head past the windowsill. The scene inside was much what he'd expected.

A woman and two wide-eyed children were huddled against the far wall. The two cowhands were guarding them, and Isaac Coleman was positioned near the door. In the center of the room, Allison kneeled astride a man on the floor. The man's features were a mask of blood, and his head lolled from side to side. He groaned as Allison swatted him with a stinging backhand.

"C'mon, Griego! Wake up and gimme some answers!"

Griego's eyes fluttered open. *"Por favor, señor."*

Allison cocked his fist. "Quit beggin', you goddamn greaser. Where's Donaghue?"

"No sé."

"Who you think you're shittin'? You understand English plenty good, so speak it!"

"Please, señor," Griego said with a thick accent. "I cannot tell you what I do not know."

"You know Cruz Vega, don't you?"

"Sí."

"He says you helped him kill Reverend Tolby."

"Dios mio! I killed no one!"

"He says you and him and Manuel Cardenas rode out to Cimarron Canyon. You ambushed the preacher there and rigged it to look like robbery—*bandidos.*"

"I swear on my mother's head! I would not kill a man of God. Never!"

Allison popped him in the mouth. "You lyin' son of a bitch! Vega spilled the whole story. He told us everything."

"Where is Vega, señor?"

"What's that to you?"

"Take me to him," Griego implored. "You will see then that I speak only the truth."

"How would that prove anything?"

"He will not lie to my face. He would not dare!"

"Vega's in jail," Allison said with a crafty smile. "We don't have time to haul you back to Cimarron."

"But I am innocent, señor! You must believe—"

Allison slugged him twice in rapid succession. Griego's nose flattened and his head bounced off the dirt floor in a puff of dust. Blood streamed down his face as Allison grabbed him by the shirtfront.

"Cut the crap! I wanna hear about Donaghue—pronto!"

Griego moaned, caught his breath. "I know nothing—nada."

"Horseshit!" Allison cuffed his head back and forth with hard slaps. "Vega says Donaghue hired the three of you to kill the preacher. He says you know where Donaghue's hidin' out."

"Lies," Griego said weakly. "All lies."

Allison cursed and resumed the savage beating. Outside the window, Braddock felt a tug on his sleeve and moved back a step. Colter looked worried.

"We better stop it," he whispered. "Allison's liable to beat him to death."

"I don't think so," Braddock said in a low voice. "Without Griego, he's got nowhere to turn. He's smart enough to realize that."

"You're runnin' an awful risk."

"Maybe," Braddock allowed. "But we couldn't do any better. Unless Griego talks, we'll never get a line on Donaghue. We might as well let Allison do the job."

Colter wasn't convinced. "I think you're makin' a mistake."

"We'll wait and see," Braddock said crisply. "I wouldn't want to bust in there anyway. Griego's wife and kids are over against the far wall. Any shooting starts and they'd get caught in the crossfire."

A loud oath from inside attracted Braddock's attention. He peeked through the window and saw Allison climb to his feet. Griego lay sprawled on the floor, out cold. His wife's eyes were filled with terror, and the children clutched at her skirts, wailing at the top of their lungs. Allison shouted them down, and the woman quickly hugged them to her legs. Glaring at her, Allison crossed the room and snatched up a bucket of water. Then he walked back and threw the water in Griego's face. He dropped the bucket as Griego rolled onto his side, moaning softly.

Coleman shifted away from the door. "What're you fixin' to do, Clay?"

"Hang the sorry bastard!"

"He can't talk if you stretch his neck."

"Don't worry." Allison's tone was clipped and stiff. "I'll hang him a little bit at a time. Strangle it out of him!"

"You ever stop to consider he might be tellin' the truth? Hell, maybe he don't know nothin' about Donaghue."

"Hope you're wrong, Isaac. He's all we got."

Allison motioned to the cowhands. They moved to Griego and lifted him off the floor. He sagged between them, conscious but still wobbly from the beating. Coleman opened the door and stepped aside. Allison strode purposefully across the room.

"Let's go find ourselves a tree."

Outside, Allison stopped and looked around. The cowhands appeared next, supporting Griego under the arms. Coleman followed them out and closed the door. There was a moment's silence as Allison searched the skyline for a suitable tree. Then, from inside, the grief-stricken cries of the woman and her children shattered the stillness.

"Don't anybody move!"

Braddock and Colter materialized around the corner of the house. Braddock's pistol was cocked, extended at arm's length. Colter held the shotgun at waist level, the butt snugged tight against his side. The range was less than three yards, and the bore of the shotgun looked like a mine shaft. Allison and the other men took Braddock's command in deadly earnest. No one moved.

"Listen close, Allison." Braddock gave him a dark look.

"I want a word with Griego. You just stand still and keep your mouth shut."

"Go to hell!" Allison's chin jutted out defiantly. "He's ours and it stays that way."

"How'd you like me to shoot your kneecap off?"

"You don't scare me, Braddock."

"Then keep talking." Braddock drew a bead on his right knee. "One more word and folks will start calling you Pegleg."

Allison's mouth clicked shut. Braddock watched him a moment with a bitter grin. Then, lowering the pistol, he turned his attention to Griego. There was steel underlying his voice.

"These men lied to you, Griego."

"I do not understand, señor."

"Last night they hung Cruz Vega."

"Muerto!" Griego choked out the word. "Vega is dead?"

Braddock nodded, his face expressionless. "These men will hang you too, and I won't stop them unless you accept my offer."

"Offer?"

"Tell me about Donaghue. If you do that, I'll escort you to jail and personally guarantee your safety. Otherwise, I will stand aside and let these men hang you."

Griego blanched. His eyes glazed and his Adam's apple bobbed. "How do I know you will honor your words, señor?"

"What choice do you have?"

Griego glanced at Allison out of the corner of his eye. His features went taut, and his gaze quickly returned to Braddock. "I have never met Donaghue, señor. I know only what Cruz Vega told me."

"And what was that?"

"We were talking one day, and he mentioned that Donaghue owns a saloon in Raton. He said it was a secret, that another man operates the saloon for Donaghue. He thought it a strange thing."

"What's the man's name?"

"He did not say."

"And the name of the saloon?"

"Something about *el toro.* I do not recall the exact—"

The door opened and Griego's wife started outside. He took a step toward her, arms flung wide to stop her. One of the cowhands seized on the momentary distraction. As Griego moved past him, the cowhand pulled his pistol and shifted aside for a clear shot. Colter triggered the shotgun and a load of buckshot sizzled across the yard. The blast caught the cowhand high in the chest, shredding him with a widespread pattern of lead. He stumbled backward, dropping his gun, and pitched to the ground. A stray ball struck Griego directly behind the ear. The back of his skull exploded in a cloud of blood and brain matter. He slumped forward and fell facedown in the dirt.

Isaac Coleman reacted out of blind panic. As the shotgun roared, his hand streaked toward his holster. Braddock shot him the instant his pistol cleared leather. The slug drilled through Coleman's breastbone and impacted on his heart. He stood there a moment, dead on his feet, then slowly toppled over like a felled tree. The pistol slipped from his grasp and his left leg jerked in afterdeath. All in the same split second, Colter cranked another shell into the scattergun and covered the remaining cowhand. Braddock's arm moved in a slight arc as he thumbed the hammer. His pistol was pointed directly at Allison.

A deadened silence settled over the yard. The woman's hand was clamped to her mouth in a look of stifled horror. Allison and the other man stood stock-still, scarcely breathing. What seemed an interminable length of time slipped past without sound or movement. Then Braddock motioned with his pistol.

"Drop your gun belts."

Allison and the cowhand hastily obeyed. Braddock jerked his chin toward the outskirts of town to the south. "Take off walking and don't look back."

"Holy shit!" Allison bawled. "There's nothin' out there for fifty miles! What about our horses?"

"I'll drop them off at the livery in Cimarron."

"You can't leave a white man stranded out here! It ain't—civilized."

Braddock fired and a spurt of dust kicked up at Allison's feet. "Don't talk anymore. Just move."

Allison turned away with a look of baffled fury. The cowhand fell in beside him and they walked off. Braddock stared after them until they passed the last adobe and headed into open country. Finally, he holstered his pistol and glanced around at Colter. His expression was tightlipped and grim.

"Wish it'd been him instead of Coleman."

"You might still get your chance."

"Not while you're backing me up with that shotgun. Allison plainly didn't care for the odds."

Colter appeared somewhat downcast. "There's times when a scattergun does more'n you intend. I'm real sorry about Griego. Wasn't no way to avoid it."

"Don't blame yourself," Braddock said quickly. "Griego just happened to be in the wrong place at the wrong time. He would've gone to the gallows eventually anyway."

"Yeah, but he'd have talked some more before he took the drop."

"Way it worked out, he told me everything I wanted to hear."

"About Donaghue?"

"None other."

"So what's next?"

Braddock smiled. "Raton."

CHAPTER TWENTY

The telegram staggered Mitchell.

For a moment the words blurred before his eyes. Unnerved, he sat down at his desk, trying to calm himself. He took a couple of deep breaths and read through the message a second time. His expression was one of astonished disbelief, and he stared blankly at the signature. The telegram was from Sheriff Floyd Mather.

A long while passed before Mitchell was able to collect his wits. He rose from the desk, aware that the decision he'd made was not altogether rational. Stuffing the telegram in his coat pocket, he strode through the outer office. His secretary glanced up with a look of surprise, but he went past her without a word. He hurried through the door.

Early morning was the busiest of times on the plaza. Mitchell pushed through the crowds, remembering now that he'd forgotten his hat. Several passersby greeted him, turning to stare strangely as he rushed along without acknowledgment. He rounded the corner onto a side street and walked directly to Stephen Elkton's office. Inside, he barged past the secretary, waving her off as he moved to the private office at the rear. He closed the door behind him.

Elkton appeared startled. "What's the meaning—?"

"Here." Mitchell handed him the telegram. "Read this."

Mitchell dropped into a chair. Elkton unfolded the slip of paper and quickly scanned the message. His mouth tightened and he was silent for a time. He finally placed the telegram on his desk top.

"You appear to have lost your nerve, Warren."

"What's that?" Mitchell snapped.

"Half the people in town must have seen you storm in here. I would imagine the other half will know it before noontime."

"Good God! Didn't you read—?"

"Please don't change the subject. We were discussing your lapse of sound judgment. Why didn't you follow our usual arrangement?"

"I couldn't wait till tonight to contact you. Don't you understand that?"

"I ask for a reason and you offer me an excuse."

"The reason is right in front of you."

Elkton frowned, wagged his head like a schoolmaster confronted with a backward pupil. He leaned forward and studied the telegram a moment. "Who is Cruz Vega?"

"Donaghue's hired killer—an assassin."

"And apparently rather inept at his job. From this, I take it he was paid to kill McMain."

"Yes."

"But he failed and got himself hung in the process."

"So it appears."

"Mmm." Elkton traced a line in the message with his finger. "I gather he talked before he was hanged. Otherwise why would Donaghue have gone into hiding?"

"That's how I interpret it."

"A messy situation, indeed. What we have is a botched murder and Donaghue on the run. To compound matters, he's being pursued by two different factions. Is that correct?"

Mitchell seemed to recover a measure of his composure. He sat straighter and nodded. "Allison and Coleman are the largest ranchers in Colfax County. Along with McMain, they were the original organizers of the coalition."

"Which brings us to the Reverend Jacoby." Elkton tapped the telegram. "According to this, he's not a minister after all. How does the sheriff phrase it—'a lawman of some sort operating in disguise.' "

"Yes, but that's rather vague. Is he a Deputy U.S. Marshal or what?"

"Good question. We can only surmise that the coalition somehow got him involved. Of course, after last night he would seem to represent a disruptive influence."

"How do you mean?"

"Well, quite obviously he's at odds with these ranchers. And I suspect that might very well create problems for McMain. So long as they're fighting each other, we gain a little breathing room."

"You seem to have forgotten that both sides are chasing Donaghue."

Elkton appeared distracted. He slowly shook his head, his gaze fixed on the telegram. "Extraordinary. You'd think a sheriff would know better than to put all this in a wire."

"He had to advise me somehow."

"Then he should have come here, done it in person. This represents a very incriminating document."

"Not really. Everything there will be reported in today's newspapers. It's public information."

"You fool! It's a direct link to you, quite clearly a report. Suppose the newspapers got wind of it? Wouldn't that make a story!"

"I hadn't stopped to consider that. I was only thinking of what it said."

"No, Warren, you weren't thinking at all. You simply reacted."

Elkton was suddenly weary. He saw himself surrounded by incompetents and dullards, men lacking either initiative or foresight. All the years of scheming and planning had ended in yet another crisis. He felt weighted by command, sorely burdened. His grand design seemed to him a cross that he alone bore.

A Missourian, Elkton had come west in 1864. After settling in Santa Fe, he had established a lucrative law practice, specializing in civil litigation. Later, using Mitchell as a front, he had set in motion a far-reaching conspiracy. To exert political leverage on a broad scale, he put together an organization of businessmen, financiers, and influential Republicans. It was a diverse group, united by a common interest in the exploitation of New Mexico's resources. Out of the conspiracy emerged the Santa Fe Ring.

The land-grant scheme was intended as Elkton's boldest masterwork. Yet from the very outset resistance in Colfax County posed a major obstacle. At bottom, the conflict with the Cimarron Coalition was one of ideology. The homesteaders and ranchers held that frontier lands were public domain, open to settlement. Elkton saw it in Old World terms, with himself as the *patrón* and therefore master of a realm. He was willing to enforce that view with whatever measures the situation demanded.

Watching Mitchell now, it occurred to him that his confidence had been sadly misplaced. But today, as so many times in the past, the situation demanded hard decisions. The most immediate decision involved Florencio Donaghue, and clearly there was no one to make it but himself. He stared across the desk.

"How reliable is Donaghue? Would he talk if he was caught?"

"Not likely," Mitchell said hesitantly. "He wouldn't risk implicating himself in murder."

"Perhaps. But, then, that's a risk we can't afford either. Your men—what are their names?"

"Johnson and Ortega."

"How quickly could they reach Cimarron?"

"Possibly tonight. No later than tomorrow."

"Order them to find Donaghue."

"And then what?"

"Silence him."

"You mean kill him."

"Exactly. While they're about it, have them kill our bogus holy man, Jacoby. No unturned stones, hmmm?"

Mitchell passed a hand across his eyes. "Where will it end, Stephen?"

"I beg your pardon?"

"The killing! We can't go on murdering people ad infinitum."

"There would be no need"—Elkton paused for emphasis—"if you had handled it properly to start with."

"No, that's not true. I'm not responsible for what's happened. All I do is transmit orders!"

"How nicely you dodge reality."

"What do you mean by that?"

"Come now, Warren. You can't divorce yourself from the act by saying 'All I do is transmit orders.' You're no less culpable than the thug who pulls the trigger."

"I regret to say you're correct. I'd probably sleep better if I pulled the trigger myself."

"Then I fail to take your point."

"I meant I'm not responsible for what's happened in Cimarron. After all, you're the one who ordered McMain killed."

"And?"

"And now it's no longer a matter of legal actions or the courts. We've convinced the coalition that murder is the most practical way to settle disputes. So they've turned into vigilantes—hangmen."

"To our great benefit, I might add. Vigilantes represent indiscriminate violence, and that frightens people. I suspect the coalition will be roundly condemned for taking the law into its own hands."

"You're wrong, Stephen. If anything, they've won even more public support. God help us if they ever form an alliance with the Democrats."

"Well, that's a philosophical discussion for another day, isn't it? At the moment we're faced with more mundane matters."

"Donaghue?"

"His name certainly heads the list. I suggest you attend to it immediately."

"I suppose you're right. We'd all swing if he ever talked."

"And none quicker than you, Warren. Everything he's done would be laid at your doorstep."

"Very well. I'll talk to Johnson and Ortega within the hour."

"Don't forget to mention the good reverend."

"I think you should reconsider on Jacoby. It would be a great mistake to kill a lawman."

"It would be a greater mistake to let him live. He's much too close to the truth to risk leaving him alive. So just do as I ask."

"Of course, I always do."

"And, Warren."

"Yes?"

"Impress on your men that they mustn't fail. You see, in the end you are responsible—to me."

The threat needed no elaboration. Mitchell bobbed his head and rose hastily to his feet. As he turned toward the door, Elkton's voice stopped him.

"One last thing."

"Yes?"

"Never again are you to come here during office hours. Never!"

"I understand."

The door opened and closed and Elkton was alone. He steepled his hands, slowly tapping his forefingers together. For a moment he considered the possibility that Johnson and Ortega would fail. By extension, he was forced then to assess the direct link to his own doorstep.

All of which led him to a personal consideration of the logistics of murder. The most efficient means by which to silence Warren Mitchell.

It was an interesting problem.

Mitchell stared blankly at his desk top. His thoughts were turned inward and he seemed lost in dark introspection.

A knock sounded at the door. His secretary ushered Slim Johnson and Pedro Ortega into the office. Ortega, unlike his rawboned partner, was short and stout, with a handlebar mustache. The men removed their hats as the door closed behind them.

"I have a job for you," Mitchell informed them.

Johnson and Ortega alerted at the tone of his voice. Like all predators, they were attuned to mood and telltale behavior. They somehow sensed that Mitchell was repelled by violence, unnerved by death. They enjoyed his discomfort.

Johnson grinned. "Anybody we know, boss?"

"Yes," Mitchell said quietly. "Our man in Cimarron . . . Donaghue."

"You want him roughed up"—Johnson let the thought dangle a moment—"or buried?"

"Don't play games with me, Slim. You know what I want."

"Why, sure thing, boss. You just go ahead and X him off your list. He's good as dead."

Ortega chuckled jovially. "Slim wouldn't lie to you, *patrón*. We never miss, him and me."

"How reassuring," Mitchell said in an aloof voice. "If you will allow me to finish, there's more. Another one."

"Well, God a'mighty!" Johnson cackled. "You mean to say you want somebody else killed too?"

"Exactly," Mitchell said with no great enthusiasm. "His name is the Reverend Titus Jacoby. Also of Cimarron."

"*Caramba!*" Ortega boomed. "Another son-of-a-bitch preacher!"

"Lower your voice, you fool! They'll hear you on the street."

"Sorry," Ortega apologized. "I meant no harm, *patrón.*"

"Just pay attention," Mitchell went on dully. "There's reason to believe that Jacoby is a lawman of some sort. Probably a Deputy U.S. Marshal."

Johnson and Ortega exchanged a look. Mitchell rapped his desk to get their attention. "I want you to proceed cautiously. Once you get to Cimarron, take your time and look the situation over carefully. We can't afford mistakes, not with a peace officer involved. Understood?"

"Don't worry, boss," Johnson replied. "We won't let you down."

Ortega bobbed his head. "Is the truth, *patrón.* Slim and me take care of it for you *muy pronto.*"

"*Muy pronto,*" Mitchell repeated, "but with care. Great care. No mistakes."

"*Si, patrón.*"

"It's in the bag, boss. Good as done."

Nodding and grinning, Johnson led the way out. Ortega flashed a wide smile as he went through the door. Watching them, Mitchell passed a hand across his forehead. He suddenly felt feverish, and slightly ill.

CHAPTER TWENTY-ONE

Soon after dark that evening, they halted on the outskirts of Raton. The mountains were a dark silhouette against a star-swept sky, and the night was bitter cold. Their horses snorted frosty clouds of vapor.

Braddock was once more in the guise of a Texas cattle-man. Earlier that day they had dropped Allison's horses off at the livery stable in Cimarron. To avoid delay, they had steered clear of Orville McMain. Colter waited while Brad-dock collected his carpetbag from the hotel. Some miles north of town, they stopped and Braddock had discarded his preacher's outfit. From his carpetbag, he'd donned the cloth-ing and fake mustache that transformed him into Elmer Boyd.

Their plan was loosely formulated. Braddock would enter Raton and conduct the search for Donaghue. Colter, who was known to Donaghue, would wait outside town. Based on the description provided by Colter, the man they sought wouldn't be all that difficult to recognize. In the event Brad-dock located Donaghue, he would then determine their next move. The overriding imperative was to effect the capture

quietly and without gunplay. Donaghue was of value only if
he was taken alive. He represented the one direct link to
Warren Mitchell and the Santa Fe Ring.

The main street of Raton was brightly lit by corner
lampposts. On either side of the street, the boardwalks were
jammed with men out for an evening's entertainment.
Braddock held his horse to a walk and rode slowly through
town. He was looking for a saloon with the word "bull" in its
name. Even if Donaghue had skipped Raton, it was the place
to begin the search. Yet, while his eyes scanned the street,
his thoughts were on Lise. By now word of the blowup in
Cimarron would have reached Santa Fe. Mitchell and Elkins
were doubtless aware of the danger to themselves, especially
if Donaghue was made to talk. Their normal caution would
now be multiplied manyfold, which further jeopardized Lise's
position. One slip, no matter how inconsequential, would
very likely serve as her death warrant. Time was running
out, and Braddock was driven by a growing sense of urgency.
He had to find Donaghue tonight or call it quits and return
to Santa Fe. He saw no alternative.

The Bull's Head Saloon was a block past the town's central intersection. Braddock hitched his horse out front, and
followed a crowd of teamsters through the door. He found a
spot at the bar, ordered rye, and subjected the place to a casual examination. Gambling layouts were ranged along the
wall opposite the bar, with several tables toward the rear of
the room. There was a single door behind the tables, and the
absence of stairs indicated there was no upper floor. After a
few drinks, he engaged one of the barkeeps in conversation.
He learned that the dealer at the faro layout was also the
owner of the Bull's Head. His name was Blacky O'Neal.

An hour or so later Braddock decided hanging around the
saloon was a waste of time. He'd seen nothing of anyone who
faintly resembled Donaghue's description. The only thing to
arouse his interest was the door at the rear of the room. Apparently O'Neal possessed the lone key. He had stopped the

faro game at one point and unlocked the door, waiting while a bartender fetched a case of whiskey. Braddock thought it entirely possible that O'Neal didn't trust the barkeeps with the stockroom key. He also wondered whether there was an office or some sort of living quarters behind the door. For the moment there was no way to tell.

Around nine o'clock, Braddock rode back to where Colter waited. He explained what he'd found and voiced the opinion that there was little chance of Colter being spotted. Neither of them had eaten supper, and they proceeded to a café near the railroad depot. After a meal of beefsteak and fried potatoes, they lingered over several cups of coffee. Then they walked their horses uptown and located a saloon catty-corner to the Bull's Head. Inside, they took a position at the bar that afforded a view through the front window. For the balance of the night, they nursed their drinks and kept one eye on the street. No one entering or departing the Bull's Head bore any resemblance to Donaghue.

Shortly after three in the morning, Braddock led the way outside. The saloons were closing for the night, and he wanted a better vantage spot. Halfway down the block was a pharmacist's shop, and they took up posts in the darkened doorway. Within the hour, the Bull's Head emptied of customers and a short while later the lights inside were extinguished. Blacky O'Neal emerged, locking the door behind him, and walked off down the street. Braddock left Colter to watch the Bull's Head, and trailed O'Neal by a discreet distance. The saloonkeeper led him to a modest frame dwelling on the south side of town.

A parlor lamp was the only light burning in the house. Braddock watched through a side window while O'Neal lit a lamp in the bedroom, then returned and lowered the wick on the parlor lamp. When O'Neal went back to the bedroom Braddock moved along the side of the house and stopped outside the window. He saw a woman asleep in the bed, and he noted that O'Neal was at some pains not to wake her.

Undressing, O'Neal draped his clothes over a chair and slipped into a nightshirt. He crossed to a bed and sat down, reaching for the lamp. The room went dark.

Braddock walked back uptown. He somehow doubted that Donaghue was being hidden out in O'Neal's house. The saloonkeeper's actions were too routine; his manner betrayed none of the signs of someone harboring a wanted man. That left only the Bull's Head and the locked storeroom. It was a long shot, but nonetheless worth a look. Braddock fully expected to find nothing more than a room stacked with beer barrels and cases of whiskey. Yet that in itself would eliminate one more possibility. And tomorrow was time enough to have a talk with Blacky O'Neal.

The business district was deserted. Braddock found Colter still waiting in the pharmacy doorway. They crossed the street and walked halfway down the block to an alley. Turning in, they moved to the back door of the Bull's Head. While Colter held a match, Braddock took out his pocketknife and began working on the lock. Less than a minute passed before the tumbler clicked over. To Braddock's surprise, there was no crossbeam barring the door from the inside. He wondered at the oversight, then put it from his mind. Whatever the reason, it simplified the job of gaining entry. A twist of the knob opened the door, and they stepped into a room dark as pitch. Then, somewhere very close, they heard a man snoring.

Colter struck another match. In the flare of light, they saw a room filled with crates and cases. Squat barrels were stacked along the back wall, and on their left, toward the front of the room, was an open door. Braddock pulled his pistol, and Colter held the match high, lighting the way. They cat-footed to the door and stepped into a small office. A floor safe was wedged into one corner, and nearby was a desk and chair. Beside the desk was a metal cot with wire springs and a padded mattress. A man was sprawled on the cot, his mouth agape, snoring loudly. He was heavily built, with a square, thick-jowled face, and he wore only long johns. His clothes were neatly hung on the chair.

"Donaghue."

Colter whispered the name as he snuffed the match. While Braddock kept his gun trained on the cot, Colter moved silently to the desk. He flicked a match on his thumbnail and quickly lighted a lamp. When he turned up the wick, the office was bathed in a bright amber glow. The man on the cot stirred, pulling the blanket down as he rolled onto his side. The snoring stopped and he lay there a moment without moving. Then, still half asleep, he put his hand up, trying to block out the light. His eyes slowly fluttered open.

"Wake up and join the party, Donaghue."

Braddock's voice brought him upright in the cot. His eyes widened and his gaze shuttled from Braddock to Colter. His jaw dropped open and his features contorted in a look of thunderstruck amazement. Colter grinned and leaned back against the wall. Braddock seated himself on the edge of the desk. He aimed the pistol at a spot between Donaghue's eyes.

"You remember Colter, don't you?"

Donaghue tried to collect his wits. "Who are you?"

"Take a closer look." Braddock permitted himself a grim smile. "You probably saw me around Cimarron. Or maybe your boys told you about me. Reverend Titus Jacoby."

"I—" Donaghue regarded him with profound shock. "What do you want with me?"

"I guess you heard how Allison and his crowd hung Vega?"

"So what?"

Braddock looked at him without expression. "Yesterday, Pancho Griego told us where to find you. Then Colter shot and killed him."

Donaghue's face went chalky. "Who's Pancho Griego?"

"One of the men you hired to kill Reverend Tolby. Vega and Griego both confessed before they died. And by law, a deathbed confession is admissible in court. Their word alone would convict you of murder."

"You'll never make it stick."

"I wouldn't even try," Braddock said, suddenly tight-lipped.

"What I would do is turn you over to Allison and his crowd. By sundown, you'd be decorating a tree somewhere. How's that idea strike you?"

Donaghue shook his head as though a fly had buzzed in his ear. "I don't get it. Are you offering me a choice of some kind?"

"I'll only say it once." Braddock's eyes took on a cold tinsel glitter. "I want the goods on Warren Mitchell. You cooperate and I'll guarantee immunity from prosecution. Otherwise I'll hand you over to Allison."

"Some choice!" Donaghue studied him with the sideways suspicion of a kicked dog. "Why should I trust you to keep your word?"

"Figure it out," Braddock said in a measured tone. "I want you alive and talkative. You're no good to me dead."

"How do I know you're not bluffing about Allison?"

Braddock's gaze bored into him. "The other side of the coin speaks for itself. You're no good to me alive—unless you talk."

There was no immediate response. Donaghue's eyes dulled as he turned thoughtful. The silence stretched out as he debated something within himself. Finally, with a great shrug of resignation, he nodded. His voice was strained.

"What do you want to know?"

"Who ordered you to kill Reverend Tolby?"

"Warren Mitchell."

"Who ordered you to kill Orville McMain?"

"Mitchell."

"How were the orders delivered?"

"By him or one of his men."

"What do you mean, one of his men?"

"He keeps a couple of hardcases on his payroll. They work out of Santa Fe."

"What're their names?"

"Pedro Ortega and Slim Johnson."

"Were all your orders delivered by them?"

"No." A nervous flicker crossed Donaghue's lips. "I met

with Mitchell once a month in Santa Fe. All the routine stuff was handled then."

"Are you talking about political business?"

"Yeah."

"Mitchell told you what he wanted done, and you passed along his orders to the courthouse crowd. Is that how it worked?"

"Generally."

Braddock watched him intently. "Was there ever any personal contact between Mitchell and the courthouse crowd?"

"Never," Donaghue said with a blank stare. "All the orders came through me."

"But they knew he was the boss?" Braddock insisted. "The head of the Santa Fe Ring?"

"Oh, nobody had any doubts about that."

"What was their payoff in the deal?"

"Mitchell let them run the county to suit themselves. Any graft or bribes went into their pockets. It was like having a patent on a money tree."

"And what were they expected to do in return?"

"Whatever they were told." Donaghue smiled vacantly. "Their main job was to enforce Mitchell's demands on the farmers and ranchers."

"In other words, force everyone to pay for land they'd already settled, or else get evicted. Is that it?"

"Pretty much."

"What was your job?"

"I picked the candidates and rigged the elections. Anyone who wouldn't play along never got nominated, much less elected."

"A political kingfish usually gets a hefty slice of the graft and bribes. How about you?"

"Mitchell insisted that all under-the-table money go to the officeholders. He wanted to keep them fat and happy."

"So where was your payoff?"

"I was in for a share of everything we collected on land sales."

"How big a share?"

"Three percent."

"Not bad, considering it involved millions of dollars. You would've been a rich man."

"Someday."

"One last thing," Braddock said with a casual gesture. "Sit down here at the desk and write it all out in your own words. Just the way you told it to me."

"I don't think so," Donaghue said slowly. "You wouldn't need me if you had a signed confession."

"Strictly a precaution, nothing more."

"In case something happens to me?"

"That's right."

"Then you'd better not let anything happen. I'll testify to names, dates, and places. But I won't put it in writing."

Braddock stood and motioned with the gun. "Get dressed."

"Where are we going?"

"Cimarron."

All the blood leached out of Donaghue's face. "You said you wouldn't turn me over to Allison. You gave me your word!"

"Quit squawking. With Buck and me along, Allison won't come anywhere near you. Isn't that right, Buck?"

Colter smiled. "Not unless he's tired of livin'."

Late that evening, Braddock sat talking quietly with Bud Grant. The marshal's expression was somber and worried. He kept glancing at the door.

Braddock no longer wore the mustache. Apart from his dyed hair, his appearance was his own. He seemed calm and controlled, perfectly at ease. He'd weighed the risk of returning to Cimarron, and on balance he thought it the wisest choice. Here, at least, he knew who his enemies were.

A few minutes before nine the door opened. Colter stepped inside and waved Floyd Mather into the office. The sheriff marched straight to the desk, nodding at Grant. Then he turned his head just far enough to rivet Braddock with a look. He stared down at him with a bulldog scowl.

"What happened to the good Reverend Jacoby?"

Braddock grinned. "I put him out to pasture."

"Who the hell are you anyway?"

"Nobody you want to know, Sheriff."

"Then why'd you send Colter after me?"

"Law business." Braddock gestured toward the rear of the jail. "I've got Donaghue back there in a cell."

"Donaghue!" Mather repeated, thoroughly dumbfounded. "What's the charge?"

"One count of murder. Three counts of conspiracy to commit murder."

Mather looked surprised, then suddenly irritated. "In that case, he belongs in my custody. I'll just take him over to the county jail."

"No, you won't." Braddock shook his head firmly. "Donaghue stays here while he's in Cimarron. He'll be guarded by nobody but Colter or myself. We've already worked out the arrangements with Marshal Grant."

"It won't wash," Mather said churlishly. "Not in my jurisdiction."

"Here's the deal," Braddock went on in a pleasant voice. "You'll inform the county judge that he's to set up a preliminary hearing for tomorrow morning. I want Donaghue bound over on a charge of murder."

"Who the hell you think you're talkin' to?"

Braddock ignored the outburst. "You'll also inform the county prosecutor that he's to convene a grand jury no later than day after tomorrow. The juror list is to be made up solely of ranchers and farmers."

"What d'you think that'll accomplish?"

"Three counts of conspiracy to commit murder."

"Against who?"

"Donaghue and certain parties in Santa Fe."

There was a moment of stunned silence. Mather's face paled and little knots bunched tight at the back of his jaws.

"You talk like I'm gonna follow orders like a toy soldier. Why's that?"

"A couple of reasons," Braddock announced. "For one thing, I don't believe you or your cronies were involved in the murder conspiracy. So you're off the hook on the capital offense."

"What's the other reason?"

"I'm the only thing holding Clay Allison in check. Either you go along with me or I'll turn him loose."

"You're threatenin' a sworn officer of the law!"

"I told you once before there's a difference between a threat and a prophecy. If I turn Allison loose, I predict he'll hang you and most of your pals at the courthouse. Would you care to put it to the test?"

Mather studied him for a long while before answering. "I take it Donaghue's gonna turn state's evidence?"

A wintry smile lighted Braddock's eyes. "You'll find out tomorrow. Tell the judge I want court convened at nine sharp."

Several moments elapsed while the two men stared at one another. Then Mather turned about abruptly and strode from the office. Braddock and Colter exchanged an amused look. Bud Grant let out his breath as the door slammed shut.

"You think he'll do it?"

"Wouldn't you?" Braddock lit a cigarette. "I doubt that anybody over at the courthouse wants a midnight visit from Allison."

"Were you really serious about that?"

"Never more serious in my life."

"God! You play for all the marbles, don't you?"

Braddock smiled and blew a perfect smoke ring toward the ceiling.

CHAPTER TWENTY-TWO

The morning was crisp and bright. On the horizon, the sun rose like an orange ball of fire. Scattered clouds capped the mountaintops and the slopes were tinged with vermilion. High overhead a V of ducks winged southward.

Braddock stood at the window. The street outside the jail bustled with early morning activity. Stores and shops were opening for business, and housewives were already about their daily errands. Somewhere in the distance a school bell tolled, and a gang of tardy children hurried along the boardwalk. Cimarron prepared to meet another uneventful day.

Watching from the window, Braddock knew it wouldn't last for long. The grapevine in any small town worked with lightning speed. While it was barely past eight, the word would spread along the street within a matter of minutes. People thrived on gossip, and the self-appointed gadflies were quick to make their rounds. By nine, all of Cimarron would know that Florencio Donaghue was slated for a court appearance. That the charge was murder would merely stoke the fires of their curiosity. Braddock knew the uneventful day was about to take on the trappings of a three-ring circus. He pondered on the best way to get Donaghue from the jail to the courthouse.

Overnight Braddock and Colter had taken turns standing guard. Bud Grant had spent the night on a bunk in one of the empty cells. Shortly after sunrise, the marshal had walked up to the café and ordered breakfast trays brought down. Then, one at a time, they had shaved with a straight razor Grant kept in his desk drawer. Following the meal, there had been a lull while the town slowly stirred to life. Colter and Grant swigged coffee, and Braddock waited by the window. There seemed no need for conversation.

Upstreet, Braddock saw Orville McMain hurrying toward the jail. He checked his pocket watch, noting it was a few minutes shy of eight-thirty. Much as he'd expected, the grapevine was working overtime. McMain barged into the office with a look of towering indignation.

"I just now heard you were in town."

"Good news travels fast, Orville."

"But you arrived last night!" McMain said in a waspish tone. "Why didn't you contact me?"

"No need." Braddock gestured toward Colter and the marshal. "We've got things under control."

"Is it true? Do you have Donaghue in custody?"

"Safe and sound, not a scratch on him."

"You captured him in Raton, then?"

Braddock cocked an eyebrow. "How'd you know that?"

"Clay Allison," McMain said quickly. "He stopped by the office late yesterday afternoon. Did you really leave him stranded in Rayado?"

"I figured the walk would cool him down."

"Quite the contrary," McMain remarked. "He says you murdered Coleman and one of his hands. He's threatening to bring charges against you and Colter."

"Allison's all wind and no whistle. I wouldn't lose any sleep over it, Orville."

"But you did kill Coleman, didn't you?"

"When somebody pulls a gun on me, I generally do my damnedest to stop his clock. Coleman wasn't any exception."

McMain looked upset. "You've put me in a difficult position. Allison's telling everyone I'm responsible for Coleman's death. He says you were acting on my orders."

"I imagine most people take what Allison says with a grain of salt."

"Not enough!" McMain declared. "I may have trouble holding the coalition together."

"Tell you what," Braddock said with thinly disguised sarcasm. "You worry about the coalition and I'll worry about Donaghue. Sound fair?"

"Yes, of course." McMain seemed to regain his composure. "I'm sorry I got sidetracked. How do you think it will go with Donaghue?"

Braddock briefed him on last night's conversation with the sheriff. McMain was by turns amazed and perplexed. He appeared somewhat skeptical.

"Have you talked with Mather this morning?"

"What's there to talk about?"

"I don't know," McMain said uneasily. "But it's not like Mather to give in so quickly. He's a very devious man."

"Devious maybe, but not dumb. I've got him and his buddies over a barrel. They'll sacrifice Donaghue to save themselves."

"Perhaps," McMain said without conviction. "I'd still caution you to watch your step. They're all scoundrels, to the last man!"

"I'll keep my eyes open, Orville."

Braddock walked him to the door. McMain went reluctantly, aware he was being dismissed. Finally, with yet another warning, he stepped outside and turned uptown. Braddock closed the door and quickly checked the time.

"Quarter of nine," he said, moving back into the office. "Let's get Donaghue ready to go."

Bud Grant rose from behind his desk. "How're we gonna handle it?"

"You've got manacles, don't you?"

"Sure do."

"First things first," Braddock said briskly. "We'll bring him out of the lockup and get him fitted with bracelets."

"What then?"

"Then Buck and me will escort him to the courthouse."

"Hold on a goldurned minute! I didn't hear my name mentioned."

"You're staying here, Bud."

"Would you mind tellin' me why?"

"I've already put you out on a limb. I'm not about to saw it off after you."

"What d'you mean by that?"

"We're operating outside the law," Braddock informed him. "You've exceeded your authority just by holding Donaghue here overnight. I'm beholden to you for that, but let's not make it any worse."

"I got my toes wet." Grant chuckled. "I might as well take the plunge."

"Lots of things could go wrong. For all we know, somebody might try to bust Donaghue loose. You'd be in a hell of a fix if that happened."

"How so?"

"Technically, he's not in legal custody. Would you want to get involved in a shootout under those circumstances?"

"I'm not partial to a shootout under any circumstances."

"All the more reason to stay behind."

"Well, it's your show," Grant said with a shrug. "But you're liable to wish you had a badge along for the ride. It'd damn sure look legal, even if it's not."

"I'm only trying to save you trouble."

"Lemme put it this way." Grant looked him straight in the eye. "I'd sooner go than stay behind."

"I reckon that settles it."

"So what's your plan?" Grant persisted. "How do you aim to get from here to there?"

Braddock considered a moment. "Suppose you lead the

way and clear a path on the boardwalk. I'll follow directly behind with Donaghue, and Buck can bring up the rear. That ought to pretty well cover it."

"Sounds good." Colter set down his coffee mug and stood. "I'm ready whenever you are."

"Let's get to it, then."

Braddock followed Grant through the door to the lockup. The marshal unlocked Donaghue's cell and waved him outside. Somewhat the worse for wear, Donaghue's clothes were rumpled and his jaw was covered with whiskery stubble. He joined them in the corridor, and they walked him back to the office.

Grant moved to his desk and dug a pair of manacles out of the bottom drawer. The wristbands were constructed of sturdy iron and attached together by a short length of chain. He unlocked each of the bands with a stubby key and tossed it back in the drawer. Then he crossed the room, motioning for Donaghue to hold out his hands. He snapped the manacles around Donaghue's wrists and pressed until the locks clicked. He glanced at Braddock.

"How's that?"

"Just what the doctor ordered."

"What's the matter?" Donaghue laughed, staring down at the manacles. "Afraid I'll make a break for it?"

"You better not." Colter cranked a shell into his shotgun. "I'm gonna be right behind you all the way."

Grant studied the shotgun a moment, then turned to Braddock. "What about me? You think I ought to carry a scattergun?"

"Take a rifle," Braddock replied. "Too much artillery might give folks the wrong idea. We're not hunting trouble."

Grant took a Winchester carbine from the gun rack. He worked the lever and jacked a Cartridge into the chamber. Then he lowered the hammer and cradled the Winchester over the crook of his arm. He looked back at Braddock.

"All set?"

"Lead the way, Marshal."

Outside, they formed a tight column. With Braddock and
Donaghue in the middle, they marched off at a rapid pace.
Passersby stopped to stare, and early morning street traffic
came to a standstill, clogging the intersection with wagons
and buggies. Ahead of them stores emptied as shopkeepers
and townspeople crowded the doorways for a better look.
Grant bulled a path through the throngs on the boardwalk,
ordering them aside in a rough voice. At first there was total
silence as the four men proceeded uptown. Then a buzz of
excitement swelled in their wake, steadily growing louder.
All of Cimarron turned out to gawk.

Nearing the hotel, Grant wheeled right and led the way
across the street. Braddock kept a tight grip on Donaghue's
arm as they passed between vehicles halted at curbside. A
pace behind, Colter's eyes were in constant motion, sweeping the street in both directions. On the opposite curb, Grant
veered around a wagon and headed toward a short walkway
leading to the courthouse steps. Spectators mobbed the por-
tico outside the entrance and every window was jammed
with onlookers. No one moved as the men proceeded up the
walkway.

Then, suddenly, an upstairs window in the hotel erupted
with gunfire. The curtains jumped from the muzzle blast of
two rifles and an earsplitting crack echoed along the street.
Donaghue grunted, lurching forward, as a slug drilled through
his backbone and exited high on his chest. His shirtfront exploded outward in a crimson bloodburst, and he dropped like
a stone. Braddock involuntarily flinched as a second bullet
droned past his ear. Directly in front of him, Grant took the
slug in the base of the neck, shattering his spine. The carbine
slipped from his grasp and a massive jerk of nerves knocked
him off his feet. He hit the walkway on his face, arms
splayed wide.

Braddock and Colter reacted in what seemed one fluid
motion. Colter whirled around as Braddock bent low and
scooped up the carbine. The hotel window belched a sheet

of flame and rifle slugs whizzed past them with an angry snarl. Colter let loose with his shotgun, triggering three quick blasts in a roaring blaze. The buckshot whistled across the street, spreading in a fanlike pattern, and peppered the upper wall of the hotel with lead. Only a beat behind, Braddock shouldered the carbine and levered two rounds through the window. Gunfire from the hotel abruptly ceased and the snouts of the rifles vanished from view. A deafening silence settled over the street.

"Behind the hotel!" Braddock shouted. "You take the left side."

Colter nodded and took off at a lope. The drivers of buggies and wagons were fighting to control their teams, and stunned onlookers were huddled in doorways along the boardwalk. Braddock sprinted across the street, dodging a rearing horse as he neared the curb. He swerved around the right side of the hotel and ran toward the rear of the building. A few feet from the corner he skidded to a halt and jacked a fresh round into the chamber. Edging closer, he saw two saddle horses tied to a tree in the backlot. The rear door of the hotel suddenly burst open, and two men carrying rifles rushed outside. They made a headlong dash for the horses.

"Hold it!"

Braddock's command caught them in midstride. The men skittered awkwardly to a stop and spun around in unison. Their eyes fixed on Braddock, who was standing with the butt of the carbine tucked into his shoulder. For a split second they stared at him as though weighing the odds. Then one moved, and the other followed suit, and their rifles leveled in his direction. Braddock sighted quickly and touched off the trigger. His slug struck the man on the right slightly below the sternum and killed him instantly.

Colter stepped around the opposite corner of the building. He squinted down the barrel of the shotgun and fired. The man on the left was punched backward by the impact, bright red dots spurting across the width of his chest. He lost his footing and somersaulted head over heels, landing flat on his back. His bladder voided in death.

Braddock and Colter walked forward. They halted before the corpses and inspected them with icy detachment. One man was tall and lanky, a limp bundle of knobs and joints. The other man was Mexican, with fleshy features and a sweeping mustache. After a time, Colter nudged the Mexican with the toe of his boot.

"You reckon his name was Ortega?"

"I'd bet on it," Braddock muttered. "And that other jaybird was Slim Johnson."

"Mitchell's gunhands," Colter added. "The ones Donaghue told us worked out of Santa Fe."

"It all fits." Braddock hawked and spat, his eyes rimmed with disgust. "Mitchell probably sent them up here sometime yesterday. He couldn't afford to let Donaghue be taken alive and start talking. I should've figured it."

"Not unless you had a crystal ball."

"The signs were there," Braddock said glumly. "Hell, even Orville McMain suspected something. He tried to warn me this morning."

"You mean his hunch about the sheriff?"

Braddock nodded. "That's why Mather caved in so quick last night. He knew these two were in town, and he let me serve Donaghue up on a platter. I walked into it like a blind man."

Colter was silent a moment. "You gonna call Mather out?"

"No." Braddock's mouth curled at the corner. "I'll let Allison have him. He'll look good on a lamppost."

"Since you're turnin' Allison loose"—Colter paused, his eyes inquisitive—"I take it you're gonna say adios and goodbye to Cimarron."

"With Donaghue dead, I've played out my string here."

"Where to now?"

"I've got some unfinished business in Santa Fe."

"Mitchell?"

"He's first on the list."

"I'd give a nickel to see him get it."

"You're welcome to come along."

"I guess not." Colter uttered a low chuckle. "I try to steer clear of big towns. Hard to keep lookin' over your shoulder with all them people around."

"You could ride with me as far as Raton . . . I'm gonna take the train to Santa Fe from there."

"Wrong direction," Colter observed. "The last couple of days are gonna make a splash in the newspapers. I calculate my name'll get mentioned somewheres along the way."

"You figure that might put the International on your trail?"

"I'm thinkin' it'd be smart not to hang around and find out."

"Where will you head?"

"West." Colter turned slightly, staring at the Sangre de Cristos. "I've been wonderin' what's on the other side of them mountains. I suppose it's time to go have a look-see."

There was a marked silence. Braddock followed his gaze, and for a moment there was a wordless bond between them. Neither of them could have articulated it, but they both understood its origin. It was the kinship of strong men who each saw something of himself in the other. A kinship immune to time and distance.

Braddock finally broke the silence. "You won't outrun the International. Not even on the other side of those mountains."

"Never figured I would."

"One of these days you're liable to find yourself in a tight fix."

"Yeah, that's possible."

"You've got my marker when it happens."

"You don't owe me nothin', Cole."

"Let's say I do and shake on it."

Colter took his hand and gave it a hard pump. "You know, you would've made a hell of a Cheyenne."

Braddock grinned. "I think maybe you're right."

"No maybe about it! It's puredee fact."

Their laughter seemed to linger behind them as they turned and walked toward the street.

CHAPTER TWENTY-THREE

The evening train was almost six hours late. Braddock's nerves felt raw and gritty as he lit another cigarette. He stared out the window, silently cursing what seemed a sudden run of bad luck. Santa Fe was still some ten miles downtrack.

The entire day had proved to be one delay after another. Following the courthouse shootout, Braddock and Colter had walked directly to the newspaper. There a heated argument had ensued, with McMain insisting that they both remain in town until a coroner's inquest could be arranged. His sole interest was in exposing the courthouse conspiracy, and he'd stressed the importance of their testimony. But Braddock, intent on reaching Santa Fe, had flatly refused. Colter, for reasons of his own, wanted to put Cimarron far behind him. McMain had dogged their heels from the newspaper office to the livery stable, protesting all the way. Braddock finally agreed to a compromise, promising to forward a sworn deposition. Then, with Colter at his side, he'd ridden out of town.

A mile or so up the road, Colter had reined to a halt. His way was west, over the mountains, and he had accompanied Braddock this far only to lay a false trail. Their parting words were brief, for they'd both said all that needed saying. With a final handshake, Colter struck out across country, on a beeline for the Sangre de Cristos. Braddock, watching after him a moment, had then turned his horse toward Raton. There was an afternoon train for Santa Fe, and he had several things to accomplish before departure time. While he hadn't mentioned it to McMain, he'd decided there was nothing more to be gained by operating in disguise. His name was now known, and his various cover stories had fallen before events of the past few days. He figured the best bet was to forget guile and rely instead on the unexpected. He would revert to himself.

In Raton, Braddock had discovered the train was running an hour late. He'd been tempted to pay a call on Blacky O'Neal, Donaghue's partner in the Bull's Head Saloon. On second thought, however, he had concluded it would merely complicate matters. To brace the man might very well cause a ruckus, even end in gunplay. Then, too, it seemed unlikely that O'Neal would know anything damaging about the ring. For the moment, Braddock's principal concern was to reach Santa Fe as quickly as possible. So he'd stuck to his original plan.

Uptown, he had purchased a complete change of clothing. The only thing he kept was the boots he'd worn while posing as a Texas cattleman. His next stop was a public bathhouse, where several rinsings in a steamy tub removed all the dye from his hair. After a shave, the image he saw in a mirror seemed curiously unreal. He'd been operating undercover so long it was almost as though he were impersonating himself. Upon leaving the bathhouse, he had gone straight to the depot. The train finally departed an hour and ten minutes behind schedule.

Braddock hadn't been too alarmed by the delay. But around nightfall he'd begun cursing the railroad with considerable anger. A rockslide at Glorieta Pass had blocked the tracks with a small mountain of rubble. Some four hours were then consumed while passengers and crew pitched in to clear the roadbed. Once under way, Braddock had ques-

tioned the conductor and got some disturbing news. There
was little likelihood of the train's arriving in Santa Fe before midnight. The conductor estimated it would be closer
to one in the morning.

The added delay forced Braddock to revamp his plan. His
original assessment had been based on certain assumptions
about Warren Mitchell. He knew Sheriff Mather would have
wired Mitchell earlier that morning. Though the sheriff still
had no idea as to Braddock's actual identity, the wire itself
would have been reassuring. Donaghue's death effectively
severed the only direct link to Mitchell; the death of the two
gunhands further eliminated any connection with the Santa
Fe Ring. Mitchell would reasonably assume he was now in
the clear. Apart from a phantom investigator, whose last witness was dead, he had nothing to fear from the Cimarron
blowup. He would have reported as much to Stephen Elkton.

For all practical purposes, Braddock saw it in much the
same light. His investigation was stymied, and he'd lost any
chance of grand jury indictments. Still, upon riding out of
Cimarron, his frame of mind had turned from practical to
pragmatic. He told himself that the end justified the means
where assassins were concerned. While it was an extreme
action, he had resolved to take Warren Mitchell prisoner.
The tactics he employed afterward would depend to a large
extent on Mitchell. He disliked extracting a confession by
violent methods and he seldom resorted to brute force, yet
by hook or crook, he intended to make Mitchell talk. All
other options had been foreclosed.

Braddock had thought to effect the capture immediately
upon arriving in Santa Fe. His plan was to take Mitchell un-
awares, either on the street or in the land-company office.
But a rockslide had foreclosed that option as well. By the
time he reached Santa Fe, Mitchell would have settled in at
the Tivoli Theater. To make matters worse, it was entirely
possible Lise would be seated at Mitchell's table. The risk of
taking Mitchell under those circumstances forced Braddock
to alter his approach. He had no choice but to determine

Lise's whereabouts and then insure her safety. Only afterward would he turn his attention to Mitchell. The six-hour delay had changed both his plan and his priorities. Lise was now his chief concern.

Apart from the delay, Braddock was still confident he held the edge. Mitchell knew him only as Elmer Boyd, the high-roller Texan. Further, someone in Cimarron had doubtless supplied a description of the Reverend Titus Jacoby. It was safe to assume that Mitchell was now aware that one man had played both roles. Moreover, Stephen Elkton would realize he'd betrayed himself as the leader of the Santa Fe Ring. Yet neither of them would believe they were in any immediate danger of being exposed. Everyone who might have testified against them was now dead.

Their overconfidence merely enhanced Braddock's edge. Quite logically, they would anticipate his return to Santa Fe. But they would expect him to appear in some new guise, operating undercover. It would never occur to them that he might return as himself, openly and with no attempt at deception. Nor was he worried about being recognized from photos in the *Police Gazette* and other periodicals. By virtue of doing the unexpected when it was least expected, the element of surprise was in his favor. He meant to strike before anyone realized he was in town.

The train slowed on the outskirts of Santa Fe. Braddock checked his pocket watch as the engineer throttled down and set the brakes. The time was 12:43, and he recalled that Lise's act was the finale for the midnight show. He was cutting it close, perhaps too close. But if he hurried, he could still catch her before she joined Mitchell at his table. The locomotive rolled past the depot and ground to a halt, belching steam and smoke. The moment the conductor opened the coach door, Braddock stepped onto the platform. He walked quickly toward the plaza.

Lise took a final curtain call. Her naughty ballads were still the hit of Santa Fe, and the audience tonight gave her a wild ovation. She threw them kisses with both hands as the curtain rang down.

Backstage, she avoided several chorus girls who were standing around smoking. She normally paused to chat, swapping tidbits of gossip and listening to their gripes. Showgirls were constantly bitching about something, and she'd become a sort of mother confessor. But tonight she brushed them off with a smile and went directly to her dressing room. The instant she was alone her expression changed.

She was worried and upset, her nerves frayed. Almost a week had passed since Braddock had left Santa Fe. From news dispatches she was aware of his movements and his involvement in the deadly affairs of Colfax County. Local papers continued to identify him as the Reverend Titus Jacoby, and he'd been dubbed "The Fighting Parson." One story had related the lynching of Cruz Vega and the ensuing street brawl between Reverend Jacoby and Clay Allison. The following day another story recounted details of a bloody gunfight in some remote *pueblo* called Rayado. The newspapers speculated that Reverend Jacoby was too handy with his fists, and a gun, for a mere preacher. There were intimations that he was something more than he appeared.

Earlier today, Lise had heard a rumor about the courthouse shoot-out in Cimarron. Since there were no afternoon papers, she was forced to await the morning edition for confirmation. But she'd already learned sufficient details to know Reverend Jacoby had survived yet another gunfight. All of which simply added to her general state of uncertainty. She believed Braddock had failed in his mission to capture a corroborating witness. That being true, then his concern for her safety would have multiplied severalfold. Her intuition told her that he was even now on his way back to Santa Fe. And the thought left her mired in a quandary. She wondered what to do about Warren Mitchell.

Slipping out of her stage gown, she hung it on a metal costume rack. She stood there a moment, debating whether she should change into her street clothes. Then, still gripped

by uncertainty, she shrugged into a loose-fitting kimono and
seated herself before the dressing table. She was thankful
she'd badgered Ned Ingram into giving her a private dressing room. Tonight she desperately needed that privacy,
and time to think. The courthouse gun battle in Cimarron
had put an entirely new complexion on things. So far as she
knew, she was the only remaining witness against Mitchell
and Elkton. She tried to reason out her next move and found
herself confronted by hard questions. Should she play it safe,
perhaps feign an illness, and await Braddock's return alone?
Or should she put on a happy face and continue the charade
with Mitchell?

Until today there would have been no reason to pose the
question. She'd brought her considerable charms to bear, and
Mitchell was all but bewitched. In defiance of Elkton's
orders, he still paid her court every night, seemingly glued
to his chair at the front-row table. After the last show he escorted her back to his suite at the hotel, and their nightcap
had by now become something of a ritual. Apart from a
few halfhearted wrestling matches, she had managed to fend
off his advances. By scolding and cajoling, she'd thus far
kept him in line. Then, too, his lust had waned in direct pro-
portion to the news out of Cimarron. With each report in the
papers, his nerves appeared to unravel yet another strand.
The last couple of nights he'd acted like a eunuch, scarcely
touching her. His mind was clearly occupied with weightier
matters.

Tonight, however, was an altogether different story. From
the rumors she'd heard, the news out of Cimarron sounded
favorable to him, and he was certain to be in a buoyant mood.
Once in the hotel suite, that same jubilation would rekindle
his randier instincts. There was every likelihood that he
would no longer settle for promises or accept her excuses.
She might easily find herself in an untenable position, faced
with the demand that she come across or else. While the idea
itself was revolting, she was disturbed by an even more trou-
blesome thought. She got a vivid image of Braddock arriv-

ing late sometime during the night. She saw him kicking down the door of Mitchell's suite and charging to her rescue. She shuddered as the picture formed in her mind's eye. She considered it unlikely that Mitchell would survive the encounter. And with him would die their case.

A light knock broke her spell. Then the door opened and half of the nightmare she'd just envisioned became a reality. Warren Mitchell stepped into the dressing room.

"Dora!" he said with ebullient good humor. "What's keeping you, my dear? You're not even dressed."

Lise composed herself and swiftly concocted a lie. "I sent a waiter with a message. Didn't he find you?"

"Obviously not." Mitchell crossed to the dressing table. "What message?"

"I don't feel well." Lise put her head in her hands, elbows on the table. "I think it's something I ate."

"Poor girl," Mitchell said in a solicitous tone. "You just put yourself in my hands. I have some really miraculous stomach powders at the hotel. We'll have you feeling better in no time."

Lise covered her mouth and burped softly. "I appreciate the thought, Warren. But, honestly, I wouldn't be very good company tonight."

"Nonsense!" Mitchell laughed off the objection. "I was particularly looking forward to your company tonight. Now, do hurry and get dressed. I insist."

"I'm really in no shape—"

Lise started, her eyes suddenly fastened on the dressing table mirror. She saw reflected there the other half of what she'd envisioned only minutes ago. The door opened and closed, and Braddock took a step into the room. The sound caused Mitchell to turn, and a strangely bemused expression crossed his features. He looked like a man having trouble placing a familiar face.

"Who the devil are you?"

Braddock smiled. "I go by many names. The last time we met I was Elmer Boyd."

"Boyd!" Mitchell parroted. "I don't believe you."

"I dyed my hair dark brown. I wore a fake mustache." Braddock's smile widened to a grin. "And I gave you a bogus check for three million dollars."

"Good God!"

Mitchell appeared to stagger. His imagination put a mustache in place, and turned the chestnut hair dark brown. The visage jolted him into a rude awakening. He saw the man before him transformed into Elmer Boyd.

"Don't pass out," Braddock said dryly. "I've got another little piece of information for you."

"Oh?" Mitchell paused, struggling to collect himself. "What sort of information?"

"The name I mostly go by is Cole Braddock."

Mitchell's face turned red as ox blood. His eyes froze to tiny points of darkness and his breathing quickened. His words spilled out in a choked rasp.

"You're the detective. You killed Judge Hough last year in Lincoln County."

"Glad you remember," Braddock said without inflection. "Since you do, there's no need for us to dance around. We can get straight down to business."

Mitchell recovered slightly. "I have no business with you."

"Wanna bet?" Braddock motioned toward the dressing table. "I'd like you to meet my partner, alias Dora Kimble. Her real name's not important."

Mitchell's features colored, then went dead white. A pulse throbbed in his neck and he stood numb with shock. He stared at Lise like a man gazing blindly at the moon.

"Sorry, Warren." Lise nodded, then smiled a little. "All in the line of duty."

"Y-You bitch," Mitchell stammered. "You deceived me. You lied to me!"

"She did more than that," Braddock told him. "She eavesdropped on your conversation with Elkton. You'll recollect that was the night you were ordered to kill Orville McMain."

"I remember no such conversation."

"Yeah, you do. It was the same night you implicated yourself in the murder of Reverend Tolby. She'll testify to that when you're brought to trial."

"And what if she does?" Mitchell sneered. "It's her word against mine and that of Stephen Elkton. The word of a saloon tart who sings dirty songs! She'll be laughed out of court."

"No, she won't." A broad grin spread across Braddock's face. "We've got corroborating evidence to back up her testimony."

"I don't believe you."

"What if I told you Donaghue spilled his guts?"

"I still wouldn't believe you."

"How about Donaghue's own words?"

"Don't be absurd," Mitchell countered. "I happen to know that Donaghue was killed in Cimarron. Do you propose to raise the dead, Mr. Braddock?"

"After a fashion," Braddock replied. "You see, a dead man's words are still admissible in court. Leastways, they are if it's in the form of a signed deposition."

"Deposition!" Mitchell looked as though he hadn't heard correctly. "Donaghue made a deposition?"

"A real doozy," Braddock lied, grinning wider. "He wrote it all down the night before your boys killed him. When he got around to naming names, yours was right at the top of the list. Damn shame he stopped there."

"What are you talking about?"

"Well, he never made any mention of Elkton. Hell, how could he? So far as he knew, you were the head of the ring. All his orders came straight from you."

"That's ridiculous," Mitchell snapped. "No one will believe a word of it."

"A jury will." Braddock's mouth tightened. "You'll be tried and convicted, and you'll hang for murder. Course, I reckon Elkton will have the last laugh."

"Elkton?"

"Why, sure," Braddock said soberly. "He wasn't named

in the deposition, and Dora's testimony alone won't convict him. He'll walk free and leave you to swing by yourself. Hell of a note, but I guess there's no way around it."

"You're bluffing!" Mitchell raged. "You're just trying to trick me into implicating Elkton. There's no deposition!"

"You'll see it for yourself in a couple of days."

"Why not now?"

"I mailed it to Dora before I left Cimarron. Sent it to her in care of the hotel. Figured if anything happened to me, she'd see to it you took the drop. So either way, you're a cooked goose."

Mitchell struck without warning. His left hand darted out and grabbed Lise by the hair. He yanked her to her feet and pulled her tight against his chest. His arm snaked around her throat.

Braddock was halfway across the room when he abruptly stopped. Mitchell's right hand dipped inside his coat and reappeared with a bulldog pistol. He pressed the muzzle to Lise's forehead and slowly cocked the hammer.

"Stand away from the door!"

CHAPTER TWENTY-FOUR

Braddock saw it was futile to act. He didn't dare draw his gun, and any attempt to jump Mitchell was out of the question. He moved aside.

Mitchell kept an armlock on Lise and backed across the room. He fumbled the door open with his gun hand, then put the muzzle to her head and stepped outside. One of the chorus girls standing nearby shrieked and ran off through the wings. The others remained perfectly still, their mouths round with silent terror. Mitchell ignored them, tightening his chokehold around Lise's throat. He backed toward the stage door.

Braddock walked from the dressing room. He appraised the situation at a glance and muttered an inaudible curse. Outside the stage door was a dark alleyway. In one direction it led to the street and in the other it continued on past the Tivoli. Once outside, it was almost certain that Mitchell would turn toward the inky darkness behind the theater. There was also a strong possibility he would murder Lise and escape into the night. If he was to be stopped, then Braddock had no choice but to stop him now. He walked forward.

"Hold on, Mitchell."

"Stay back!" Mitchell shouted. "Take one more step and I'll kill her!"

"No, you won't," Braddock warned with cold menace. "Because if you do, you're a dead man. I'll shoot you down on the spot."

Mitchell edged toward the stage door. "I have nothing to lose, Braddock. You'd kill me anyway! So just stay where you are."

"Here's my last word." Braddock advanced another step. "Let her go and you can walk out that door unharmed. It's the only way you'll leave here alive."

Mitchell hesitated. "Will you come after me?"

"I'll give you a five-minute head start."

"Not enough!" Mitchell yelled. "I want at least—"

The door beside the orchestra pit banged open and Ned Ingram rushed backstage. Mitchell instinctively looked toward the theater owner, and Lise reacted with remarkable presence of mind. She wrenched free of the chokehold and threw herself sideways to the floor. Mitchell's reflexes were quick, and he tried desperately to recover. His pistol swung downward even as she fell.

Braddock seemed to move not at all. The Colt appeared in his hand and spat a streak of flame. He worked the hammer and triggered another shot within the space of a heartbeat. The slugs stitched a pair of bright red dots on Mitchell's shirtfront and he slammed backward into the stage door. He hung there a moment, as though impaled by some invisible force, then his knees buckled and he slumped to the floor, his eyes fixed on infinity.

A chorus girl screamed and fainted. Ned Ingram stared at the body a moment, then turned and bolted back through the orchestra-pit door. Braddock moved forward, holstering the Colt, and knelt beside Lise. Her kimono was pulled down over one shoulder and her hair had come undone. She smiled an upside-down smile.

"You had me worried, lover."

"Yeah?"

"Yeah," she replied with a sudden sad grin. "You weren't going to let him out of here, were you?"

"Not till he turned you loose."

"And if he hadn't?" she asked in a small voice. "What would you have done then?"

"I would've killed him."

"What about me?"

"Here or outside"—Braddock shrugged—"you were a goner unless I got him first."

"You mean he would have killed me either way?"

"What do you think?"

She slowly shook her head. "I think show business beats the hell outa the detective business."

"No argument there."

"I also think"—she gently touched his face—"I wouldn't trade you for all the tea in China."

Braddock grinned. "I'll second the motion."

"You damn sure better!" She took his arm and let him assist her to her feet. "So what's next, chief? Where do we go from here?"

"The hotel."

"Hotel?" She looked confused. "What about Elkton?"

"I want to get you under lock and key. Then I'll tend to Elkton."

"Are you worried he'll send someone after me?"

"Better safe than sorry," Braddock said solemnly. "Once he hears about Mitchell, he'll know you've been working undercover. I'd prefer to have you tucked away somewhere just in case."

"Well, lover," she said as she straightened her kimono and dusted herself off, "you won't believe your ears, but I agree. One gun at my head is enough for tonight. Let's go lock me up."

"That's him! The one there with Dora!"

Ned Ingram appeared in the doorway. His finger was leveled at Braddock, and behind him were two deputy town marshals. The lawmen squeezed past Ingram, their guns drawn, and approached cautiously. Braddock cut his eyes at Lise, and his face congealed into a frown. He carefully raised his hands.

"Looks like we're both gonna get locked up."

The interrogation lasted most of the night. Town Marshal Harold Croy was understandably zealous. He viewed the death of Warren Mitchell as a once-in-a-lifetime opportunity. A case that would establish his name in the pantheon of western lawmen.

There were several aspects of the shooting that lent it an aura of sensationalism. The deceased was both a prominent businessman and a powerful figure in territorial politics. He was also widely acknowledged as the front man, perhaps the leader, of the Santa Fe Ring. As for the man who had done the killing, he was, by his own admission, none other than Cole Braddock. His reputation as a manhunter automatically guaranteed front-page coverage throughout the West. And Santa Fe's marshal envisioned his own name emblazoned in those same headlines.

No political neophyte, Harold Croy was a staunch, dyed-in-the-wool Democrat. Aside from personal publicity, he also perceived a chance to deal the Republicans a mortal blow. The list of those rumored to be involved with the Santa Fe Ring formed a virtual roll call of the Republican elite. His interrogation was therefore politically motivated and, as a result, all the more tenacious. Yet he quickly discovered himself matched against an opponent who was versed in the finer points of law. Braddock was by turn reticent, taciturn, and downright uncooperative. He admitted nothing beyond the bare bones of the shooting. He claimed self-defense on behalf of himself and Dora Kimble.

Croy resorted to every trick in the interrogator's handbook. He questioned Braddock and the girl separately and in exhaustive detail. Afterward, he compared their stories and found himself holding two peas from the same pod.

They both claimed a lovers' triangle, ending with Mitchell's threat to kill the girl. The marshal next grilled them together, attempting to trip one on some statement made by the other. Neither of them stumbled, and he came away with the impression that they had rehearsed their stories somewhere between the theater and his office. However many times he made them repeat it, the result was always the same. They professed complete innocence, grounded in the right of self-defense.

To Croy's great disgust, their story was borne out by eyewitnesses. The chorus girls, as well as Ned Ingram, all admitted that Mitchell had indeed held a gun to Dora Kimble's head. Further, it was established that Braddock had fired only as a last resort, to save the girl. She was purportedly Mitchell's mistress, and that too tended to substantiate the story. But the marshal nonetheless thought it a fairy tale, pure invention. He was convinced Cole Braddock had not traveled to Santa Fe merely to settle a lovers' quarrel. He believed, instead, that the manhunter and the singer were working together on a case. He felt reasonably certain the case somehow involved the Santa Fe Ring.

Still, there was no evidence to support Croy's theory. Braddock and the girl adamantly stuck to their version of Mitchell's death, and the facts supported them in every particular. The upshot was that neither of them could be charged with anything. Croy advised them that there would be a coroner's inquest, but it was a hollow threat for he knew the jury would return a verdict of justifiable homicide. Then, albeit reluctantly, he released them from custody. Braddock walked out with the girl on his arm and a smile like a cat with cream on its whiskers. The marshal stood at the window, watching them cross the plaza as the first blush of daylight tinged the sky. He knew he'd been made to look the fool, and yet, despite himself, he felt a grudging sense of admiration. The first tenet for a private detective was that the details of an assignment, as well as the client's name, would never be revealed. Braddock had kept the faith.

Ten minutes later, Frank Kirkland walked through the door. An early riser, the lawyer had stopped for breakfast at a nearby cafe. There he'd heard the news of Mitchell's death and Braddock's arrest. Apparently he had run all the way, for he appeared out of breath when he entered the marshal's office. All the more suspicious were his agitated manner and his questions about the shooting, which seemed motivated by anything but simple curiosity. To Croy's inquiries, he turned evasive, offering no explanation for his interest in the affair. Upon being informed that Braddock had been released, he rushed out of the office and hurried toward the hotel. He acted like a man desperate to hear the truth about some earth-shattering event.

Harold Croy was no mathematician, but he could add two and two without counting on his fingers. He knew Frank Kirkland was the lawyer for the Cimarron Coalition and an avowed enemy of the Santa Fe Ring. He also recalled the news items about a mysterious preacher who had taken up the coalition's banner in Colfax County. Moreover, he was aware that Braddock operated undercover, generally in disguise. The sudden appearance of Frank Kirkland was the last factor in the equation. However it was figured, the marshal told himself, the answer was plain as a diamond in a goat's ass. Cole Braddock was working for the Cimarron Coalition. His assignment was to break the Santa Fe Ring.

Ergo the death of Warren Mitchell ceased to be a riddle.

Marshal Croy called a news conference at nine sharp. The reporters scribbled furiously as Croy recounted the events surrounding last night's shooting. Their mouths dropped as he added a dash of conjecture about the Santa Fe Ring and a dab of speculation about the Cimarron Coalition. Then he stirred into the broth the name of Cole Braddock and let the news hounds draw their own conclusions. He gave them everything but proof, which seemed highly irrelevant under the circumstances. Sensationalism, as he'd learned in past dealings with the press, demands no hard facts.

The story went out over the telegraph wires late that

morning. Harold Croy, chief law enforcement officer of Santa Fe, was given prominent mention.

Braddock and Lise walked directly from the marshal's office to the hotel. He saw her to her room and waited while she checked the loads in her Derringer. His orders were to stay put and shoot to kill in the event anyone attempted forcible entry. He delayed in the hallway until he heard her lock the door. Then he went in search of Stephen Elkton.

Leaving the hotel, Braddock spotted Frank Kirkland entering the marshal's office. He cursed, all too aware that the lawyer had somehow got wind of the shooting. He'd been rather pleased with the way he had misled the marshal, avoiding any hint of his mission in Santa Fe. Now, simply by showing up and asking questions, Kirkland was certain to let the cat out of the bag. But, then, in the overall scheme of things, it probably made little difference. Stephen Elkton would have long since gotten the word.

Hindsight, Braddock reminded himself, was a thing of wondrous clarity. Last night he'd figured he had the situation under control. While it surprised him to find Mitchell in Lise's dressing room, he had capitalized on the moment and turned it to advantage. He would have sworn he had Mitchell on the verge of confessing. Then, to his astonishment the cornered rat turned and fought. Somehow he hadn't credited Mitchell with the stomach for personal violence. Those who hired killers generally found the act itself repugnant. And that lapse in judgment last night had very likely cost him the case. He'd silenced the wrong man for all the wrong reasons.

Across town Braddock stopped outside Elkton's law office. He rattled the doorknob and peered in the window, and finally concluded the place was empty. Considering the early morning hour, he hadn't really expected to find anyone there. But a hunt had to begin somewhere, and apart from Elkton's law practice, he knew nothing about the man. Farther downstreet, he noticed a corner café already open for the breakfast trade. He had a cup of coffee and managed to buttonhole the owner while paying his check. His questions were framed in a casual manner, and the owner was happy to oblige. He walked out with Stephen Elkton's address.

Some while later he approached a house several blocks north of the plaza. He had no set plan in mind, but he'd already decided how it would end if Elkton was at home. After pounding on the door, he saw a frump of a woman pad down the hallway in a flannel bathrobe. She identified herself as the housekeeper and informed him in no uncertain terms that Elkton wasn't home. When he persisted, her gossipy nature won out. She told of a knock late the previous night and a whispered conversation at the door. Afterward, Elkton had hastily packed a suitcase and vanished into the night. Further probing revealed that Elkton had no wife, no children, and no family known to the housekeeper. She had no idea where he'd gone or by what means he had traveled. Nor would she venture an opinion as to when he might return. The latter comment was unsolicited, an answer to a question Braddock saw no reason to ask. He'd known the answer the moment she opened the door.

Stephen Elkton would never return to Santa Fe.

A few minutes before nine Braddock entered Frank Kirkland's office. The lawyer grinned, rising from his chair with an outstretched hand. Braddock ignored the handshake.

"You lied to me, Kirkland."

"What?"

Braddock fixed him with a baleful look. "When you hired me, you said my assignment was to bust the Santa Fe Ring. What you really wanted was somebody to do your killing."

"That's not true!"

"The hell it's not," Braddock said, jaw clenched. "I accused Orville McMain of the same thing, and he all but admitted it. He damn sure didn't deny it."

Kirkland sat down heavily. "If that's so, then he lied by omission—to both of us."

"Cut the double-talk," Braddock said sharply. "Just give me a straight answer."

"Before I came to Denver," Kirkland asserted, "I met with McMain. We agreed the ring took priority over all else. There was no discussion of recruiting a hired killer. None!"

"You're saying McMain conned you?"

"I'm saying I *did not* retain you under false pretenses."

Their eyes locked. Braddock's expression was cold and searching, and he stared at the lawyer for several moments. Finally, convinced he'd heard the straight goods, he inclined his head in a faint nod.

"I'll take your word," he said gruffly. "I broke the ring as of this morning, and I'm still owed five thousand. Write me out a check."

"This morning?" Kirkland said, baffled. "I went by the hotel, and the desk clerk said you'd gone out. Where were you?"

"Stephen Elkton's house."

Kirkland appeared even more perplexed. "What does Elkton have to do with it?"

"Mitchell and Elkton"—Braddock held out two joined fingers—"were just like that. Only Elkton called the shots and gave all the orders. He masterminded the whole operation."

"Incredible!" Kirkland was visibly astounded. "The last man I would have suspected was Stephen Elkton. He was so unsociable, almost scholarly."

"A scholar of murder," Braddock grunted. "By rough count, nine men got snuffed out because of Elkton. He missed being number ten by the skin of his teeth."

"What happened?"

"I've just come from the depot," Braddock explained.

"He hopped a late night freight bound for Denver. Bribed the stationmaster to sneak him aboard the caboose."

"Why Denver?" Kirkland asked. "Wouldn't he know that's your home base?"

"I'd judge it's a stopover to somewhere else. He'll run a

long way before he stops. Or maybe he won't ever stop, not if he's smart."

"I don't understand. You've broken the ring and driven him out of Santa Fe. Your assignment's completed."

"The assignment might be completed, but the book's not closed. Not yet."

"What book?"

"The book on Elkton."

"That sounds vaguely personal."

"Nothing vague about it. Elkton owes me and I aim to collect."

"Owes you what?"

"A life."

Kirkland began a question, then stopped. Something in Braddock's eyes told him to pursue the matter no further. He wrote out a check for five thousand dollars, and Braddock stuck it in his pocket. Then, without any great ceremony they shook hands and Braddock walked from the office. Kirkland was still staring at the door when it closed.

He wondered how far Stephen Elkton had run. He considered a moment and decided it would never be far enough. Not while Braddock was owed a life.

CHAPTER TWENTY-FIVE

Lise was like an exuberant child. The case had been long and grueling, and Braddock figured she'd earned a holiday. When he asked where she wanted to go, there was no hesitation. She squealed and clapped her hands.

"New Orleans! Ooo, please, Cole. New Orleans!"

The trip consumed the better part of a week. By rail, they traveled from Santa Fe to Denver, and then on to St. Louis. There they boarded a riverboat for a pleasant interlude down the Mississippi. On a warm autumn day, their boat steamed around a bend and slowly reduced speed. The sun was at their backs, and before them the mighty sweep of the river was like molten fire. Arm in arm, they stood in silent wonder.

New Orleans was considered the most spectacular port on the globe. For sheer size and the density of ships lying at berth, it was unrivaled by any anchorage on the world's great oceans. The wharves, which curved with the river, were lined with steam packets and windjammers flying the colors of a dozen nations. Along the levee, which extended downriver for some five miles, were row upon row of flatboats and keelboats and twin-stacked paddle-wheelers. The waterfront teemed with sailors and stevedores, and everywhere on the wharves bales of cotton were stacked in massive blocks. The sight was far grander than anything Lise and Braddock might have imagined.

Their boat docked at the Canal Street landing. Once the gangplank was lowered, a porter carried their luggage ashore and arranged for a hansom cab. Their hotel was located in the heart of the Vieux Carré, the famed French Quarter. With its many theaters and restaurants, the Vieux Carré was home to the city's Creole community. Descendants of French and Spanish émigrés who had intermarried, the Creoles seldom set foot across Canal Street, where the Anglo district of New Orleans began. Their language was French, their culture was Parisian, and their world centered on the Vieux Carré. It remained a continental outpost of grace and sophistication.

For the next four days, Braddock and Lise surrendered themselves to the languorous pace of the French Quarter. They slept late and ate breakfast in bed and made love as though there were no tomorrow. Their afternoons were spent sightseeing, from the waterfront to Jackson Square to the elite Creole residential district beyond Esplanade Avenue. One entire afternoon was devoted to exploring the area around Jackson Square, which was dominated by the Cabildo and the Presbytère and a three-spired cathedral. Their nights were an unending succession of epicurean restaurants and stage plays and after-hours suppers in intimate cafes. They gorged themselves on seafood and gumbo and a variety of exotic Creole specialties. Then they went back to the hotel and ravaged one another until exhaustion overtook them with sleep. Quite literally, they gave themselves over to the pleasures of the Vieux Carré.

On the fourth night they dined at Antoine's. The restaurant was renowned for its cuisine and catered almost exclusively to the Creole trade. The men were immaculately attired in formal evening wear and their ladies were gowned in the latest Paris fashion. The maître d', who viewed Braddock and Lise as foreigners, treated them with polite civility. They were shown to a window table, which looked out on the street and kept them somewhat removed from the regular clientele. Yet the service was impeccable and the meal was worth the slight affront. They dined on crawfish bisque, followed by *court-bouillon* and *boeuf* Robespierre. The highlight was a specialty of the house called *café brûlot*. Brandy and sugar were mixed with cloves, orange peel, and cinnamon sticks. Then the ingredients were set afire. Coffee was next poured into the bowl, and while the concoction blazed, a waiter deftly ladled it into cups. The end result was a heady brew unlike anything they'd ever tasted.

Over coffee, Braddock steered the conversation around to Buck Colter. He had told her sometime previously of the young half-breed's role in the Cimarron investigation. But he'd never talked about Colter the man, about his personal side. Lise sensed there was more to the story than he had revealed initially. For Braddock to extend his trust at all—something he'd rarely done—indicated that Colter was very unusual indeed. Yet she'd wisely just listened, asking few questions. She knew he had to tell it in his own way, in his own time. Tonight, for whatever reason, he apparently felt some need to talk about the events surrounding Colter's life. He told her everything.

"How terrible," she said when he finished. "And it's so unfair! He lost his girl and any chance he had for a decent life. I've never heard anything so sad."

"Funny about that," Braddock remarked. "He doesn't feel the least bit sorry for himself. I guess maybe it's his Cheyenne blood. He's just too proud to wallow in self-pity."

She took a sip of coffee. "You admire him, don't you, Cole?"

"Yeah, I do," Braddock admitted. "He got a rough break and he took it in stride. Not many men would show that much grit."

"I think you might envy him too."

"Envy?"

"Yes." Her voice had a teasing lilt. "He's like a wild thing. No ties, no responsibilities. He's free to pick up and go whenever he chooses. I think you miss that."

A smile tugged at Braddock's mouth. "I've got no regrets. Not yet anyway."

"Aren't you gallant!" Her eyes sparkled with suppressed mirth. "Now stop being diplomatic and tell me the truth about something."

"What's that?"

"I caught it in your voice. You were intrigued by the idea of being the hunted rather than the hunter. I got the feeling you wouldn't mind trading places with Colter."

Braddock rocked back in his chair with a belly laugh. "I wasn't intrigued by it very long. Hell, with the International on his trail, it's a good thing Colter's part Indian. He'll need a whole bag of tricks just to stay one jump ahead."

"Won't the International ever stop hounding him?"

"Not till he's dead." Braddock studied his nails, thoughtful. "Nobody kills the head of a cattlemen's association and walks away. I suppose you might call it the cardinal sin, the one unpardonable offense. Colter's a marked man the rest of his life."

"You have influence," she said softly. "Isn't there some way you could make an appeal and get him a new hearing?"

"Wouldn't work." Braddock sighed heavily. "The International's a law unto itself. There's no appeal—ever."

"So Colter will be hunted down and eventually killed?"

"Tell you a secret," Braddock said, smiling. "I damn sure wouldn't want the job. He's just about the toughest thing I've ever run across."

"Oh, my God!"

"What's wrong?"

"There!" She pointed past him. "The man crossing the street!"

Braddock twisted around and looked out the window. He saw a man step onto the curb and pass beneath a lamppost.

In the glare of the light, the face was distinct and familiar. It was Stephen Elkton.

"Here." Braddock pulled a wad of cash from his pocket. "Pay the check and have the doorman flag a cab. I'll meet you back at the hotel."

"Cole?" Her voice was a low, intense whisper. "What are you going to do?"

"Don't ask."

Braddock hurried to the cloakroom. He reclaimed his hat and walked from the restaurant. At the corner he turned onto a side street and saw the stocky figure less than a half block ahead. Braddock's stride lengthened, and he closed the gap some yards short of the next corner. His hand was inside his jacket, gripping the Colt.

"Hello, Elkton."

Elkton jumped at the sound of his name. He swiveled around and his face momentarily drained of color. He remembered the voice, and he'd seen Braddock's photograph in recent newspaper articles. A look of recognition was stamped on his features.

"How did you find me?"

"Outhouse luck," Braddock said truthfully. "Course, some people might call it divine intervention. What made you pick New Orleans?"

"Why should I tell you anything?"

"Why not?" Braddock replied. "You're through running."

Elkton was silent a moment, then shrugged. "I booked passage for South America. The ship is scheduled to leave tomorrow."

"Looks like you're gonna miss the boat."

"Would you be open to an offer?"

"Try me."

"I managed to get most of my money out of Santa Fe. I could make you a rich man."

"How rich is rich?"

"A hundred thousand—perhaps more."

"I'll think about it while we walk."

"Where are we going?"

"The waterfront."

"See here now—"

Braddock showed him the gun. "Walk."

Some minutes later they passed a warehouse and emerged onto a darkened wharf. Upshore, there were lights and laughter from a row of waterfront grog shops. Before them, the black sheen of the river stretched endlessly into the night. They halted at the edge of the wharf and turned to face one another. Braddock slipped the Colt from its holster.

"I decided to pass on your offer."

Elkton cleared his throat. "Killing me won't accomplish anything."

"Do you remember a man named Bud Grant?"

"I've never heard of him."

"He was the marshal of Cimarron."

"I don't understand." Elkton shook his head. "What was Grant to you?"

"Nothing," Braddock said quietly. "Leastways, he wasn't till he took a bullet meant for me."

"Are you talking about that affair at the courthouse?"

Braddock nodded. "Those two gunhands were supposed to get me and Donaghue. One of them missed and got Grant instead."

"They were Mitchell's men, not mine!"

"You gave the orders."

"I still deserve a trial," Elkton protested. "You have no right to appoint yourself judge and executioner."

"Bud Grant wouldn't agree."

Elkton's forehead beaded with sweat. "Don't I get any kind of chance?"

"Are you heeled?"

"No," Elkton declared. "I never carry a gun."

"Let's give it a try and see."

Braddock dug a coin from his pocket. He balanced it on his left thumb and forefinger and motioned upward. "You can make your move anytime before it hits the dock."

"I told you," Elkton pleaded hoarsely. "I'm not armed!"

"Here goes."

Braddock flipped the coin. Elkton's gaze followed it upward for a mere instant. Then he jerked his eyes down and his hand darted inside his coat. Braddock shot him.

A surprised look came over Elkton's face. He stood perfectly still, a great splotch of red covering his vest. His hand opened and a pistol dropped from beneath his coat, clattering to the dock. He took a shuffling step back and his heel caught the edge of the wharf. He tumbled headlong into the water.

There was a loud splash, then silence. Braddock stood looking down at the river for several moments. He saw the body bob to the surface and drift away in the swirling current. At last he holstered his Colt and turned from the wharf.

He walked back toward the Vieux Carré.

"Are you all right?"

"Never better."

Braddock moved through the door. Lise closed it behind him, watching as he pegged his hat on a hat tree. He crossed the room and took a seat on the sofa.

"God!" Lise said on an indrawn breath. "I was scared stiff!"

"You know better than to worry."

"You're absolutely, positively all right?"

"Fit as a fiddle."

"Was it really Elkton?"

"If it wasn't, I made a hell of a mistake."

"What happened?"

Braddock smiled. "The Santa Fe file is closed."

Lise understood there would be no further explanation. His statement was purposely vague, for he never spoke of the men he killed. Yet, in his own cryptic manner, he'd told her Stephen Elkton was dead. To her that was enough; the details were unimportant. A man had died tonight simply because justice would have otherwise gone begging. She knew he'd killed only as a last resort.

"You know something, lover?"

"What's that?"

"I think we ought to celebrate!"

"You name it," Braddock said agreeably. "We've barely scratched the French Quarter's nightlife."

"No." A slow smile warmed her face. "I won't settle for anything less than the best show in town."

Braddock chuckled. "And where do we go for that?"

"Nowhere!"

She joined him on the sofa. Her eyes were heavy-lidded and smoky, and she snuggled close in his arms. Her kiss was soft and lingering, and acted like an aphrodisiac on him. His hand caressed her curving buttocks and drifted higher to the round swell of her breasts. Her hips moved and her mouth opened in a long exhalation. A low cry drifted from deep within her throat.

"Oooh, Cole. Take me to bed—now!"

Braddock took her.